KISSED
BY
SHADOWLIGHT

BOOKS BY KRISTA STREET
SUPERNATURAL WORLD NOVELS

Fae of Snow & Ice
Court of Winter
Thorns of Frost
Wings of Snow
Crowns of Ice

Supernatural Curse
Wolf of Fire
Bound of Blood
Cursed of Moon
Forged of Bone

Supernatural Institute
Fated by Starlight
Born by Moonlight
Hunted by Firelight
Kissed by Shadowlight

Supernatural Community
Magic in Light
Power in Darkness
Dragons in Fire
Angel in Embers

Supernatural Standalones
Beast of Shadows

KISSED
BY
SHADOWLIGHT

paranormal shifter romance

SUPERNATURAL INSTITUTE
BOOK FOUR

KRISTA STREET

PREFACE

Kissed by Shadowlight is a paranormal shifter romance and is the final book in the four-book *Supernatural Institute* series. The recommended reading age is 18+.

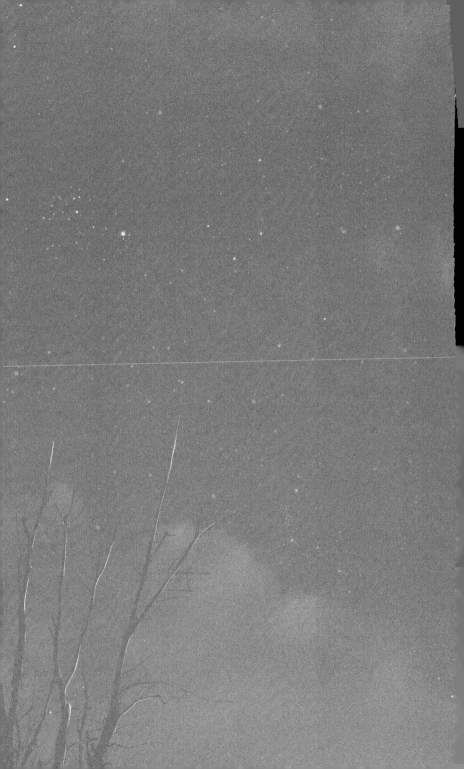

CHAPTER ONE
WYATT

"No! No!" I barreled through the trees in the direction the elf lord had taken Avery. Her scent clung to the breeze, her lilac fragrance as fresh as a newly cut bouquet of flowers.

Behind me, the battle raged at Shrouding Estate. The potent scent of magic filled the air, and screams and shouts from the Fae Guard and SF members carried through the wind.

Amidst the sounds of clanging metal and twisting branches, the earth rumbled when the trees shifted and swayed. The forest fought us, following the elf lord's bidding as the powerful warlocks cast deadly spells.

We were losing even though an entire battalion had been fighting to protect my mate.

My mate who had just been abducted.

A flash of Avery's dark hair appeared in the trees. "Avery!" I yelled.

The sight of them disappeared again, and I sprinted faster, frantically searching the thick swamp of trees.

There! The elf lord had stopped. Rage seared my skin when his arms wrapped around her. That glazed look coated her eyes, the thrall from Nicholas's compulsion still fogging her mind.

I launched myself toward them, a guttural roar bellowing from my lips, but at the last moment, the trees shifted, their branches locking in front of me as they attempted to halt my progression.

I ripped through them, bark and shards of wood cutting into my skin, but the trees fought back, holding me in place even though I hacked and clawed.

My eyes widened when a portal appeared only feet away from the elf lord.

No!

Lord Nelifeum Godasara spun, whispering to Avery before magic flowed from his fingertips and penetrated the skin on her neck.

She gasped, her eyes rolled back, then she slumped against him.

I snarled and exploded through the branches, but new tree limbs twisted and curled around me just as fast, snapping at my ankles and ensnaring my wrists. "Avery!"

A wicked grin streaked across the elf lord's face. Triumph gleamed in that cruel expression.

We made eye contact, and a tidal wave of my alpha magic shot off me, shredding the trees encasing me.

The elf lord stepped into the portal with Avery in his arms.

"NO!" I launched myself the remaining ten feet of distance, arcing through the air in one giant leap.

But the portal closed, the elf and Avery disappearing into it, and all that was left was a rustle of leaves and the sway of trees as the magical door faded.

I slid on the dirt right where they'd stood only a second before, my knees collapsing as disbelief coursed through me.

That didn't just happen.

That did not just happen.

But it had.

"No! Fuck! No!" I slammed my fist into the ground.

I leaned back on my haunches, and a howl of fury coupled with fear tore from my lips. My wolf stretched my skin, his hairs sprouting through the backs of my hands. My fingers plunged through my hair, yanking on the strands as terror coiled inside me. *Where did they go?*

Where had he taken her? How do I get her back? And how did this happen?

My heart beat erratically, like a thundering beast raging inside me. *How?*

Avery had been seconds away from safety. I'd just handed her off to an SF member whose job had been to whisk her back to headquarters, on earth, and safe from the elf lord that hunted her. I knew there was a health risk by her leaving the fae realm, but I'd been willing to take that chance since being captured by the elf lord was so much worse.

But we'd failed. *I'd* failed. He'd taken her after all.

I ripped at my hair again, trying to process my colossal mistake. Lord Godasara had come from out of nowhere and snatched Avery right from our hands. We hadn't even known he was there.

My fist pounded into the earth again, the skin on my knuckles splitting from the impact as a terrible primal scream ripped from my throat.

The sound of it cut through the forest, sailed through the breeze, and rocketed to the stars.

I'd failed. Failed so badly.

Avery had been taken.

I *hadn't* kept her safe.

"Wyatt!" Bavar flew through the trees, running at full tilt. Wild eyes met mine. "Where is she?" He came to a sudden stop beside me, swinging around in a circle, his dagger in one hand, a sword in the other. Blood streaked across his face and through his hair. "Where's Avery?"

"He . . . he took her." My entire body shook, and my chest heaved. It still didn't seem real. *None* of this could be real.

Bavar's face paled.

Inside my chest, my wolf howled, his rage firing through me.

More hairs sprouted on the backs of my hands. Heat shimmered over my skin. My bones crunched. Fire licked my insides.

In an explosion of magic, I leapt from the ground and shifted. My huge wolf landed on all fours on the forest floor. Snarls and vicious growls tore from his throat.

The elf took our mate.

He'd *taken* her to some location we didn't know.

And the pain that thought provoked . . .

My wolf tilted his head back and howled again. The long agonizing sound flew from his throat with so much pain and raw fury that Bavar backed up.

"Wyatt, we'll find her. We'll get her back—"

My wolf tore past him, his paws thundering on the ground as blood lust consumed his thoughts.

Kill.

Destroy.

Torture.

The warlocks would pay for what they'd done. They would die. My wolf would tear apart their limbs. He would devour their entrails.

The world became a blur. Streaks of twisting branches and fluttering blue leaves flew past our sides. The forest didn't try to stop us. The trees' limbs had grown completely still.

The second we reached Shrouding Estate, the stench greeted us—smoke, magic, blood, and scorched skin, yet nobody was fighting.

Pentacles of ruined rubble lay on the castle's west side. Only three of the castle's wings had survived the battle.

"Where did they go?" someone shouted.

The Fae Guard and SF members breathed heavily, bewildered expressions on their faces.

I blew past them, searching for the warlocks, *hunting* for the men who'd taken my mate. I circled the castle again and again. Pursuing. Chasing. Raging.

But they were gone.

"Wyatt!" Bavar called again. He blurred to my side, a sorrowful expression rippling across his features. "You need to shift back. You need to gain control!"

But my wolf was too far gone.

He wouldn't listen.

Rage soaked every cell of our being, and the need to kill and maim those who'd hurt my mate consumed us.

SF members leaped out of the way when we surged past them. The Fae Guard that was still standing, limped to anything that would support them.

My wolf circled the perimeter of the estate again and again and again. His form became a blur, his massive body a streak of magic and despair.

But nothing remained to destroy.

Not one warlock.

My wolf ground to a halt on paws shredded from stone chips and shards of glass. But we welcomed the pain. We deserved nothing less. Another howl ripped from my wolf's chest.

And it was only when the realization hit us that there was nobody to kill, that my wolf's frenzied mind finally allowed me to shift back to human.

In a flurry of twisted limbs, I reappeared, crouched to the ground, my body naked and streaked with blood. Bavar was there in an instant, draping his cloak over my back.

But my chest still heaved, and my insides roiled.

Avery was gone, and nothing I had done had kept her safe.

CHAPTER TWO

AVERY

I awoke with a start, jolting up to a sitting position. Frantic breaths filled my chest. The power inside me hummed and swelled. Streaks of electrical energy zapped my skin, making the hairs on my arms stand up.

It was so dark I could barely see.

I brought a hand to my forehead and used the other to feel the area around me. Cold, damp rock met my fingers.

My breaths eventually slowed, and I became aware of my numb butt which was wedged against a cold, hard surface.

And . . . *fuck!* My head pounded. It throbbed like a steady bass drum.

What the hell?

Was I in the castle?

"Wyatt?" I whispered.

No response.

"Nicholas?"

Silence.

I rubbed my temple, barely suppressing the moan as an intense headache pounded my skull. The pain was so strong that my stomach churned, its contents threatening to heave up my throat.

But I swallowed the feeling down and sucked in large breaths of dank, humid air.

Dank, humid air?

I reached a hand out to the wall again as the icy tendrils of panic set in. *Where am I?*

Fuzzy memories filled my mind.

Air.

Wind.

A battle.

Hands on me.

Hands that belonged to a tall elf with huge pointed ears—

"Oh my Gods!" My fist flew to my mouth.

The powerful elf, Lord Godasara, had abducted me.

"Oh shit! Oh shit! Oh shit!"

I reached out again. My hand encountered more coarse grainy rock. I felt along its surface. It was rough, cutting my skin at times when my fingertips grazed over needle-like ridges.

Wincing, I brought my hand back to my side as panic threatened to choke me.

"I see you've woken up."

I shrieked when an eerily gravelly voice spoke from behind me. Heart pounding, I whipped around as a dim fairy light burst to life, illuminating a robed man. He stood three yards away, an endlessly black cavern behind him.

My jaw dropped. *I'm in a cave.*

Wet rock loomed in the vast underground chamber. I breathed in the musty, oppressive air, as the sound of trickling water reached my ears.

The hood of the man's robe was so long that it draped over his features, hiding him.

"Who are you?" My question came out all wrong. It was filled with fear, yet I wasn't powerless. The power of Verasellee, the Goddess of Time, hummed inside me. I could access it and wield it. Hopefully. "Where am I? Why did you take me?"

"So many questions." The man hunkered down, his robe covering his limbs.

My hammering heart picked up a rapid beat. Everything in me screamed to run away. But where?

An image of the dome I'd built around myself appeared in my mind. That magical impenetrable dome that I'd created when I'd woken in the field only a few days ago beckoned me.

The man straightened and stepped forward, his face still hidden by the hood of his robe.

I squeezed my eyes shut, determined to build that fortress around me once more.

"I'm afraid that won't work."

My eyes flew open to see him only feet away. He gazed down at me, his face a black hole of nothingness.

"You see, we've learned a thing or two since the last time we tried to take you. Our lord has woven a spell over you. It won't allow you to access the goddess's power, not until the ritual."

"Ritual?" I echoed.

"Yes, the ritual." He crouched again and entwined his fingers.

I recoiled when I saw his hands. Gray skin with blood-red veins streaked through the backs of his hands. His skin didn't look normal, not of fae, human, or supernatural descent. Not even of demon descent.

"What are you?" I inched back farther toward the jagged cave wall.

He laughed darkly before he lifted those awful-looking hands and slipped the hood from his face.

And when I saw him, my breath sucked in before a blood-curdling scream surged from my throat.

CHAPTER THREE
WYATT

I paced back and forth on the ruins of Shrouding Estate. The scent of ash and smoke burned my lungs, and coarse rubble skittered over the burned grass every time I took a step.

I'd been sending messages back and forth with Wes for the past sixty minutes, mobilizing more squads and working to procure a seer.

Bavar had been helping, too, but his squad needed to recuperate. The other two squads who'd fought with us were in a similar shape. Two SF members had fallen today, and countless more were injured.

"Major Jamison?"

I whipped around to see a fairy from Squad Nineteen. Soot coated his features, and his suit was torn at the sleeve.

"Nicholas Fitzpatrick is asking for you, sir."

A growl rumbled in my throat, my wolf on the brink of breaking through his restraints. I was still fuming that Bishop had pulled the vamp to safety. "I have no interest in speaking to that . . . *consultant*," I snapped.

The fairy shuffled his feet. "He's insistent he can help, sir."

My teeth ground together. "What we need is a seer, not a vamp intent on saving his name or salvaging his career by trying to fix what he did!"

"Sir." He dipped his head, then scurried away, taking care not to trip over the ruined wing that lay in a wreck of crumbled stone, exploded furniture, and jagged tree branches.

Since Lord Godasara had left, the Shroud Forest had grown quiet once more. Memories of the large trees swinging and fighting against us still seared my mind. I'd never seen anything like it.

But now, the towering trees were still and serene, as if they'd never played a role in the siege. Even the forest's creatures stayed hidden as though terrified they'd be commanded too.

A glint from something dark flapping in the breeze near the ruined castle caught my eye. I prowled toward it and bent down. A tuft of material was trapped between a block of stone and a shattered wooden picture frame.

I rubbed it between my fingers, then pried it free. It was the same material our SF suits were made of.

Lifting the fabric, I inhaled. The scent of sage filled my senses.

Lex.

His scent clung to the fabric, indicating it had been his suit. A heavy ache filled my chest, and I balled the fabric in my fist.

We'd lost him. Lex had been hit by a binding spell from one of the warlocks, effectively paralyzing him, before the warlock had unleashed a death curse.

I hadn't seen it happen, but Charlotte had witnessed the entire event.

I hung my head. Charlotte had already returned to SF headquarters at Bavar's insistence. She'd seen more horrifying events in her first week of active duty than most new members saw in their entire first year.

A lump formed in my throat. Some of the racing panic that had filled my veins since Avery had been taken abated. It wasn't just my mate who'd been compromised today. Lex and a wolf from Squad Nineteen, not to mention dozens of Fae Guard members, had been killed.

It'd been a bloodbath, but all of the blood had come from *our* side.

Not only was Lord Godasara still alive, but every single warlock had escaped.

I uncurled my palm, then carefully folded the material from Lex's suit before slipping it into my pocket. Even though Lex's body had already been recovered, I would give the material to Wes, in case the family wanted it. If not, I would add it to the pile to be burned as was protocol following a bloody battle.

I inhaled, my breath stuttering. It was a dark day for the Supernatural Forces. We'd lost two members who had been with us for years. *Two* brothers had fallen today.

My ears pricked when the sound of quiet footsteps came from behind me. Given his scent, I knew who it was before he spoke.

"Nicholas is emphatic that he has useful information," Bavar said quietly. "You need to talk to him."

Fury rose in my gut, like a raging inferno that threatened to destroy everything in its path. "I won't speak to him. He's the reason my mate was taken!"

Bavar crossed his arms. "How so?"

"He compelled her and fogged her mind. She would have been more aware, even able to fight if he hadn't done that."

"It's still not definitive that Nicholas was to blame for her condition."

I snarled. "According to who? Him? What's he still doing here anyway? He should be gone."

"He refused to leave." Bavar's heavy sigh followed, and I finally looked at my friend—really *looked* at him.

Bavar's orange hair was streaked with dirt and soot. And for once, he actually appeared his age. Tired lines streaked from the corners of his eyes, and pain was evident in his features.

Guilt hit me. He'd lost a squad member today. One of his men had fallen. He didn't need my shit on top of it.

"I'm sorry." I tore a hand through my hair. "I don't mean to take it out on you. With Avery gone, I'm losing my mind." I ripped at my hair. "I'm sorry, friend."

Some of the weariness lifted from Bavar's features. "I know, and we'll find her." He tapped his fingers on his thigh, then opened his mouth before closing it.

"What is it?"

Bavar sighed again. "You know, Nicholas is insistent that he didn't compel your mate."

I locked my jaw, forcing myself to take another deep breath, but a growl still vibrated up my throat because Nicholas had *bitten* my mate. *Touched* her. *Fed* from her. Under normal circumstances, I would have killed him for that. I almost had.

"And you believe him?" I bit out.

Bavar placed a hand on his dagger's hilt. "I do. You need to hear him out. I think he's innocent."

Innocent. I scoffed. I'd heard that line from Nicholas before.

Irritation flashed in Bavar's gaze, and in a blur his hand shot out, gripping my forearm as he reappeared beside me. He squeezed, effectively capturing my attention.

"You need to *stop* being a wolf right now, Wyatt, and return to being a commander. I know you're looking for someone to blame, someone to take revenge upon, but Nicholas said Marnee drugged them, and I believe him because she's gone." He loosened his grip, if only a little.

"Gone? What do you mean, she's *gone?*"

"We can't find her. The last time Marnee was seen was near the Jeulic wing."

"Is she dead?"

"No. Her tracking signal picked up an hour after the battle. It registered her location along with her vital signs. Her heart was still pumping, and she was three miles out. All of that was recorded *after* the elf and his warlocks disappeared, so we know she survived the fight."

"She abandoned her squad?"

Tight lines formed around Bavar's mouth when his lips thinned. "It appears so."

I curled my fingers into my palms. I was brimming for a fight even though we'd just finished a battle, but I reined in my temper. "Marnee actually left her squad." I said it more to myself than to Bavar, but only because that was unheard of in the SF.

"From what I can gather, yes, which means Nicholas's accusation could be true. We both know she's been acting unusual on this assignment, that she's due for a soak, and we also both know she was jealous of what you and Avery share. Given her previous odd behavior, her jealous antics, and now this—abandoning her squad—his accusation isn't that far-fetched. I think he's telling the truth."

"Motherfucker," I whispered as my wolf snarled inside me, but just as quickly, I suppressed his anger.

Bavar was right. I needed to control my wolf nature and return to being a cool-headed commander. I took a deep breath, then another.

Ever since Avery had been taken, I'd been letting my emotions get the better of me, but she'd been gone for two *hours*. Every minute that passed decreased our chances of finding her.

But that didn't excuse my behavior. I'd allowed my wolf's need for revenge to cloud my judgment. I was acting irrationally, and that wouldn't help me find my mate.

"Okay," I finally said. "I'll hear him out."

Bavar's shoulders relaxed, his death grip releasing on my arm. He beckoned for me to follow him.

We carefully traipsed over the wreckage. A few times, Bavar cast sorrowful glances at the ruined castle. For hundreds of years, this estate had stood against wars and sieges. Until today.

"I'm sorry about your family's home."

Bavar inclined his head. "My mother will not be happy, but quite frankly, I don't give a damn about the castle. We lost two lives today, and we didn't protect your mate. That's what matters."

I dipped my head in agreement. Every fiber in my body was focused on Avery and Avery alone, but she wasn't the only victim of this siege.

Every time we lost someone in the SF, we all mourned. Even though there were thousands of members in our elite organization, who didn't necessarily know one another, we were still brothers and sisters.

We were bound by duty—a duty that had called to all of us. We knew death was a risk when we took our vows to save and protect, and every time we woke up and donned our SF suits, we all knew that day could be our last.

But some days, that reality was starker than others.

"Has Wes told their families?" I asked when we rounded the Daphnis wing. I didn't envy Wes's job. He personally delivered the news to the family of each fallen member.

"He's going to hold off until tomorrow. He wants to make sure we have a plan in place to rescue Avery. Although, I imagine the families may already know since news has broken out in the capital about this battle. Twice, Lex's comm device has activated with calls from home. His wife has been trying to reach him."

"Shit," I muttered. "Do they have kids?"

"One. A boy, aged three."

My heart sank. "I hope Wes gets there soon, so they're not left wondering."

"Me too, brother."

"And I hope he tells his widow that we'll avenge Lex's death."

Bavar's jaw locked, and a flash of retribution shone in his gaze. "Yes," was all he replied, but that one word said it all.

My nostrils flared when we rounded another wing and Nicholas's vampire stench carried toward me on the breeze.

Every muscle in my body tensed when I set eyes on him.

He sat beside Terry in the sun, both seated atop boulders of broken stone. The trees around the estate had all fallen. Patches of bright sunlight now hit the ground.

Terry and Nicholas engaged in quiet discussion, and their soft words drifted to me.

"Tell me again what happened after you drank the beverage," she prodded.

Nicholas shook his head. Streaks of blood-matted hair hung across his forehead. It was his blood that coated the strands, after I'd beaten the shit out of him.

My fingers curled into my palms when images of him feeding off Avery again clouded my mind.

"We both felt the effects after we'd had a few drinks," he said quietly. "Avery said she began feeling dizzy, and I felt funny too. That's when I knew we'd been drugged."

Bavar and I stopped, letting them finish their conversation. I devoured every word, taking deep breaths the entire time. I needed to stay calm.

When finished, Terry lifted her eyes to mine and then Bavar's. Nicholas's shoulders grew rigid, and he slowly turned to face us with an apprehensive expression.

He'd already healed from the beating I'd given him.

The only evidence of my ferocious attack lay in the dried blood caking his face, hair, and body.

I'd nearly torn him limb from limb. If Bishop hadn't stopped me, I would have, and I wouldn't have regretted it.

Because seeing him atop my mate, between her soft thighs, while he feasted on her neck, had born a rage inside me that I'd never experienced before. And that rage had only flamed hotter when I'd heard her moaning and seen her writhing at his touch.

In that singular moment, my wolf hadn't cared that Avery still hadn't fully accepted us as her mate. In his mind, she was ours, and all he'd seen was another male grinding against her, wanting to claim her.

To my wolf, that had sealed Nicholas's fate. He would die.

Bishop had stopped me, but the pain evoked from seeing them together . . . so much fucking pain.

Because the truth was that unless the day came that Avery firmly told me our mating was never going to happen, which would force me to release my desire to claim her—to walk away from her—I would always view her as mine.

Slamming a hand through my hair, I looked away from Nicholas's carefully blank expression.

Terry finally stood and broke the silence. "I think

he's telling the truth, commanders. We haven't retrieved the thermos that holds the drink he and Avery shared, but my gut is telling me he's being truthful."

"Can his blood be tested?" I asked curtly. "For this supposed drug?"

Terry shook her head, and a flash of pain filled her eyes.

I cursed inwardly, berating myself for being so insensitive. It would have been Lex's job to test Nicholas for drugs, but Lex was gone.

Terry cleared her throat as a veiled mask descended over her features, her expression clearing. "As a vamp, he would have metabolized any drugs by now anyway. No trace would be left, so testing is pointless."

I nodded. "Of course."

"We'll find the thermos eventually and test the drink," Bavar added. "But right now, digging through the rubble for a thermos isn't a priority."

"No, it's not," I agreed. "Finding my mate is."

"There's another reason that I think he's telling the truth." Terry's eyes flashed daggers. "Why would Marnee disappear if she hadn't done anything wrong?"

Bavar and I shared a contemplative look. Terry's logic was solid. To have Marnee abandon her squad, especially after her bizarre behavior during the past few days, did paint her in a bad light. She very well could have drugged Nicholas and Avery, hoping the exact situation that had occurred would happen.

Because if we *hadn't* lost the battle, and instead I'd returned to the cell later than I did, to tell them of our victory, I could have walked in on Nicholas fucking my mate.

My breath sucked in.

Even if Avery had been drugged, even if Nicholas wasn't to blame, I would have murdered him.

"Terry's right about me being innocent, Wyatt." Nicholas's clipped comment snapped my attention to him.

My jaw locked as my gaze swept between Nicholas, Terry, and Bavar. I stepped closer to the vampire and inhaled, scenting for traces of deceit. I found none.

Still, I couldn't stop myself when I grabbed him by the lapels of his shirt. I hauled him clear off the ground until he was eye to eye with me.

He didn't try to fight. Not once.

I searched his eyes, his expression, his scent—I searched *everything* for a hint of trickery.

But all I found was remorse, and for a moment, the rage inside me faltered.

"I didn't mean to touch her, Wyatt. You can choose to believe me or not, but that's the truth. Just like it's the truth that I never raped or intentionally harmed your little sister."

My nostrils flared when he spoke of Lassa, my fingers curling more around his shirt.

For years, I'd carried burning fury inside me for the vamp. Even though the courts ruled that he'd never raped my sister, which I eventually agreed with, he'd still taken her virginity and seduced her. Lassa had only been sixteen. She'd still been a *child*. And Nicholas was old enough to know better than to believe everything a young woman told him.

But as a vamp, all he'd seen was an attractive female and easy sex.

He'd taken advantage of her adolescent flirting.

And *that* was what I'd carried with me, was what had made me hate him . . . until recently. I'd finally started to forgive him and had been ready to move on.

And now this.

"If it wasn't for the thrall she was under, this wouldn't have happened." I growled and gave him a rough shake. "Avery would have been able to fight back, and maybe that would have been enough for her to break free of *him*."

Nicholas still dangled from my hands, not even trying to physically defend himself. "Maybe that's true. Maybe if she hadn't been *drugged* she could have broken free from Lord Godasara, but your anger is misplaced. *I* didn't drug her, and *I* didn't compel her. *I* am not to blame for her fogged state. What you witnessed wasn't my thrall. It was the effects of a potent aphrodisiac."

A fire lit behind the vampire's eyes, and I scented his rising anger, finally sparking to life. "It was that siren who drugged us. She gave me the food and drink, telling me that it'd been packed for Avery and me in case we were stuck in that room for days. If anyone should be angry here, it's me. I'm a victim of her malicious actions, too, not just your mate. And furthermore, if you're looking for someone to blame, how about yourself? *You* wouldn't let Avery fight. *You* guilt-tripped her into going into that room with me. If she'd never been there, she wouldn't have drunk the drugged beverage. She would have been clear-headed enough to fight back. You play a part in this too, Wyatt. It's not all on me."

I abruptly released him, stumbling back. My chest heaved as his accusations cut deep. *You play a part in this too.*

For a moment, stunned silence surrounded us. Bavar and Terry stood motionless.

My wolf snarled inside me, begging me to rip Nicholas's head off, as my human mind sorted through his comments at lightning speed.

You wouldn't let Avery fight. You guilt-tripped her into

going into that room with me. If she'd never been there, she wouldn't have drunk the drugged beverage. She would have been clear-headed enough to fight back.

Gods.

He was right.

Absolutely *right.*

I hadn't wanted her to fight even though she carried that great power. I hadn't wanted her anywhere near the battle. But she'd wanted to be there.

And what if, for once, I'd suppressed my instinct to protect her and didn't beg her to stay out of harm's way? Nicholas was right. She was strong, so very strong.

Yet I hadn't allowed her to fight.

Fuck. I speared my fingers through my hair, balling the strands in clumps.

I wasn't blameless, far from it. But Nicholas had still bitten my mate and drunk from her.

I squeezed my eyes shut, the rage inside me threatening to return. As much as my human mind was trying to rationalize and accept that *I* was as much to blame for Avery's fate as anyone else, my wolf's was feeling anything but rational.

All he saw was another male on top of our mate right before she'd been abducted.

His mournful howl rose within me, and I knew when I opened my eyes that my irises were glowing.

Nicholas took an abrupt step back.

But it wasn't just Nicholas my anger was focused on. I shouldn't have forced Avery to do anything. I shouldn't have locked her in that room.

I dropped my chin, forcing down my wolf's anger as I struggled with the bitter feelings blazing through my soul.

I finally looked up, meeting his trepid expression. Our gazes locked and held. An eternity seemed to stretch between us. I took a deep breath, then another, before finally saying in a stiff voice, "If it's true that you didn't compel my mate, then I'm sorry for what was done to you."

Bavar's eyes popped, as Terry's mouth dropped open.

But I kept my wolf in check and didn't succumb to his bloodlust. No. It was time I faced some hard truths.

I wasn't blameless in this, but perhaps Nicholas was.

I waited for the vamp to respond, but my reaction had apparently robbed everyone of speech since neither Nicholas, Bavar, or Terry replied.

I gritted my teeth together. "I may be a wolf, but my human side is stronger than most wolves. I'm not a beast. My wolf doesn't control me. And if you remember, I fought my wolf nature for three months while Avery was my new recruit. For three *months*, I pushed her away even though all I wanted to do was keep her at my side." I grumbled. "So you can all stop looking so surprised that I'm capable of being rational."

Bavar at last snapped his eyes back to normal. "Nobody thinks you're irrational, Wyatt. We've all worked with you long enough to know that you're level-headed to a fault, but you're also a mated male werewolf now, and well . . ." He held his hands up in surrender. "We all know what happens to a male wolf's mind when that occurs. Rationality isn't always a bonded wolf's strong point, not where his mate is concerned."

My lips thinned. "Well, I'm going to prove you wrong." I eyed Nicholas carefully. "Bavar said you can help regarding Avery?"

Nicholas straightened, then brushed at his shirt. The image was almost laughable, since we were all covered in blood, dust, and grime, but I also knew he was still grappling with my rational response. Hell, only a few hours ago, I'd tried to tear his throat out.

Nicholas finally finished tidying his attire. "Possibly. I'm fairly certain that I read somewhere in the scrolls about Lord Godasara's favorite dwelling, but I can't remember the exact location. I'll need to return to the library to find it since I can't help but wonder if that's where he's taken her."

My heart pounded as hope surged through me. "Do

you think he'd still use the same dwelling that he did thousands of years ago?"

Nicholas shrugged. "Honestly, I don't know, but right now, unless the seer is able to give us a firm location for where Avery's located, it's all we have to go on."

"And there's no guarantee the seer will be able to locate Avery at all," Bavar added.

"How long until she arrives?" I asked Bavar.

"Within the hour. She was dealing with a case that couldn't be left unfinished, but that gives you an hour to travel to the library and back."

"Do we have portal keys?"

Bavar pulled a handful from his pocket. "More than enough. My uncle sent more."

Terry's eyes widened at the treasure in Bavar's palm and for good reason. Portal keys were precious and hard to come by, but Bavar was a royal. He had access to wealth we couldn't even contemplate.

My jaw locked. "In that case, Nicholas, we leave *now*."

CHAPTER FOUR
AVERY

My scream rang around me, echoing through the cave as it bounced off the walls. I scooted back on the rock, getting as far away from the grotesque *thing* as I could because the warlock that stared back at me made gargoyles look like fluffy teddy bears.

He wasn't natural.

He wasn't supposed to exist.

Sorcerers who turned this far dark were no longer products of nature.

They were abominations, a perversion of magic twisted so savagely that they were worse than demons walking in the underworld.

I finally stopped screaming, my throat dry and tight, but my chest still heaved. *Fuck, fuck, fuck!* I needed to get out of here!

The warlock watched my attempts at scrambling away with barely controlled glee. He obviously enjoyed the response he'd caused.

Sick fucker.

But how could I have stopped it? He was hideous, and everything about his appearance was created to provoke horror.

Blood-red veins crisscrossed his face, and his skin was a mottled gray and purple that looked like death. Sunken eyes with solid pitch-black irises watched me eerily from a face that resembled a skull. His skin was so thin that he looked like a walking corpse. And when he smiled—as if done just to terrify me further—I was awarded a view of needle-like teeth that appeared decayed and rotten, yet I had a feeling that they were strong enough to tear through flesh.

He was the thing of nightmares.

A twisted curse of death and magic.

I *knew* that I was facing a sorcerer who should have died long ago. Only terrible magic could explain why his soul still walked in this realm and how his body hadn't turned to rot.

"How old are you?" I finally managed through my raw throat.

His grin grew. "More centuries than you would probably believe."

"Are you as old as him? As that elf lord?"

His gaze grew sharper, colder, and all humor left his face. "You do not speak of my lord."

I swallowed, but it did nothing to relieve the sandpaper in my throat. The pounding picked up in my head again, my headache returning with a vengeance, and for the second time, I thought I was going to be sick.

"How?" I whispered. "How is it possible you're still alive? No sorcerer can live thousands of years."

"But I'm not a sorcerer. I've evolved. I've *become*. We all have." He waved toward the cavern behind him.

In the darkness, a group of obsidian eyes flashed.

My jaw dropped. *Oh Gods! They're all here.*

Roughly a dozen set of eyes watched from behind the hideous warlock crouched in front of me.

I dragged my gaze back to him. "You've all turned to dark magic to stay alive." I shook my head, the horror of that realization making me want to puke my guts out. "But that would take hundreds of human or supernatural sacrifices, even *thousands* of sacrifices to wield that kind of extended life and power."

He laughed. "Perhaps." But as quickly as his dark laugh came, it went.

Energy flashed behind him. Nobody said anything, but I could feel them there, watching and waiting.

But waiting for what?

A bolt of fear ran down my spine as goosebumps pimpled my skin and dread filled my belly. My breathing kicked up. My instinct told me something bad was about to happen. "What are you going to do to me?"

The warlock's mouth turned into a thin line, all idleness vanishing from his demeanor. "No more questions. You're coming with me, Goddess incarnate, and we're finally taking that great power from you."

His hand snaked out brushing against my wrist, but I whipped my arm back just in time.

With a growl, he lunged for me, but I jumped up from my seated position and dashed to the side. Fear propelled me, making me faster than seemed humanly possible.

Suspended fairy lights abruptly burst to life, illuminating the entire cave system. The other warlocks rushed forward, and my eyes widened as terror coated my belly in churning acid.

I had to get out of here.

I couldn't let them perform a ritual on me.

Who knew if I would survive it or not, plus I had a feeling that if they harvested the godly power inside me, it would be very bad news for *everybody*. Not just me. It could destroy this entire realm.

I darted to the edge of the cave, my side colliding with the damp, sharp rock as I called upon the power inside me. It broiled and simmered, like a volcano ready to erupt, but as soon as it pushed to the surface of my skin, something doused it, as if a fountain of water drenched me and sizzled its crackling flames.

"I told you it wouldn't work." The warlock tried to grab me again, his pitch-black eyes so cold and empty, but I managed to evade his attempt.

Knowing I couldn't use the goddess's magic to fight him since it was bound by the elf lord's spell, I crouched lower as the other warlocks formed a semi-circle around the divot I'd slept in.

"The Lord will not be happy if we magically subdue her." One of the warlocks crossed his arms, looking entirely unperturbed.

I bared my teeth, still on the balls of my feet as I readied for their next attack.

One of them swiped out, but I dashed away, bumping into the back wall. I was cornered, quite literally, but I wasn't going down without a fight.

"This is growing exceedingly annoying," another snarled. "Grab her."

Four of them came at me at once.

Instinct took over.

When one grabbed for my wrist, I dipped and rolled, then hissed in pain when the sharp rock floor needled my back, but I didn't let it deter me.

Another snarl of displeasure came from the warlocks as they tried to capture me, but I darted a foot out, catching one of them completely unaware as I swept his feet out from beneath him.

He fell with a groan, hitting the rock hard, and I shot to my feet.

Before the others could react, I kicked, catching one of them in the chin, before dipping low and coming up with a sharp uppercut to the stomach, right in the solar plexus.

A strangled breath escaped that one, and he stumbled back.

Somewhere inside me, I was vaguely aware that I was fighting these men. Truly *fighting* them.

Wyatt had said I'd been trained to fight at the SF even though I didn't remember it, but some part of me must have been aware. I didn't question my instincts. I followed them as I tried to claw my way out of this pit.

"Enough!" one of the warlocks yelled.

He swirled his hand, and a blast of magic seized me midrun, freezing me in place. Pain flared my nerve endings, and the goddess's power rumbled and exploded inside me, but as before, I couldn't work it free.

"The Lord will be most unhappy that you did that." Another warlock crossed his arms. The sleeves of his robe drifted up, and I got a glimpse of mottled skin with crimson spiderweb veins crisscrossing over his wrists.

"Perhaps, but the effects will wear off soon enough. Then we can conduct the ritual."

I remained immobilized, suspended mid-air. Only the tips of one of my toes touched the ground. The warlock's immense magic had literally frozen me.

My lips tried to twist into an ironic smile. Only days ago I'd frozen *them*. But I couldn't move my mouth. I couldn't move anything other than my eyeballs.

I fought against his paralyzing binding spell, but I didn't stand a chance. Dread again welled up inside me. With the goddess's power trapped and unable to be accessed, all I had were my wits and the apparent fighting skills I'd once been taught. But unable to move my body, I couldn't use my fists or legs.

"Move her to a more secure location. I will confer with the Lord as to when we will reconvene for the ritual," one of the warlocks said.

All of their robes were still securely in place, so they were merely the gravelly, chilling voices that spoke through the dark cave of their hoods.

My body lifted farther from the ground, and I swallowed a scream of terror. I wouldn't give them the satisfaction of hearing my fear.

I floated in the air under their command. Trickling water trailed down the cave walls, and my eyes widened when the entire cavern came into view. Tunnels dipped in every direction. Nooks and crevasses appeared down others. We were far underground. I knew that much.

Good Gods. I was truly trapped here.

The warlocks dispersed, most leaving down a tunnel in the opposite direction from the way I was being floated.

Only two warlocks accompanied my hovering body, neither of them speaking. My eyeballs frantically whizzed around as I searched for a way out.

One of these tunnels had to go up. One of them had to lead out of here.

I didn't know when they would release the binding spell, but the second they did I would be fighting and running again, which meant that I needed to get my bearings.

The dream I'd had at Shrouding Estate—the feeling of floating above the fire while seeing my body empty and cold beneath me—came back to me. Had that been a ritual?

If the ritual went ahead, I knew I'd be a goner. I *couldn't* let it happen.

The warlock in front of me abruptly took a turn down another tunnel in the cave. He maneuvered through a narrower portion, my body floating behind him.

A flash of color on the right caught my attention, and I managed to catch a glimpse of something lying on the floor in another divot.

A shroud.

The outline of a body.

Then it was gone.

"What was that?" I called shrilly, my words garbled since I couldn't move my lips.

Neither warlock answered. They continued down the tunnel, their footsteps silent, as if they didn't even touch the ground.

"Who's under that sheet?" I screamed.

One of them *tsked*. "So many questions. It is most annoying."

The other one grunted.

I screamed again. Who had been under that sheet? And how long had they been down here? Were they dead? Alive?

I clamped down on my frustration. If I wasn't alone down here, that meant they'd abducted others. But why?

Were there others in this realm who harbored powers from the gods? Were they going to harvest their powers too? Perhaps the ritual they wanted to conduct on me, was only one of many.

Shit. Shit. Shit. I had to escape.

The warlocks stopped when the tunnel walls grew too narrow for us to continue.

The one commanding the spell moved my body with a wave of his hand, and I glided over to the wall before being laid down in another divot. Similar to the area I'd woken up in, the ceiling in this area was low and round, yet sharp rock grazed my skin.

"Leave her, Malis." The taller one spoke in a gravelly voice similar to the one who'd woven the spell over me.

With a grunt, the magic evaporated.

My arms shot up, the magic no longer restraining me. With a jolt, I was on my feet. I lunged for them, but at the last moment, a shield erupted.

I slammed into an invisible wall, pain shooting through me. I hit it so hard that I bounced back and landed on my butt.

The sharp rock cut into my pants, poking my skin painfully. I still bolted to standing again but approached the invisible barrier more carefully.

The warlocks turned away, as if not giving me a second thought.

"Where are you going?" I yelled after them.

Of course, they didn't answer me, but at least I could move again.

I reached forward, then hissed in pain when my fingers connected with the shield they'd put around my newest prison cell.

I snatched my hand back, but my skin still burned. At least the binding spell no longer held me frozen, but I didn't understand what had just happened.

I'd been *certain* that they were going to take me to whatever ritual they'd spoken of, but then they'd cast that binding spell on me when I'd fought back. One of them had sounded displeased about that. He'd said something about the Lord, about how he wouldn't like the setback.

So what did that mean?

It felt as if my brain was moving at one million miles an hour. Panic creeped into my chest again, and I struggled to breathe.

No. Stay calm. Think!

I took several breaths of the dank, humid air and tried to piece together what I knew.

I'd fought back. They'd cast a spell on me. That had created a setback.

Okay. So warlock spells cast on me caused problems for them. Good to know. As for why that was, no idea, but I could definitely cause all sorts of problems next time they came back, which would force them to cast another binding spell and hopefully postpone the ritual again.

I just needed to keep fighting. Sooner or later the SF would find me, so I needed to stay alive until they did.

And if the SF didn't—

No.

I couldn't think like that. One step at a time.

Knowing I wasn't completely helpless quenched some of my fear. And thankfully, the pounding headache had abated, allowing me to think more clearly.

So what else did I know?

Before ending up here, I'd been at Shrouding Estate with Wyatt.

Wyatt. My heart squeezed. Where was he now? Did he know I was gone?

Yes! More memories slammed into me, not quite as fuzzy as before.

I'd been in the Whimsical Room with Nicholas. We'd been waiting, talking, and agonizing over all that was happening on the estate.

But then . . .

Things grew fuzzy again. I cocked my head, trying to remember.

We'd had something to eat and drink. Right?

Yes!

Oh Gods, the fairy beverage. We'd been *drugged*.

I squeezed my eyes shut, trying to concentrate, but everything after that turned murky. I only got flashes and feelings.

Arousal. Lust. Someone kissing my neck—no, *sucking* my neck. Nicholas must have drunk from me.

Then the door had banged open. Someone's rage had coated the room. *Oh Gods, that was Wyatt.* Then I'd been flying up and up, around and around. I'd gone outside. A battle had been waging around us. Wyatt had been holding me, but he'd been cursing. He'd been angry. So angry.

Wyatt had handed me off to someone, telling them something about getting me away. And then other hands had grabbed me, and I'd been flying again.

My skin chilled.

That's when the elf lord took me.

We'd whizzed through the forest, Wyatt calling for me. Wyatt had almost caught up with us, but then the trees stopped him and something pricked my neck, stinging me, and then everything had gone black.

The sting! That's when the elf lord had placed the curse on me that bound the goddess's power.

I lowered myself to the cave floor, my heart

pounding as I realized that I'd first been drugged by Marnee and then spelled by the elf lord.

Gods. WTF.

Neither of them had the right to do that to me.

I stomped my foot on the ground. If only I'd never been in that damned Whimsical Room. If I hadn't, I never would have been drugged, and then maybe I could have fought back using the goddess's power.

I swallowed the urge to scream in frustration. But dammit, if only I hadn't been in that damned underground room.

Fucking hell, Wyatt. Why did you guilt-trip me like that?

It didn't help that I didn't know if my friends had survived. For all I knew, Charlotte, Nicholas, and Bavar were all dead.

Fear clawed up my throat, but I forced it down and focused on my anger. I seethed inwardly, cursing Wyatt and his stupid overprotectiveness. Even though my body innately desired him, I was royally pissed at him.

Nostrils flaring, I stood again and approached the invisible barrier. The goddess's power buzzed inside me. If only I could reach it and use it. Her power was strong enough that I could smash my way right out of here.

Closing my eyes, I mentally reached inside my chest to where her power resided. It was there, swimming in its potency. I tugged at it. Pulled. Called. Clawed. Begged.

But as before, it didn't rise past my skin's surface.

"Shit!" Panting, I opened my eyes and cursed every single swear word I could think of.

Then I began pacing, needing to do *something*.

It didn't help that I still didn't fully understand how the goddess's power had gotten inside me, and I had no idea how to use it. But according to Wyatt, it infected me after the Safrinite comet shot past the fae lands, and then weeks later, it'd erupted, her power being born within me when the planetary alignment occurred.

I ground my teeth together at my lack of memories. I still didn't remember *any* of those details. Instead, my memories only started from the moment I'd woken up in the field outside of the capital with Wyatt and Nicholas hovering over me.

An image of Wyatt appeared in my mind again, snagging my attention. His dark hair, brooding moss-green eyes, and square jaw formed so readily.

"Wyatt," I whispered, my feet grounding to a halt on the rough rock floor. An ache hit my chest, despite my absolute irritation with him.

Because even though I was so mad at him that I could spit, I still craved him.

Mate.

That's what he'd called me. His *mate*. So did that mean my body also felt he was my mate?

How typical. So not only did I have no say in what I could or couldn't do around the SF, but I also had no say in who I got to be with?

Red-hot annoyance flared inside me. I wanted to shake my fist at the universe and all of her controlling mate-driven antics, but more than that, irritation hummed through me that was one hundred percent self-directed.

Because despite everything that had happened, I still had an irrational desire to be with him when all I wanted to do was slug him in the shoulder.

"Gods." I abruptly sank to the ground again, my fingers digging into my hair.

So much had happened in the past few days. I still didn't remember my life or the people I cared about. I still didn't know who I was or why I'd been chosen by the goddess. But I did know that I had to fight to get back to the life I'd once led, even if I didn't remember it.

A memory of Wyatt's tender embraces and soul-shattering kisses stole over me. *Fucking mate bond.* Even here, when I was possibly waiting to be executed in some sick ritual, my body still drifted to him.

How was it possible that in only days I'd begun

falling for him? Even though I didn't remember him, I was drawn to him as if I'd always known him.

As though my body remembered what my mind could not.

Shivers danced up my spine.

"I have to get out of here!" I lurched to my feet once more from the cold stone floor.

Vibrations from the invisible barrier skittered along my skin, making goosebumps rise. *Just use her power. Call upon all of it, and break through the elf lord's spell!*

The goddess's magic pulsed inside me despite the binding spell trapping it. I closed my eyes, concentrating again on her power. It flowed through my chest, down my limbs, and awakened my senses. Power strummed along my arms, growing and growing until electric energy crackled along my nerves. I just had to grasp it.

Heart beating fast, I concentrated on extending her power outside of me to the barrier. I imagined it hurtling out of me, into the glass-like wall and shattering the magic that kept me encased.

Breaths coming quick, I opened my eyes and coiled her power, letting it build and build, growing and burning, until it felt like it was going to explode.

Now!

I threw her magic with everything I had, arcing it through my body, to my hands, and out of my fingertips.

Hope exploded in me that for once maybe I could control it. Power rushed through my limbs as fast as lightning traveling across water.

Yes!

An explosion of her power reached my fingertips and—

An invisible shield slammed into my senses, knocking the goddess's power back inside me with so much force that I blew clear off my feet and was thrown to the back of the cave.

I hit the wall, my head cracking against it so hard that I saw stars.

Falling to the ground, my vision went dark before I slumped into nothingness.

CHAPTER FIVE

WYATT

The portal key dropped Nicholas and me off in a hallway. Only the corridors between the five gigantic libraries could be accessed if clearance had been preapproved to bypass the protective wards.

The underground libraries sat nestled under the city of Sofia. Humans that inhabited the streets above had no idea what lay beneath their feet.

"This way." Nicholas didn't waste any time. He whizzed toward the Sacramentum Library, one of the five humongous libraries that were protected in these ancient walls.

Around us, large columns rose, soaring thirty feet above. At their tips waited smooth stone. None of the gargoyles slept upon them, which meant it was still daytime here on earth.

Thank the Gods.

I didn't say anything as I followed Nicholas. Time was of the essence since the seer was on her way to Shrouding Estate to see if she could detect anything about Avery's whereabouts.

If she couldn't find my mate, the only clue we would have lay here, in this underground monolith, and from the previous abduction cases I'd dealt with I knew the longer Avery went unfound, the more likely it was that she wouldn't be alive when we located her. *If* we did.

My stomach seized, and everything inside me went cold.

No, I couldn't think that way. I would find her.

We reached the doors to the Sacramentum Library, and Nicholas pushed his way through them.

Inside, several gargoyles were working with other gargoyle representatives and their clients. A few lifted their heads. Those that did sucked in a breath when we passed.

Their reaction wasn't surprising. I was wearing my SF suit, which usually got a double-take, but I imagined Nicholas's appearance was what really caused the stir. The vamp's clothes were dirty and bloody. Not to mention, his hair was a mess. That was probably a first in centuries for the vampire.

Considering the man normally looked like a men's fashion magazine model, I begrudgingly realized he hadn't once complained about his soiled clothes.

"Master Godric!" Nicholas called when we neared the large stacks of ancient documents.

The gargoyle startled. He'd been standing by one of the stacks, perusing a shelf. A long cobalt-blue robe hung from his shoulders. He swiveled around toward us, the scroll in his hand forgotten. "Yes, Mr. Fitzpatrick?"

We came to a halt in front of him.

"I need the scroll that spoke about Lord Godasara's favorite dwelling." Nicholas put his hands on his hips. "Do you remember the one I'm talking about? We need it now. He's abducted Avery Meyers, and it's possible he's taken her there. Do know where that scroll is?"

The gargoyle's black eyes widened before he dipped his head. "I believe I do. I shall retrieve it immediately."

I stood behind Nicholas, my heart thrumming wildly as the gargoyle scurried away. Waiting. I was waiting again. It made me feel so goddamned helpless.

An image formed in my mind. It was of those warlocks surrounding Avery, hurting her, using her. I growled, the sound nearly turning into a whine as my wolf once again threatened to break free.

Nicholas gave me a sympathetic look.

"What do you think they're doing to her?" I asked. "Do you think we're too late?"

The questions slipped out before I could stop them. I knew better than to think this way. I knew better than to let my head get trapped in the game of *what if's*, but she was my mate. She wasn't a normal protectee. As hard as I was trying to, it was impossible to detach myself completely from the emotions ripping through me.

"She hasn't been gone that long." Nicholas's features softened. "She's strong, Wyatt. Don't forget that. You underestimate her. She'll fight."

I snapped my head back. "I don't underestimate her."

"Yes, you do." He sighed when a warning growl cut from my throat. "I'm not saying this to anger you, but it's the truth. I know you wolves are always so protective of your women, but most of them are not damsels in distress. It would serve your kind well to remember that."

Shock rippled through me, and I had the nearly uncontrollable reaction to punch the vamp in the face. "Is that what you think of us?"

Nicholas clasped his hands behind his back and stared at the tall bookshelf in front of us. His cool act didn't fool me, though. The tips of his fingers were twitching. "It's not what I think of you, it's merely an observation. I don't think there's anything wrong with wanting to protect your mate, but when those protective instincts become smothering, that's when it's a problem."

"Smothering?" I forced my hands on my hips 'cause now I was *really* close to punching him. "Is this coming from you or Avery?"

It suddenly struck me that she and Nicholas had been in the Whimsical Room for several hours. Just the two of them. And considering the scene I'd walked in on had only just commenced, that meant they'd had several hours to talk to one another before the aphrodisiac had kicked in.

What exactly had they spoken about?

Nicholas kept his attention on the scrolls, fingering a few at times. "My comments aren't coming from Avery. Not really. Although she did voice resentment about being in that room."

I stopped breathing, feeling as if I'd been kicked in the gut. Were those the last feelings my mate had toward me? Anger and resentment?

Gods, how could I live with myself—

"But I've seen similar scenarios play out over the years," Nicholas continued, none the wiser to how close I was to clawing my hair out. He eyed me, his blue eyes

54

as bright as crystals. "I've lived more centuries than you, Wyatt. You're not the first male wolf to act irrationally around his mate. And you're certainly not the first wolf whose possessive nature ended in a detrimental downfall."

My eyes narrowed, my anger at myself lobbying back to him. "I didn't realize I asked for your opinion on my character."

"You didn't, but you also attacked me this afternoon when I had done nothing wrong. Yes, I fed from your mate, and for that I am truly sorry, but I was not in control of my senses when it occurred. Believe it or not, until Avery and I had drunk that poisoned beverage, I'd made an effort to stay away from her. I'd even declined her offers to sit on the bed beside her."

"She invited you to the bed?"

He rolled his eyes. "Not sexually. She merely felt bad that I was sitting on the floor."

"You stayed on the floor?"

"I did. Believe it or not, I meant you no disrespect, commander. I still don't, and for once in your damned life, it would be nice if you recognized that."

His venomous tone left me speechless.

He cleared his throat, his gaze flicking back to the scrolls. "Just like I never intentionally hurt your sister."

My breath sucked in, but he continued.

"I'm not your enemy, Wyatt. The sooner you realize that, the better off we'll all be. I'm here to work with you, not against you. Yes, I'm a vampire. Yes, I would love nothing more than to fuck your mate—" He held up his hand when a growl tore from my throat. "But I won't do that. Would I have done that a few months ago when I first met her? Yes, I would have. In fact, I tried to, but that was before you had claimed her. She was still ripe for the picking then, and she responded to me most deliciously—"

"If you're trying to repair things between us, you have a really funny way of doing it." I advanced toward him.

He held his ground but raised a hand again. "I'm merely speaking the truth, commander. You've unfairly targeted me for years following that complete debacle regarding your sister. I've put up with it, only because I knew your intentions came from a good place—you wanted to protect Lassa, just as I know you also want to protect Avery. But again, I am *not* your enemy. I didn't deserve how you treated me in the Whimsical Room, even if you were acting on instinct. I didn't deserve that beating, and quite frankly, I'm sick and tired of being your scapegoat."

He smoothed back his hair, his fingers catching in the strands still slicked with dried blood.

I kept my hands on my hips as I mulled over his words. I still didn't know what to think of everything he'd said, but I didn't get a chance to ponder it further because Master Godric hobbled toward us from a deeper place in the library.

"I've found the document you seek." He held up the scroll in his clawed hand. "Let me show you."

The gargoyle hurried over to one of the many tables dotting the areas between stacks.

I shot Nicholas another glance, still reeling from the tongue-lashing he'd given me. My wolf growled. Of course, he had focused on Nicholas's crude comments about my mate, but my human side focused on the rest.

The part that said I'd used him as a scapegoat, and it was time I stopped.

It was possible the vampire had a point, but I didn't have time to think about that now.

Nicholas and I flanked the gargoyle as he rolled out the scroll. My tablet buzzed in my pocket just as his clawed finger trailed down the parchment to an area with a picture of mountains, rocks, and trees.

I pulled out my tablet, a message from Wes appearing as the gargoyle said, "It says here that Lord Godasara spent most of his time in the Elixias Mountains near the end of his life. Those mountains held intricate cave systems. Some say the elf lord conducted hundreds of rituals there, spilling the blood of humans and fairies alike to feed his dark magic."

My insides squeezed. My mate could have been taken to a remote location in the fae lands where human sacrifices had been made.

I finally read the message from Wes.

> The seer has arrived at Shrouding Estate. They're taking her to where Avery was abducted. Hopefully she'll see where your mate is.

Mate. Wes had called Avery my *mate*.

A lump formed in my throat, making it hard to swallow. In a gruff voice, I said, "The seer's at Shrouding Estate. I need to go back. Do you have maps of the cave system?"

Godric dipped his head. "We do, but I cannot guarantee how accurate they are."

"Send what you have to the SF's database immediately. Time is of the essence."

"Of course. I'll retrieve them now."

After the gargoyle departed, I rounded on Nicholas. "Where exactly are the Elixias Mountains?"

"They're three days travel from Bavar's estate, in the far north. It will be cold this time of year, and that area is nearly uninhabitable."

"Sounds like the perfect place to make sacrifices for dark magic."

Nicholas inclined his head. "Indeed."

"It also sounds like the perfect place to take a woman you've abducted. If nobody lives there, nobody will be a witness to anything."

Icy shards grew in Nicholas's eyes. "And if it's where they conducted rituals previously, it does beg the question—"

He let his words hang, and it felt as if the wind got knocked out of me.

Because he was right.

If that was where the elf lord had resided thousands of years ago in order to conduct sacrifices to strengthen his dark magic, then one couldn't help but wonder if that was what he intended to do with my mate.

I slipped my tablet back into my pocket, my hands shaking as alpha magic rolled through me. "We need to go. We've already wasted too much time here. If that's where he's keeping my mate, we don't have a moment to spare."

CHAPTER SIX
WYATT

Within seconds, the portal key transferred Nicholas and me back to Shrouding Estate. Dozens of Fae Guard still sat among the ruins nursing nasty cuts and battle wounds. Fairy healers dashed about, using magic to heal those they could and easing the pain of those they couldn't. Many more would die today. It was inevitable.

"You're back." Bavar hurried toward us. Clean orange hair curled around his ears, and his clothing looked new and spotless. Even his dagger was blood free. He'd no doubt used fairy magic to cleanse himself. Bavar inclined his head toward one of the estate's remaining wings that hadn't been completely destroyed. "The seer is here. She just arrived."

"Good. Let's see what she can find." Bavar led the

way as I filled him in on the visit to Bulgaria. "The information the gargoyles found in the library alludes to the Elixias Mountains. If the seer is unable to pinpoint Avery's location, we go there."

Bavar cocked his head. "The Elixias Mountains are days away from here. Lord Godasara and his warlocks must have used portal keys or advanced magic to transport themselves that far."

An image filled my mind of Lord Godasara's grin before he tumbled with Avery into a foreign-looking portal. The usual glowing red doorway conjured with portal keys had been absent. Only a circular void had appeared from thin air.

"I think he created his own portal when he took Avery." My heart kicked up, beating faster.

"He *is* an ancient elf." Nicholas's perfectly waxed eyebrows drew together. "He probably has enough magic to do that."

Bavar's expression turned grim. "The very few fae old enough to remember the elf lords' magic say it was terrifying in its strength. We saw only a hint of that in the battle. But we'll still get Avery back," Bavar was quick to add when he caught my expression.

"That's *if* she's there." Gods, my heart was beating so fast.

"I think she very well could be," Nicholas said. "The

cave system beneath those mountains was where Lord Godasara spent most of his time before his death, as has been confirmed by the scrolls. It's not unreasonable to believe he's there again."

"This way." Bavar took a sharp turn around a crumbling pillar of stone. "The seer's waiting near Merimum wing."

The three of us jumped over rocks and rubble as the scent of smoke filled the air.

The seer stood near a tipped over wall, a plush turquoise-colored couch in tatters behind her. Hair the color of onyx hung down her back, and a long skirt flowed from her hips. Her top billowed around her, reminding me of a flapping sail on a boat.

She turned when we approached, her crystalline blue eyes sharp and focused.

Bavar bowed. "Nolene, this is Major Jamison and our gargoyle representative, Nicholas Fitzpatrick."

Nolene dipped her head. "I hear you're looking for the woman who was abducted from this location earlier today."

"That's right." I placed my hands on my hips. "And we don't have a moment to spare. She's already been gone for hours."

"I've heard, and I'm sorry it took me so long to get here. I was working with a demon lord, and he wasn't inclined to let me leave until I finished what he'd paid for."

"Not a problem," I replied curtly. "Now, what do you need to locate Avery?"

Nolene brushed a lock of hair behind her ear. "Do you have an item of her clothing? Or a lock of her hair? Or something that she recently touched? I need something of her essence, the more recent she was in contact with it the better."

"I have something." Bavar pulled a piece of clothing from a bag he'd been carrying. "I figured you would need as much." He held up the bright pink sweater, almost guiltily. "While you were at the library, I retrieved this from the chambers you and Avery shared. It carries her scent, so I'm guessing she wore this recently?"

My gut tightened. "She wore that yesterday." My nostrils flared. Avery's fresh lilac fragrance wafted from the swath of fabric. "Will that work?" I asked Nolene.

"I believe so. Now, I might just move away from the commotion." She walked carefully over the rubble away from other SF members who cast us curious glances. The healers hurried about, not paying us any attention.

We followed Nolene to the forest's edge. Tree branches and broken roots littered the ground.

Once we reached a clearing, she stopped and

fingered the fabric between her hands. "I will need silence while I try to find her location. Please don't interrupt me."

None of us replied, yet the tension that oozed around us was palpable. Even Nicholas stood rigidly while my hands stayed balled at my sides.

Nolene closed her eyes and rubbed the fabric more. She stood quietly, her eyeballs moving rapidly beneath her closed lids, as if she were in REM sleep. A moment passed, then another. She shifted slightly from foot to foot, her body swaying as her long skirt flowed around her ankles.

In the distance, moans came from the wounded and shouts carried from those attending to them, but my attention stayed focused on the seer.

Nolene frowned, her eyebrows drawing together in a dark line. Her lips parted, then she said in an even-toned voice, "I see a forest and mountains. The sun isn't bright there. It's behind clouds. No. Wait." Her frown deepened. "The sun is completely hidden." Another moment passed, and her eyeballs moved faster. "I'm going down and down, far beneath the ground. There's no sun here. It's dark and cold, and I see rocks. So many rocks. She's surrounded by them." She opened her eyes. Her irises had turned milky, as if unseeing, yet I knew she was seeing so much.

I held my breath, and my heart beat faster. Unable to help myself, I bit out, "Are you able to identify anything more concretely? A landmark or a village near this underground area?"

Bavar grabbed my arm and squeezed, effectively silencing me, but damn it was hard to stand by and remain quiet when the seer's information was so vague.

She continued staring around us, her gaze staying fixed far away. "It's cold and dark. So very dark. And she's bound, trapped. Something holds her. It's keeping her from breaking free."

A growl rumbled in my chest, and magic flowed hotly beneath my skin. I would tear apart the men who took her, limb from limb, and I would enjoy every minute of it.

"Fear surrounds this place and so much dark magic. It travels through the rocks and around her. Something evil envelops this place, like a shroud." She blinked, and her eyes abruptly cleared. Once again, blue irises regarded us. She took a deep breath and then another. Placing a hand against a nearby tree to steady herself, she said, "I'm sorry, but that's all I can see. I don't have anything more."

I gritted my teeth together so I wouldn't vent my annoyance. Mountains. Trees. Rocks. Coldness. Underground. That was all we had to go on. That was it.

And that could have been hundreds of places in the fae lands.

Bavar, Nicholas, and I shared a frustrated look.

"Are you sure you can't see anything more specific?" I prodded. "Perhaps a landmark that's unique? Like the shape of the mountains?"

Nolene shook her head. "I'm afraid not. I just saw mountains. They could be anywhere, but wherever they are, it's far away and not near habitation. I know that much."

Nicholas crossed his arms, his fingers tapping his bicep. "It must be the Elixias Mountains. They're days away from any villages, and they're surrounded by trees."

Bavar nodded. "And there are cave systems, too, beneath the mountains. Nicholas is right. It's quite possibly the place, and right now, it's all we have to go on."

But what if we're wrong?

That nagging fear stole over me again, like a bad rash. We were taking a gamble again, only going off minimal information and hoping it was right, just as we had done after Avery had fallen ill from the Safrinite comet.

Nicholas's and my last hunch had turned out correct, when we'd whisked Avery to the fae lands at the cusp of the alignment.

Hopefully, this hunch would be right too.

"Thank you for your time," I said to Nolene. "Does Wes need you elsewhere?"

She gave a wan smile. "I'm always needed elsewhere. If there's nothing more for me to do here, I shall leave you for my next assignment."

"No, nothing further, thank you." Bavar gave a final bow.

After Nolene left, I faced Bavar. "We're going to need at least three squads. When I spoke with Wes earlier today, he said two would be arriving about now. Have you heard about a third?"

"No. In our last communication, he was still working on getting a third free. That damned fighting in Jakarta. It's taking so many of our resources."

My wolf rumbled. He paced within my belly, growling and snarling. His agitation seeped into my veins, making my heart race and my muscles flex. Because hearing that Avery was being kept somewhere underground which was dark and cold, and that she was being held against her will surrounded by dark magic . . . *Fuck*, it made both of us see red.

"We need to go. We can't wait for them." A part of me knew I was losing it again, but dammit, *hours* had already passed since my mate had been taken. Every moment she was gone, she was more at risk. "Who knows what they're doing to her. We need to get to her."

"And we will," Bavar said calmly. "But we can't go without proper backup. You saw how strong those warlocks are. Look at what they did to the Fae Guard." He swept his hand toward the wounded guardsmen, many of whom were still bleeding and sporting horrific wounds.

"It was the forest that did that. That damned elf lord can control the trees."

"And the Elixias Mountains are surrounded by forest," Nicholas chimed in. "Bavar is right. You shouldn't go without the right kind of backup."

It was on the tip of my tongue to ask him when he'd become an SF commander, but then I remembered what he'd said in the library—how he'd spoken so candidly and honestly about his actions toward Lassa and then Avery.

He is not your enemy.

Hana's soft words breezed through my mind. The Bulgarian libraries' healer, the witch who was nearly four hundred years old, had sensed the turmoil that constantly ran between me and the vamp.

But even she had known that Nicholas wasn't to blame for everything.

I took a deep breath, trying to stem my bone-deep

rage, and to reason with my irrational desire to run headfirst toward my mate. Because Bavar and Nicholas were right. If the Elixias Mountains and the surrounding forest were where Avery was being held, we needed a careful and covert plan.

It was the only way we could defeat the elf lord.

"I think we should go now and scope out the area." My nostrils flared as my mind whirled. I looked toward Bavar. "Just the two of us, so we know what we're getting into, and when the third squad arrives, all the squads join us, and then we attack."

Bavar nodded, a gleam shining from his eyes. "Yes, that works. You and I go now, and when the teams are ready to be mobilized we not only attack, we destroy."

CHAPTER SEVEN
AVERY

The warlocks stood around a large fire pit. Above us, the galaxy blazed in blinding colors of fuchsia, crimson, and turquoise. Magic bathed the realm, power from the great universe sparking my nerves as the Safrinite comet burned across the sky.

The warlocks joined their hands. Robes draped from their shoulders. They shifted and swayed, their chanting rising above the realm as the night sky was suffused in magic.

I screamed and fought against their restraints. My power was bound because that tall elf lord had tricked me. I'd come to this land, believing that my love walked in this realm.

But he hadn't.

And I'd realized that too late.

The elf lord joined the other warlocks, coming from the darkness to complete the sacred circle. His voice rose both low and high, deep and soft. A smile curved his wicked lips as my spectral form rose higher and higher.

I tried again to access my power, to freeze time, to stop the progression of this perversion of magic.

But it didn't work.

My power was ensnared by him.

And when my spectral form reached the apex above the fire, when the Safrinite comet bathed my spirit in fiery purple light, an explosion ripped the power of the Gods away from me.

My power shot from my chest, rushing toward the universe as the elf chanted higher, his magic creating a net around it.

Rage pummeled through me. All-consuming, soul-lashing rage. I gripped and clawed for the power that was mine. I would not let him take it.

But the sacred circle's great dark magic wove around me, capturing me as easily as a babe. I was as helpless to resist it as a human, as a mere mortal.

I lunged again, fighting my restraints, and I managed to snare the smallest bit of my power, just a tendril of what my kind commanded, but it was enough.

I threw my power at the elf lord, cursing him to a long and painful death, then thrust the remainder of my Godly power through the net, joining it to the Safrinite comet and the galaxy's magical systems.

When my curse hit the lord, he fell.

A smug feeling filled me as the comet zoomed across the sky, capturing the rest of my escaped power from the elf's net. It would spread my power into the galaxy. It would birth my prophecy, and he . . . I cast a scathing glance his way. He would—

The elf's chest rose.

No!

He hadn't died. My power hadn't been great enough to kill him. Instead, his eyes stayed rolled back in his head, his form frozen.

But his heart still beat.

Agony ripped through me.

He was still alive, but he didn't move.

And then it struck me, what my curse had done. It had tied his life to mine in a twist of fate, keeping him alive. Because I wasn't strong enough to fight him, not without my full power —my power that was currently streaking across the galaxy, joined with the comet, which would spread my power throughout the solar system. It wouldn't see this land again for thousands of years.

My spectral being drifted higher, my body still on the ground, but a tiny feeling of satisfaction filled me that even though I hadn't succeeded, the elf hadn't either.

My power would remain in the heavens, floating through

the stars. It would remain untouched until my curse birthed a prophecy of the heir who was worthy.

And when she was born, then I would rise.

And my vengeance would begin.

I shot upright from the stone floor, the dream barreling through me. Grimacing, I brought a hand to the back of my head. Thick wetness greeted my fingers. Congealing blood.

Damn. I'd taken a bad blow to the head, enough of one to knock me out.

Darkness surrounded me, only a flickering fairy light illuminating this part of the cave. I was still here. Trapped.

Head pounding, I wiped the blood off my hand on my pants and took a few deep breaths. Slowly, the pounding in my skull dulled.

"Gods," I whispered. The dream had felt so real, so *alive.*

I licked my lips, wishing I had a glass of water, but perhaps the warlocks and elf lord were so out of touch with humanity that they'd forgotten normal supernaturals had to eat and drink. Then again, they didn't seem to be the types that cared.

Despite my thirst, the dream tugged at me.

It'd been so *vivid.* And it seemed important.

More important than being abducted by a psycho elf lord?

My lips parted as the crashing realization hit me that the dream was similar to the others I'd had since waking up in the field, except this one was in exact detail and perfectly clear.

My eyes popped.

Because these dreams weren't just dreams. They were memories.

The goddess's memories.

Yes!

I squeezed my eyes shut, recalling the dream. Relief swept through me that for once I was able to remember it clearly.

It came back to me like a movie, the image reeling through my brain. The goddess had shot her power into the galaxy, and that power had glued itself to the Safrinite comet and the rest had dispersed throughout the solar system.

She'd believed that her power would return to be born inside someone who was worthy, because she didn't want the elf lord to have the power. No. She wanted to recapture her power so she could enact her revenge.

So what does that mean? That I now had her power inside me because I was the lucky winner of the Safrinite comet's poisonous blessing? The heir?

But the goddess had done that on purpose. She'd

flung her power into the galaxy to keep it away from Lord Godasara and had spelled it to be born again.

But why?

And then it hit me.

She'd done that because she *wasn't* dead. If she was in a dormant sleep—as Nicholas had said she could be—she could be awoken, just like Lord Godasara had woken.

Nicholas's findings in the Bulgarian libraries returned to me in a flurry. *"Verasellee, the Goddess of Time, was rumored to have touched down in this realm where she was captured and enslaved by a circle of supernaturals, and was then forced into a dormant state."*

And she wanted her power to be born again, because she wanted to reclaim it.

I didn't know if I was right, but it was a logical guess, which meant that I needed to not only escape here, but I needed to find *her*.

I didn't know how I knew that, but the knowledge hummed to the center of my soul. Verasellee had been trying to show me what had happened. She'd wanted me to figure this out.

As if realizing that I now understood, her power throbbed and zapped against my skin, trying to break free yet still trapped inside.

I pushed to a stand and began pacing inside my

rocky cell, my feet scurrying over the rough floor. The goddess had been trying all along to show me her plan.

My head throbbed anew from the weight of this new knowledge.

I eventually stopped pacing and stood silently by the barrier. I had no idea how much time had passed since the two warlocks had deposited me here, but it'd been long enough for me to have that dream.

I tried to see around the corner, to where the figure we'd passed—the one lying in another rock enclosure and covered with a sheet—waited.

"Hello?" I called to them quietly. "Can you hear me? Please say something if you can."

Silence.

Who was under that sheet? Another prisoner? A dead person?

The goddess?

It seemed almost too good to be true that she could be so close.

I shifted where I stood, trying to see into that cell again when a figure emerged from the darkness of the intricate cave tunnels.

I yelped and nearly fell over. It was *him*, the elf lord.

Giant ears rose alongside his head, and his dark eyes regarded me steadily from an olive-green face as he stepped closer to my cell. Two warlocks followed behind him.

Gods, he was ugly.

"Malis." The lord dipped his head, and one of the warlocks came forward to stand next to him. "Unlock your shield."

"Yes, my lord." The warlock's tone was full of reverence.

I scrambled to the side of the enclosure, my eyes darting about as I tried to think of a way to run and escape the second his shield fell.

Malis lifted his hand, and a shimmer of magic erupted from his fingers. He did it so quickly and easily. I didn't even hear him mutter a spell.

Damn, these men were so powerful.

The barrier to my cell crackled, then disappeared, and I knew it was my only chance.

I launched myself at the elf lord, calling upon whatever training I'd once been taught.

Lord Godasara held up a hand, but he was too late, obviously not anticipating that I'd fight back physically and so violently, but fear was making me desperate.

I crashed into him, both of us going down in a tangle of limbs.

Those terrible-looking ears, so large and alien-like, brushed against my hand.

His lips peeled back in a wicked grin, but before he could say anything, I punched him in the face, my fist connecting with his flesh like it was a punching bag.

An awful crunching sound followed, and the lord's grin disappeared as he howled in pain.

A roar of rage erupted from Malis as the warlock reached for me.

But I anticipated that too. Kicking out, my feet swept underneath him, catching him at his Achilles tendon. His legs buckled beneath him.

He began to fall at the exact moment I pushed up.

Before either of them knew what had hit them, I was on my feet and running.

I dodged down the tunnel, my hair flying behind me as the cold rocks pressed in on me. A snarl rose from behind, and I knew I only had seconds until they caught up.

Sprinting, I searched wildly for a way out, but all I saw were snaking tunnels and dark corners.

I was going so fast I nearly forgot about the other person who was trapped down here.

I passed their cell a second later, intent on seeing if they were awake too. If, by any luck, fate was on my side, perhaps they wouldn't be dead and we could fight off the warlocks and elf lord together and make our escape.

Yet when I reached their cell, the sight left me even more shocked than before.

The cell was empty.

A deep, dark chuckle rose from behind me, and I didn't give the prisoner another thought. I began sprinting again because I had to escape. Run. Get out. *Now!*

The tunnel reached the cavern I'd been in previously, where the other warlocks had all encircled me before I'd fought them off.

It was dark, the fairy lights absent. My eyes widened, searching for any light that would help me navigate this underground tomb.

Footsteps came from behind me.

I lunged to the left just as a rush of air kissed my back.

Another wicked chuckle followed.

I nearly gagged. Good Gods, he was enjoying this.

Of course he is. He's a hunter, and you're his prey. Every hunter loves a good chase.

I reached another tunnel in the cave. The light was almost completely gone now, the little that had been illuminating the tunnel outside of my cell not able to reach these darker regions.

"Fuck!" I whispered, then snapped my lips closed

when I realized all sound carried in this underground system.

"You're going to pay for breaking my nose," a sinister-sounding voice called from behind me. "I'm going to enjoy making you scream."

Bile rose in the back of my throat, but I didn't stop moving. I bumped into a cold rocky wall, the light completely gone here. Inky blackness surrounded me, yet I kept moving.

I reached my hands out in front of me, so I didn't collide with another rock, but I wasn't running anymore. I couldn't. I was blind. Only darkness surrounded me.

Keep going. Don't stop!

Terror clawed up my throat, threatening to tighten my windpipe and slow my breath. My heart felt like a battering ram in my chest, hammering over and over and over again.

Trickling water reached my ears, growing louder with every second. The trickle turned into a streaming sound, then a churn.

"I wouldn't go that way if I were you."

I stopped midstride, my heart thumping when the sound of rushing water grew so loud it nearly drowned out the elf lord. *Shit!*

Plastering myself against the wall, I stopped and

waited. Panting breaths rushed out of me, and I slapped a hand over my mouth, trying to quiet my sounds.

I listened.

Waiting.

The rushing water continued to my left, and the sickening realization came that it was probably a river. A horrible, rushing river in this underground cave that most likely flooded some of the tunnels and went to who knew where. If I fell into it, it wouldn't matter that the elf lord had taken me. I'd be dead from drowning.

Straining, I tried to hear past the rushing water, but I couldn't.

Knowing that I needed to do *something*, I inched along the wall again, my palms flat against the rock wall behind me as I felt for another tunnel away from the river.

I crept closer to where I'd run from, my ears pricked for the slightest sound.

A hand abruptly wrapped around my throat, then hot breath rushed against my ear.

The heavy scent of radishes—the elf lord's godawful scent—flooded my nose. "Did you really think it would be that easy to escape?" he whispered in my ear.

I kicked and thrashed but it was as if I wasn't even trying. His grip didn't budge.

"You will never escape from me. *Never.*"

His hand tightened around my throat, his palm so large that he encircled my entire neck with one hand.

I choked, my lungs squeezing when my air was cut off. Panic bloomed inside me, and I clawed desperately at his grip, but the elf lord wouldn't let go.

He squeezed harder.

Stars crept into my vision. I couldn't breathe. *Couldn't breathe!*

"After I take the power from inside you I'm going to enjoy ending your life. You shouldn't have fought me. If you hadn't, I would have made your death quick, but because you did, I'm going to make it hurt."

The last thing I heard was his dark laughter before unconsciousness claimed me.

I AWOKE to the feel of cold air flowing over my limbs. A shiver struck me and then another. My eyes cracked open to see three glowing orbs above me.

With a scream trapped in my throat, my stomach muscles curled as I tried to sit up, but I couldn't move.

A spell trapped me. I recoiled internally, remembering the feel of the elf lord's hand wrapped around my throat. Aching pain shot through me when I tried to swallow.

How long ago had that been? Minutes? Hours?

Breathing heavily, a crackling sound came from my right, and my eyes shot that way. A fire rose from a pit in the earth.

Oh, Gods. No!

Above, the glowing orbs took shape. Moons. Behind that, the galaxy.

The ritual.

Oh, shit.

Everything around me looked eerily familiar, the dream come to life.

No, no, no! I mentally thrashed as hard as I could, trying to break whatever spell Lord Godasara had placed on me, but my limbs wouldn't move.

"Now, now, none of that," a cold voice said on my left.

I tried to turn my head, to see who had spoken, but nothing would move. Nothing!

A hooded face appeared above me, and I choked on a sob. Gray-colored hands lifted and pushed the hood back. A terrifying grin spread across the warlock's face, and fear that burned as hot as acid scorched my skin.

"Is she awake?" the elf lord asked. He stood just beyond the warlock, his hood also pushed down. Large, curved ears rose from the sides of his head. Whatever damage I'd inflicted on his nose no longer showed.

He'd healed. Gods, he'd *completely* healed since I'd punched him square in the face.

"She's awake, my lord."

"Good. Bring her to me. It's time we begin."

The warlock lifted his hand, swishing his fingers precisely through the air. As before, I didn't hear him say a spell. His magic was either so strong that he no longer needed spells or he whispered it so quietly I couldn't hear him.

Cold, icy fear raced down my spine. It was just like the dream. The moons and stars shone throughout the galaxy, and I was powerless.

I knew what was to come. I knew what they were going to do. They were going to take the goddess's power and then kill me.

Damn you, Wyatt! Damn you for not letting me fight!

Tears threatened to fill my eyes.

I'd never felt so helpless.

CHAPTER EIGHT
WYATT

A cold northern wind blew around us as we crouched at the edge of the Derian Forest. A hundred yards ahead, the cave entrance waited at the base of a mountain.

The Elixias Mountain range rose ominously, its peaks swirling in the clouds which drifted in front of the three moons. Snow blanketed the highest tips, yet here at the base, late autumn weather still prevailed.

Northern fae flower species sprouted among the short grass in the field, their little buds of purple and black reminding me of night and frost.

The forest's dark trees rustled in the breeze, their bright leaves shining like silver in the moonlight. I eyed them warily. The elf lord could control trees, and right now, we were surrounded by them.

Bavar crouched at my side. We'd staked out the area earlier and were now ready to attack.

Behind us, three full SF squads waited. Twenty-five SF members made up our team.

Like me, Bavar was too invested in this assignment to sit on the sidelines, even though the rest of Squad Three was on a mandatory break after the attack at Shrouding Estate.

That also meant the squads at our backs were all fresh and ready to fight. We'd placed them strategically so they had the best view of the cave entrance, scree field, and forest.

"The so-called sacred circle obviously feels safe up here, since they haven't cloaked their scents." I growled. "Smug bastards."

"Indeed," Bavar replied quietly. "But we'll still need to move quickly, and you'll have to lead."

"There's no way I wouldn't be leading this." My wolf was itching to run free again. Ever since we'd picked up Avery's scent near the cave's entrance when Bavar and I had scoped the place out, he'd been fighting to break free. Bloodlust clouded his mind, and he wanted nothing more than to rip Lord Godasara to shreds.

"Are we ready?" I asked curtly.

"Almost." Bavar shifted, tapping something on his tablet. "Wes received the information the Bulgarian libraries had on the cave system. He's now scouring the SF database for additional info. The more intel we have, the better. I'm expecting a reply from him within a few minutes, but if they don't find anything new, we'll be relying on you and the other wolves to track their exact location."

I grunted as hot blood pumped through my veins. "I won't have any problem doing that."

Avery's and Lord Godasara's scents were all over the cave's entrance, along with the warlocks' odors. Lucky for us, they hadn't bothered with their cloaking spells, which meant they didn't think anyone knew they were up here.

My fingers curled into the dirt beneath me, my fingernails already turned into claws.

"Ah, here's his reply." Bavar tapped his screen again. Magic shimmered from the device, cloaking its glow so anyone who happened to look upon us wouldn't see the tablet being used.

"Anything?" I asked.

"Yes, the maps are downloading now."

Our wristbands vibrated when the download was complete. I pulled it up, my eyes scanning the intricate channels. A route had already been mapped out for us. In lightning speed, I memorized the twists and turns, remembering which forks led to what. They snaked downward, deep into the ground below the mountain. Large chambers waited near the bottom of the tunnels.

I pointed to a series of natural occurring indentations. "That's most likely where she's being held. Those would be easy to block off to become cells."

"Agreed," Bavar replied.

I whipped my suit off until my naked body gleamed in the moonlight. "So it's agreed that you'll stay out here with Squad Seventeen to cover us should any of the circle escape and try to ambush us when we exit?"

He gave a curt nod. "We'll have your back."

"Squads Five and Twenty-seven," I called over my shoulder. "We're moving out. Cloaking spell, now."

The two witches in our group activated the spell. A shimmering dome descended over us.

The squads and I emerged swiftly from the trees. I shifted mid-run, the other wolves in the squads doing the same. We moved so quickly we turned into a blur.

Within seconds, we were at the base of the mountain, the gaping entrance to the cave waiting. Inky darkness greeted us, but Avery's scent called to me. It was so much stronger here.

My wolf whined, his paws slapping silently against the rock as we entered the cave and loped through the tunnels. Nothing greeted us. Nobody stood watch. No warlocks patrolled the ground.

They'd either grown complacent or they knew something we didn't.

My mate's scent grew denser the deeper we moved into the tunnels. I could only hope we weren't too late.

Squads Five and Twenty-seven followed behind me, the fairies and other wolves keeping my pace. The tunnels sloped downward as the humidity in the air increased.

The squads' sorcerers and witches brought up the rear but still moved quickly using a combination of levitation spells and propulsion blasts from their SF suits. We all kept together.

A snarl rumbled in my wolf's chest as we wove deeper into the caves, moving steadily downward. Seconds turned into minutes. Down and down we went.

Avery's scent grew riper, and my wolf's eyes illuminated the dark cave systems, automatically grabbing any light in the air and projecting it so I could see.

A few fairy lights had been left alight. They grew more abundant the deeper we went.

A whimper worked its way up my wolf's throat. Avery's scent was so rich now it smelled as if I were in a lilac field.

Trickling water danced down the walls, and my wolf's ears pricked forward as our frantic run slowed. We were close to where they kept her. I could sense it.

The squads moved silently, our feet and paws like one. Years of honed practice infiltrated our movements.

I ground to a halt when we reached a fully lit chamber. Silence greeted us.

My ears pricked again, searching for heartbeats.

My wolf found none.

An anxious whine erupted from his throat. My human mind, which was still functioning parallel to his, revved into full panic mode. Avery wasn't here. *She wasn't fucking here.*

But I could scent her. She'd been here recently.

My nose met the cave's floor and began sniffing. My wolf broke into a jog, then a run, tracking my mate's scent through more dizzying twists and turns.

Within seconds, we were moving upward again.

"There's another exit!" Major Reichman, Squad Twenty-seven's commander, seethed from behind me. "Dammit! How did we not have that on the map?"

Anxiety laced through my wolf's senses as his movements picked up. Avery had been here. But now she was gone. She'd been moved again. She was no longer here.

Oh Gods. No. What if they'd moved her to a second location? How would we find her if they'd portal transferred her elsewhere? We only had this one location. The seer hadn't seen anything else, and the libraries had provided no further guidance.

"We'll find her, brother."

Major Reichman's comment cut through my senses like a knife, and with a jarring realization, I became aware of the high-pitched whine that had been emanating from my wolf.

"So there are two entrances." Major Reichman moved beside me, still running as I tracked our way through the tunnels. "But that wasn't in the information from the Bulgarian libraries or the SF database. We obviously need to update our maps."

She continued to sprint, easily keeping up with my wolf. Standing a foot shorter than me in my human form, with short hair and a pixie-like face, one could easily overlook her. But her small size was deceiving. Many had underestimated her because of her diminutive stature and feminine looks, but the female vampire was entirely lethal.

"Strengthen the cloaking spell!" she commanded to the witches at the back who controlled it.

The hazy dome shimmered as we moved swiftly toward the surface. We didn't have backup out here if the warlocks were waiting. *Shit.*

Avery's scent grew stronger the closer we got to the cave's second entrance. I could barely keep control of my wolf's mind. He was nearly psychotic with need to find her.

Fresh air flowed through the tunnel, prickling my senses. Moonlight beams appeared next.

The cave's hidden second entrance appeared.

"Fan out," Major Reichman commanded.

Under the witches' cloaking spell, with weapons raised, we departed the cave in formation.

But the elf lord, warlocks, and Avery weren't here either.

The Derian Forest waited. Moonlight shone through the trees, and something flickered in the distance. I slowed, taking in the forested land north of the mountain, as my wolf chuffed with the need to keep running, but that flickering light drew my attention again.

My wolf's hackles rose as I assessed what looked to be a glowing fire pit about half a mile away.

Something wasn't right. There wasn't supposed to be anybody around here to light a fire. Not a single soul resided in these woods, nor were there any nearby villages. Bavar and I had thoroughly staked out this entire landscape before the three squads were called in.

I ground to a halt, dirt kicking up around my wolf's paws as everyone's movements stopped around me. Major Reichman paused at my side.

My wolf whined, inclining his head toward the flickering light.

"I see it." She cocked her head. "It looks like a fire."

I shifted in an explosion of magic until I was in human form again, not caring about my nakedness, then held out my hand to her. "Ocular lens."

She whipped it out of her pocket and handed it to me. The device was a tiny circular lens the sorcerers had created. They were lightweight, indestructible, and allowed one to zoom in to an area with 1000x focus.

"Why the hell would someone be lighting a fire all the way out here?" I brought the lens to my eye. "And more importantly, where did they come from?"

I zoomed in on the area.

A large fire rose from a pit in the earth. Around it, robed men stood, their hands joined as they formed a perfect circle. My blood ran cold. "Shit. All of the warlocks are there." I took in the surrounding area. "But I don't see the elf lord or Avery—"

Avery's body lay motionless on the ground.

"She's there! They left the cave system right from beneath our nose."

"Fucking hell," Major Reichman muttered. She tapped her comm device. "Major Fieldstone? Get Squad Seventeen here now. We found Avery. They're not in the caves. They've taken her to the north side of the mountain."

I kept the lens on my eye, tracking the lord's and warlocks' activities. My wolf growled inside me, urging me to shift again and protect our mate. Nostrils flaring, I forced myself to take deep, even breaths as I willed myself to stay in control and not to lose it.

But fuck, it was hard. Everything in me screamed to go now and save Avery, but at this moment the elf lord and warlocks were oblivious to our impending attack, and it needed to stay that way. One wrong move could cost my mate her life, and we would be at our strongest if all of us were present when we attacked.

"ETA?" I asked Major Reichman.

She tapped her wristband. "Less than ten minutes. They're moving fast."

"We move fast and hard when Squad Seventeen arrives. Are the cloaking spells going to hold?" I barked at the witches.

The two witches from Squad Five were working together. They wove their hands through the air. The cloaking spell brightened. "Yes, sir," one of them replied.

My gaze shifted back to where Avery was, and I lifted the lens again.

Lord Godasara stood over her. His hood dropped back, revealing his hideous face and huge pointed ears. I cocked my head. His lips were moving, but he was too far away for me to hear what was being said. He and the warlocks were chanting in unison.

My gaze narrowed.

The lord moved closer to Avery and placed his hands over her body, hovering them above her chest.

"He's doing something." I grew rigid, then rose to my full height, knowing we were too far away for them to see. I watched for a moment longer, then a chill raced down my spine. "It's a ritual. The fire, the joined hands, the chanting . . . they're doing a fucking *ritual*. We move now."

Major Reichman shook her head. "We wait for Squad Seventeen to arrive."

"We don't have time to wait for backup!" I snarled. "If they finish that ritual, it could be too late!"

"Shit," she muttered under her breath. "You're right. Okay, Ranger, Lopez, McConnel, Abara . . ."

She began issuing orders to her squad as I shifted instantaneously again. My wolf emerged in an explosion of vengeance.

"Change of plan," Major Reichman said into her device to Bavar. "We're attacking now. They're doing a ritual on Avery. Move as fast as you can."

"Dammit!" came Bavar's reply. "We'll be there in five minutes."

I growled and nudged the vampire commander's hand. I knew for at least a few minutes we wouldn't outnumber the warlocks and elf. We'd just have to move fast and quietly to catch them unaware and hope that

Bavar was able to mobilize the other squad behind us quick enough.

"Go!" Major Reichman ordered.

We flew from the mountain in a burst of speed, moving silently and unseen under a strong cloaking spell.

The wolves, fairies, Major Reichman, and I flew to the front of the group. The six remaining SF members of witches, sorcerers, and a half-demon fell behind us.

Cold air whipped across my face. I held onto control of my wolf's mind just enough to keep him from doing anything rash. I'd never had to restrain him like this before during an assignment, but then again, I'd never had my mate at the center of an assignment before either. He was straining to break free of me as bloodlust again threatened to consume him, but I controlled him tightly.

Despite that, blood still pounded through his ears as the ground thundered beneath his paws. In less than a minute, we'd covered the ground to Avery's captors and their pit, and we broke into a circle around them, moving slower as our training kicked into action. Our cloaking spell still hid us, and our presence seemed to be undetected by them, which meant that they hadn't bothered with enchantments around their perimeter which would have alerted them to our approach.

As before, they weren't bothering to hide themselves, which meant they were incredibly arrogant, or simply so powerful they didn't need to.

A low growl rumbled in my wolf's belly, but I stopped him from letting it reach his throat.

The warlocks continued chanting, their words a low hum as they spoke in an ancient tongue. The hoods of their robes hid their faces, but I imagined that their eyes were closed. They all appeared completely lost to whatever dark magic they were weaving.

The elf lord stayed positioned over Avery, his eyes closed as his large ears rose above his head. Potent energy shot from his hands in an explosion of sparks, and Avery's body abruptly shuddered. Her back arched, her lips parted, but no sound came from her.

Rage exploded inside me as Squads Five and Twenty-seven moved into place.

Magical scents flooded my wolf's nose. Interweaving fragrances of magic and spells assaulted him, but it was enough to give us a clue as to what was happening.

It wasn't a binding spell that trapped Avery, something else did. Its oily scent reminded me of sulfur mixed with heady Russian sage. It stung my wolf's nose it was so strong.

A flash of a memory reached me, that scent triggering the moment the lord had abducted her. Just before he'd taken Avery, the elf lord had placed his fingers on her neck, muttering a spell. Before they'd disappeared, the same scent had come from his magic.

It was extremely powerful magic. I knew that much.

When the last squad member slipped into place, I was about to issue the order to attack, using the comm device attached to my wolf's leg which was woven with spells that allowed telepathic communication, when a Squad Five member's message abruptly came through.

We have another victim at three o'clock. They're under a sheet. Species and gender unknown. But they're breathing. I just saw movement from the chest area.

My wolf paused, the words to attack dying in my mind. His lips curled back to reveal his lengthy canines as he struggled to resist my domination and attack regardless.

I held onto my wolf enough to reply, *Do we know it's a victim and not one of them? It could be a volunteer for this ritual.*

A pause that felt longer than a millennium passed before the SF member replied. *I don't know for certain, sir. I just know we have another body on this side that's covered in a sheet. They appear alive.*

Something scratched at my mind, something that felt a lot like guilt, but I shoved it down. We didn't know if the figure under the sheet was another victim or one of them, and right now, all that mattered was Avery. I needed every inch of manpower to get her out.

Then we focus on Avery and Avery only.

Another pause came and went before the SF member replied. *Yes, sir. Attack at once?*

Yes. On my mark. My wolf crouched lower as I sent out the signal to those around us. Everyone readied. We would attack fast and hard, catching the warlocks and the lord entirely unaware.

A signal came from Bavar just as I reached the end of my countdown. They were two minutes behind us.

Two, one, I communicated. *Now!*

In an explosion of magic and weapons, we leapt toward the sacred circle.

CHAPTER NINE
AVERY

Lord Godasara stood over me, his hands hovering above my chest. Bone-clenching, all-consuming fear exploded through my body when something abruptly ripped me apart. I screamed, yet no sound came from my lips. I clawed and fought, but I didn't move.

Instead, a fracturing feeling sawed me in two, splitting my chest at the breastbone as searing pain engulfed me like fire.

I was being cleaved.

Hacked apart.

I was dying under his spell and couldn't stop him.

I thrashed and yelled again, the pain so great it threatened to annihilate every fiber of my thoughts. It burned. Oh fuck, it burned! Such raw flaming torture scorched my soul that scream after scream of agony ripped from my lungs, but as before, no sound came out.

An explosion rocked my chest.

The goddess's power erupted to the surface of my soul, bathing me in her strength as the force of the Gods seared my being.

A moment of hope surged through me. Her power was free! It was no longer contained.

I stretched and reached for it. If I could manipulate her power again, I could stop time. I could run away. Escape. Break free.

But my mental efforts only clawed air.

No!

And that was when I understood what he was doing.

The elf lord had ripped my soul from my body, yanking it from my flesh and bones until I hovered as a spectral entity above my lifeless form. Yet without my body, I couldn't wield the goddess's magic. I was simply a vessel. My soul would transport the goddess's power to them, but *I* couldn't use it.

A sob wracked my chest, but it was only an emotion, a feeling. Without my body, I was nothing but an entity that was weak and powerless. I wasn't a goddess. I couldn't fight back. Not like she had done all of those millennia ago.

What was happening now was just like the dream,

only now, I wasn't a spectator. I was the victim, and damn if that didn't make earth-shattering *rage* consume me.

My spectral form rose higher and higher, drifting toward the warlocks and fire pit, clearing the air above their heads. On the other side of the pit, a figure lay on the ground draped in the sheet. Their chest rose.

Alive. That person is alive.

A flash of awareness shifted in me. The goddess's power yearned for what lay under that sheet. I could feel the body beneath calling to it, begging the power to enter its form.

Oh Gods. I'd been right.

It's her. Verasellee is under that sheet.

But as soon as that thought came to me, it went. I was drifting closer to the warlocks now, heading toward the fire. The lord and warlocks continued to chant and sway, and I knew that when I reached the apex of the fire it would be all over.

I would be dead. My soul would be obliterated, and the elf lord would have won. The goddess's power would transfer from me into him, and then darkness would cloak this realm as he rose to power.

I wanted to close my eyes, so I wouldn't have to witness the destruction of myself and this world, but in this spectral form I had no control over anything, and I continued to see it all.

A flash of movement came from my left. Then my right. Then all around.

An explosion of beings shot toward the circle— werewolves, fairies, witches, sorcerers, a half-demon, and a vampire. They moved so incredibly fast that they blurred into a motion of color and fur.

It happened so quickly that I barely had time to process it just as a warlock fell. A huge wolf had jumped onto his back and ripped his head clear from his body in less time than it took to blink.

Then another warlock fell when a fairy yanked the hood from his head, revealing the awful skull-like face and mottled skin. A blade glimmered in the moonlight, then cleaved the warlock's head clear from its body. Black blood gushed from the decapitated warlock before he slumped to the ground amidst flashing fangs and sword-wielding hands.

My spectral soul slammed into a wall before I reached the apex, as though hitting a concrete block.

Behind me, another wolf—this one even bigger than the last—leaped onto the elf lord, a blur of fury and snarls. My eyes bulged when a sense of knowing, of recognition, nearly overwhelmed me.

Wyatt!

I'd never seen him in his wolf form before, at least not that I could remember. I screamed internally for him, hoping he'd see me, but no sounds came out.

Wyatt took the elf lord down, his massive jaws going for his throat. Like the others, he was using the element of surprise to his full advantage, going for the kill shot immediately and not taking any chances.

But at the last moment, the elf turned and Wyatt tumbled to the ground, turning into a ball of rolling fur before he was back on his feet and attacking the lord again.

A blast of magic shot from the elf's hand, yet Wyatt surged to the side as the curse shot past him and exploded into the ground.

Rage erupted inside me just as my spectral form moved unexpectedly toward my body, my soul naturally seeking my corporeal form now that the elf lord no longer commanded me.

And then I slammed into it.

I AWOKE to the sound of snarls, screams, and the potent scent of magic. Life breathed back into my body as my eyes flashed open.

The elf lord and Wyatt were battling next to me.

They were a blur of dueling magic and potent alpha power as each tried to tear the other apart.

Waves of alpha energy rolled from Wyatt, hitting the lord again and again.

To his credit, the elf lord didn't fall. He stayed on his feet and continued to shoot curse upon curse at the massive werewolf intent on destroying him.

Wyatt dodged each spell, his movements impossibly fast as guttural snarls rose from his throat again and again.

But despite Wyatt being incredibly strong and a gifted battle strategist, I knew he wouldn't win. The elf lord's dark magic was too strong, too powerful. The element of surprise was wearing off. He kept pushing Wyatt back, gaining the upper hand. But then a shift of movement suddenly came from the north.

I sat up, my limbs finally in my control again.

Another hint of motion came from the north. The trees. They were . . .

Dear Gods, they were *moving.*

A massive branch from a tree abruptly shot out. It swiped into an SF member, knocking him clear off his feet as he sailed fifty yards through the air before landing with a bone-sickening crunch.

I leapt to my feet, not realizing that doing so would distract Wyatt.

An ear-piercing yelp reached my ears, and Wyatt fell to the ground just as a burst of bodies came from the trees as more trees shifted and fought.

It was absolute chaos.

But then I caught sight of Bavar's orange hair, which shone auburn in the moonlight.

A sharp sense of relief stole over me. He was alive, and he was here!

Wyatt and the elf lord continued to battle just as Bavar's sword rose in his hand. The long metallic blade glinted in the moonlight as the fairy commander's other hand raised his dagger.

He and a dozen other SF members leapt into the skirmish just as the elf lord drew his arm back. A curse was balled in his palm.

"Wyatt!" I shrieked in warning.

Wyatt dodged at the last moment, my scream alerting him to the curse that had been aimed at his head.

Another thump came from behind me when a tree walked—actually *walked*—into the fight. Its giant roots heaved from the ground as the monstrous forest became alive, working as a silent army.

Good Gods!

A head rolled from a warlock when Bavar sliced it clear off his shoulders from behind. The fairy arced through the air, his body moving and twisting in a graceful dance as Wyatt rushed the elf lord again.

I whipped back and forth, not knowing which way to look or where to stand. No matter where I turned, bloodshed was spilling all around me. I scrunched my eyes closed, willing myself to pull on the goddess's power.

Come on, come on, work!

It burned and zapped inside me, but like when I'd trained with Charlotte, I didn't know how to readily pull it to the surface to use. At least it wasn't bound anymore. Whatever spell had trapped it before was gone, the ritual no doubt needing it free.

But I still couldn't readily control it.

My eyes flew open. *Dammit!*

I searched for a weapon or stick, or *something* that I could use to fight with. I grabbed a partially burned branch from the fire. Even though the end was burned, it felt sturdy. It would have to do.

Hackles raised, Wyatt leapt again at the elf lord, catching him square in the chest.

The lord stumbled back, but dipped at the last moment and avoided Wyatt's snapping jaws.

I circled them, looking for a way to jab at the elf while avoiding getting in Wyatt's way, but they were moving so fast.

Wyatt snarled, his wolf crouching low again as his snapping teeth went for the lord's ankle.

I screamed when the elf lord threw another curse Wyatt's way, and in retaliation I slammed my stick into his back. It was enough of a surprise for him that the spell misfired, missing Wyatt by inches.

Wyatt lurched out of the way, just as the elf rounded on me, but then Wyatt lunged upward in a frenzied burst of speed, clamping his jaws down on the elf's hand.

With a vicious tear, he tore the appendage clear off the lord's arm as blood sprayed across his muzzle.

My jaw dropped as a wretched cry rose from the lord's throat. Another cursed spell balled in his good hand. Red murderous fury shone from Lord Godasara's eyes.

Wyatt jumped back, his lips curled in a ferocious snarl as the magic grew around the elf.

I tried to hit the elf with my stick again, but another tree moved and dipped, blocking me. Branches suddenly came from everywhere, shifting and hitting at the SF members who were fighting so valiantly that I would have cried at the beauty of it if it wasn't for the threat to their lives.

I ducked at the last moment when another branch came at me, managing to avoid being hit, but a small female vampire wasn't so lucky. A tree's wickedly sharp branch impaled her clear through the stomach. Her eyes bugged out, her face paling in the moonlight.

Another tree swung, hitting Bavar from behind, catching him completely unaware.

The fairy commander pitched forward, righting himself at the last second just as a warlock threw a curse at his chest.

I hurtled my stick at the warlock, knocking him in the head as I screamed a warning to Bavar.

The warlock hunched forward, but it didn't stop his curse from flying.

Bavar spun, his body dipping just as the curse shot past him, missing him by millimeters. It exploded into the ground, leaving a black crater full of rock shards and crystalized dirt in its wake.

Rage again bubbled up inside me at how closely a friend had come to death. Energy zoomed down my arms and through my senses, and that deep, all-consuming power vibrated inside me. But still it wouldn't unleash.

Fucking hell!

The trees didn't stop coming. They continued to move, advancing toward the group, and I suddenly remembered that Bavar had said that the ancient elf lords could commune with the forests.

They could control them.

Another snarl tore from behind me. The elf lord lifted his arm, the stump a mess of congealed dark blood. Despite the vicious wound, he didn't appear weakened or deterred. Already the bleeding had stopped as he continually battled Wyatt again and again.

Each curse, each spell, each movement from every participant in this fight was designed to murder and kill.

There were no second chances here.

This battle was for blood and vengeance.

And only the side that won would have any living left.

Wyatt leaped again, his massive body twisting and spiraling in a powerful explosion just as the elf lord unleashed another curse.

My scream got trapped in my throat when the curse kissed Wyatt's fur, alighting one side of his body on fire. But it didn't stop Wyatt. He slammed into the elf lord, knocking him clear off his feet as his wolf opened its mouth, intent on going for the throat again.

Flames licked one side of his body, the scent of scorched fur followed by flesh reaching my nose.

But Wyatt wasn't letting that stop him. I knew he'd let himself burn to death if it meant saving me from the elf lord.

Panic suddenly birthed itself inside me, feeling like death.

Before I knew what I was doing, I was running toward Wyatt, leaping and dodging the spells and branches that hurtled through the air like explosive confetti.

A deep, primal instinct rose inside me to protect him, to protect what was *mine*, and a fury unlike anything I'd ever felt rocketed down my nerves, over my skin, and into my pores as though giving birth to life itself.

A rattling and vibrating sensation grew in my chest. The ancient, terrifying power that had been locked in my veins skittered and skated along my nerves like electrical currents rushing over my skin.

The elf lord's remaining hand clamped down on Wyatt's jaws, just as Wyatt bit into the elf lord's neck.

A chilling whine rose from Wyatt as the lord's hand singed his fur and skin, more flames crawling up his body as they both tried to destroy one another.

Over his bloody muzzle, Wyatt's eyes met mine.

Time seemed to slow even though I knew I hadn't done it.

A keen intelligence reflected in his wolf's irises, and I knew it wasn't just his wolf I was looking at. It was Wyatt. A millisecond of silent communication passed between us.

He was going to die to save me. He would take the elf lord down now, but in the process, the elf would kill him too.

And that knowledge of Wyatt's intentions birthed a flurry of speed and rage through my soul and into my body until the world became a blur around me.

A blast rocked my chest as the goddess's power erupted out of me of its own accord. Purple light bathed my sight. Ire blossomed like blooming petals of hate and malice.

The realm stopped.

Time ceased.

Movements froze.

All-consuming power washed over me again and again.

I flew through the paralyzed world until I reached Wyatt and the elf lord. The goddess's power roiled from me in steady waves. I soothed the flames on Wyatt's body, dousing the fire which would have killed my mate if I hadn't stopped it. The flames were silent and unmoving, not one flicker as time held still. With a burst of my power, I managed to smother them completely.

Because Wyatt was my mate.

He would die to protect me, and I would die to protect him.

That thought was there and then gone.

I pried Wyatt's massive lupine body from the elf lord's grip, picking his wolf up as if he weighed two pounds instead of hundreds. In a blur of movement, I darted to the far side of the mountain, my stomach churning when the scent of Wyatt's scorched flesh and burned fur reached my nose. He was hurt, injured. Perhaps beyond full repair, but he would live.

Still, he could be scarred. And he'd done that all for me.

I'm sorry.

Laying him down gently, at least fifty miles away from the battle, I breathed heavily from the exertion, then raced back to the mountain's base.

One by one, I removed the SF members from the scene, whizzing and running in movements so fast I knew I was a blur, all while keeping this realm frozen in time. My body ached and my mind screamed for rest, but I wouldn't stop.

Because I was time itself.

A goddess incarnate.

And nothing would stop me from protecting those I loved.

I carried them all, over and over and over. Miles of land passed underneath my soles. Then hundreds. There were twenty-five SF members to transport, and I would move them all, living and dead, until every last one of them was out of harm's way.

When the last member of the squads was safe, I returned to the silent scene, knowing that my work wasn't quite done. Fatigue rolled through my body, but I didn't slow.

The sheet was still draped over the body that had been placed on the other side of the fire—the body that some kind of ancient instinct told me was *her*.

Slowly, I approached the draped form, and the power inside me hummed and swelled. *Yes*, it seemed to say, *yes, go to her.*

I pulled the sheet from the body, my breath catching at what I would find underneath.

A woman lay as still as stone.

Her chest no longer rose, but a part of me knew that was because time had stopped all movements in her, too. Because her powers were not in her body. They were in *mine*.

My gaze traveled over her brown skin, the glossiness of her black hair, and the perfect shape of her features. She was beautiful. Magnificent. Utter perfection cut into flesh and blood. A beauty that was not to be possessed by mortal man or magical supernaturals. Her beauty was reserved for the Gods and the Gods alone.

A fierce protective instinct surged through me.

I wouldn't allow her to die, not at the hands of such evil beings who threatened to cleave my soul in two and rip her otherworldly power away from its rightful owner.

Bending down, I lifted the goddess in my arms, slowly and reverently. She didn't stir, but the power hummed and flowed through me, as if caressing and encouraging.

In a speed of movement, I took her to where I'd lain the others. Sweat poured down my forehead, but I didn't stop. Her power vibrated and swelled inside me as a growing heaviness filled my limbs. I was growing tired and weary. I'd frozen time for so long, and my body—which was barely stronger than a human's—was not used to commanding such great power.

I knew that I couldn't keep this up, not forever, but there was one final act I had to do.

In another blur of movement, in which my limbs felt heavier and more sluggish, I zoomed back to the fire.

The elf lord and his remaining warlocks stood frozen around it. As before, when they'd attacked us at the inn, the elf lord seemed aware of what was happening. I'd felt his watchful gaze and assessing stare then, and I felt it now too.

He couldn't fight me, but he could *see* me.

But it wouldn't stop me from doing what I knew

must happen to ensure the safety of the fae realm. My stomach churned at the thought. Even though I didn't remember my past, I knew I wasn't a murderer. I'd never willingly hurt somebody, let alone taken their life.

But I also knew there wasn't another way, not if I wanted to protect innocents.

"And now you will all die," I whispered.

I picked up a sword from a fallen SF member. At least three SF members were dead, their faces pale and their bodies lifeless. They deserved proper burials, and they would have them when we returned to earth's realm.

But their deaths wouldn't be in vain.

I gripped the sword tighter and focused on the feel of it and only it. Detaching from reality was the only way I would be able to do this. Because it had to be done.

I wouldn't allow the warlocks and elf lord to live.

This would end here and now. No more blood would be spilled for the sake of Lord Godasara's insatiable hunger for power.

I went to the lord first, thinking it was only fitting to take down the leader with one swipe from my blade.

Muscles quivering, I lifted the sword. Fatigue rolled through my body, my control on the goddess's power slipping, but I *wouldn't* let him live, not even if doing so killed me right here and now.

Nausea churned in my gut. *You have to do this.*

I positioned the sword at my side and imagined it arcing toward his neck and cleaving his head from his shoulders. A twisted smile streaked across my face at the thought of ending his life so easily and so simply.

With a firm hold on the sword, I swung it toward the elf's neck as my hold on Verasellee's power slipped even more.

And when it was about to reach his neck the elf lord's lips moved, and one simple word flowed from his lips.

"Wait."

It was enough of a shock that my grip faltered and my hold on the sword slipped. Instead of slicing it down and through his neck, I hit his arm, slashing his skin wide open.

A groan came from him, then more words followed.

"You can't kill me," he said quietly.

He was talking. How was he talking when I'd frozen time?

Rage bloomed in my chest. He was stalling, trying to waste my time until I weakened more and he was able to break completely through my hold.

But I wasn't a fool. I lifted the sword again. "Yes, I will."

"But if you do, she will die."

His quiet sentence made me pause. Damn him, but it made me *pause*. "What?"

"Our souls are linked. If you kill me now, Verasellee will die too."

Sweat dripped from my forehead. I was failing fast. I needed to kill him and all of the warlocks *now*, or we risked another bloodbath. "You lie. You're just saying that so I won't kill you."

A dark laugh drifted from his lips. It made my skin crawl. "You can tell yourself that if you like, but go ahead, kill me and see what happens."

The sweat poured out of me, and I struggled to keep my breathing even. My muscles strained, the goddess's power rumbling so strongly inside me that my legs were growing weak. Another twitch of movement came from my left, from one of the warlocks.

His hand had moved.

Crap! I was running out of time.

I almost laughed at the irony of it. I was wielding power from Verasellee, the Goddess of Time, and I was running out of time.

But I didn't have her strength. My body was never designed to carry the power of the Gods.

"She will die as soon as you kill me. Killing me, kills her."

I stumbled back, the sword in my hand clattering to the ground.

I pictured the goddess again. Her pristine beauty, her flawless skin, her body that looked human yet screamed *other*, and her fierce determination not to let the elf lord take her power.

For two thousand years, she'd been kept in a dormant sleep.

"Why did you link with her? Why did you make her dormant?" I asked as another flash of movement came from my left. A second warlock had moved. I only had minutes, maybe not even that. My breathing had increased, as Verasellee's power flowed hotly through my veins.

I was failing fast, but I needed to know.

"I didn't want us linked. Her curse unwittingly started it. In fact, I tried to kill her after the ritual. With her power in the galaxy, I no longer had need of her, but that was when I learned that our souls are entwined. *She* did it. *She* cursed me when I tried to take her power. A horrible, awful curse that has plagued me ever since. In trying to take her power, she cursed me to die, but instead it linked us, so I've had to keep her alive in a dormant sleep, just as I did myself until the comet returned."

"So if she dies, you die."

He laughed darkly again. "Careful, human. If you're thinking of killing her to kill me, there will be repercussions."

I snorted quietly. Of course his first conclusion was to think that I'd kill her to kill him. Because that was what he would have done. No feelings. No remorse. Just boom. She would be dead, and he would have her power.

Another flash of movement tickled my peripheral vision. A third warlock had moved. I nodded toward them, "Well, if I can't kill you, then I suppose I'll have to settle with killing *them.*"

His eyes widened slightly, as I picked the sword back up and whizzed over to the warlocks.

"No!" he screamed.

But I didn't let his wrath deter me. Using the last ounce of the goddess's power, I severed each warlock's head one by one in a furious dance of death and blade.

Their heads didn't roll or fall. Gravity didn't work when time stood still, so their heads stayed on top of their bodies, yet I knew as soon as I released my hold on time, they would drop like rotten tomatoes to the ground.

Sweat was dripping down my face like raindrops when I finished. Black blood coated the thin sword.

But I had done it. I'd killed every last remaining warlock, and I didn't feel one iota of guilt.

The elf lord twitched, then one of his fingers moved. "You will pay for that!"

I met his gaze. Hatred swirled in his eyes like burning embers. His power was returning while mine was failing.

I have to get out of here. I had no doubt he would kill me in a flash once he was able to fully move, which meant I needed to incapacitate him. But how?

Already, his hand was healing and regenerating, but it wasn't growing fast. With a sickening swallow, I knew what would buy us time.

Raising the sword, I swung it behind my back. Shock lined the elf's face, his mouth opening in a roar, but he didn't anticipate what I had planned when I aimed low.

The force of my blow, with the goddess's power careening through me, sliced his legs off at the knee.

Howling pain ripped from his mouth.

"Have fun healing from that." A sick feeling had my stomach almost hurling. So much blood. So much gore. But I had to protect Wyatt and my friends.

I began to sprint away, knowing I would vomit if I didn't get away from here.

I whizzed through the air, getting closer to Wyatt and the others, but then I had to slow to a steady run when a sharp pain cut like daggers through my skin. Seconds. I only had seconds until my grip on Verasellee's power disappeared.

The night blew around me, even though the realm remained still. My legs felt like jelly. It seemed as though anchors had attached themselves to my ankles, making me feel sluggish and weak. Behind me, I felt the elf lord's power growing.

He would break out. My hold on him wouldn't last much longer.

Keep moving!

Air devoid of sounds whipped past me. The ground became a blur as I forced myself to push with everything I had.

And when I reached the SF squads I'd saved, still frozen in time miles away, I finally relinquished my hold on time, the world abruptly turning again.

Everyone blinked, confused expressions forming on their faces. Wyatt's wolf lunged to a stand, his eyes wild.

They were the last thing I saw before my eyes rolled back, and I fell to the ground.

CHAPTER TEN
WYATT

One second my wolf was battling the elf lord, the next he saw my mate falling to the ground. My wolf forced the shift, and I sprang toward her just as she collapsed. "Avery!"

Night-kissed wind caressed my face and naked body when I slammed into the ground beside her. Pain seared my side. I'd been engulfed in flames, but the fire was gone. Pink skin now graced my body where I'd been aflame, but the newly healed flesh tore from how quickly I'd moved.

Fuck. That hurt.

But at least I'd moved fast enough. Avery's head fell onto my palm, breaking her fall. My skin began knitting itself together again, the burns healing more as I called, "Avery!"

But my mate didn't move. She was out cold. I assessed her for injuries but only found a small injury to the back of her head, the blood cold and the wound already healing. It wasn't recent.

I whipped around, expecting to see another curse being thrown at me from the elf, but . . .

All was quiet.

The elf lord and warlocks were gone. And it was as if my wolf had known that.

"What the actual fuck?" someone said. The shuffle of feet sounded beside me. Then more cursing and additional notes of confusion.

"How did we get here?" someone else asked.

"Where are the warlocks?" a third called.

I vaguely became aware that my surroundings were unfamiliar. The mountain was no longer at my back. It lay to my west, miles in the distance.

And there was no elf lord. No warlocks. No skirmish. The trees were still. Nothing waited around us except for quiet wind, moonlit leaves, and shadows from the surrounding hills.

"Wyatt." A hand touched my shoulder. Bavar stared down at me. "I think she stopped time again."

I glanced down at Avery. She looked so pale and weak, and suddenly it all made sense. She *had* frozen time again. It was the only thing that explained why my body was no longer engulfed in fire and the split-second change of events. But Avery had sacrificed her wellbeing to do so.

Gods. She'd done it to save us.

"Yes." I cradled my mate to me, then gently stood, holding her in my arms.

Someone began handing out clothes to the naked wolves. On autopilot, I slipped on a pair of loose shorts, vaguely recalling that I'd discarded my suit before shifting, but one of the witches was already on it, using location and transport spells to retrieve our fallen equipment and SF clothing. Nothing was ever left behind.

I gazed down at Avery again as my skin continued to knit and heal. I could hardly believe that she was with me and safe again. I squeezed her, just to ensure that she was real.

Warm skin pressed into me. Long lashes rested on her lackluster cheeks, and her head lolled onto my forearm, but she was *alive*.

I inhaled her scent, her rich lilac aroma tingling my senses and making my wolf whine in gratitude. The steady thrum of her heart beat quietly. It was like music to my ears.

I took in a deep, heaving breath. Emotions clogged my throat, making it feel thick. Avery was alive and with me, but that didn't mean the threat was over. That elf bastard still lived.

A protective instinct surged through my veins, and I held her tighter to my chest. "We need to get back to the SF headquarters. She's not safe here. If her health deteriorates from leaving the fae lands, we'll deal with it."

"Agreed. We have just enough portal keys if we move in groups of three or four." Bavar began issuing orders, and I took in the scene around us.

Most of the SF members were standing. Dazed expressions covered their faces, but they were alive.

My breath sucked in. All alive except for three.

My chest tightened when I saw Corporal Hanson from Squad Seventeen. She was in her second year at the SF. Her unseeing eyes gazed skyward. A death curse had brought her down, her chest singed beyond repair.

Beside her lay two additional SF members. Each had been placed side by side, hands folded over their chests. One looked broken, as if his entire body had been pulverized. I vaguely remembered seeing someone sail through the sky, being hit by one of the giant trees before landing on the rocks. Corporal Eder hadn't stood a chance from that kind of assault.

And beside him lay another member, in service at the SF for over ten years. Corporal Zucik of Squad Twenty-seven had also taken a spell directly to the chest, a singed crater left in its wake.

"Did Avery move us?" Major Reichman staggered toward me. She clutched her stomach, a wicked wound beneath her palm. It was already healing. She was lucky. If the tree branch had pierced her heart, she would be dead. Pain was evident on the vampire commander's face. "Did Avery bring us here, and bring . . ." Her jaw locked. "Did she bring our fallen here too?"

A lump formed in my throat. Gods it had been a disastrous week for our organization, but I knew that the only explanation for the rest of us being alive was my mate.

"Yes. She must have stopped time again and carried all of us here."

Major Reichman's brow furrowed. She gazed down at my mate, her expression impossible to read, but then she nodded curtly. "She has my thanks and my respect."

Something squeezed inside me, and I was reminded of something I'd known about Avery since we'd first met. The strength that I'd seen in her all of those years ago had only grown with each year she'd aged. Her inherent magic was weak, but her soul was strong. So god damned strong.

"And this one?" Major Reichman pointed to a body

mostly covered in a sheet. Reichman's breath sucked in. "So beautiful."

The person was a woman of perhaps Indian descent. Coal-black hair spread onto the ground around her, and smooth brown skin graced her cheeks. Major Reichman was right. The woman had an ethereal beauty to her. She lay completely still even though she didn't smell of death. She smelled of . . .

I couldn't place it.

"Did Avery retrieve her too? This is the person we haven't identified. Another victim, or as you suggested, perhaps one of *them?*"

A moment of shame washed through me at the vampire commander's words. This woman wasn't one of them. I'd known that immediately, but I'd been so intent on saving my mate that I hadn't cared about her. "I don't think she's with the warlocks or elf lord. I think she's another victim."

Major Reichman's eyes widened, then she abruptly crouched down, still holding her stomach. Her gaze glued to the victim's chest. A moment passed, then she exclaimed, "There! Did you see that? She still breathes. She must be unconscious too. Does anyone know who she is?"

The SF members who heard Major Reichman's question all shook their heads, but Bavar's head cocked as he moved closer to the unconscious woman. His eyes narrowed as he gazed down at her.

"She has a . . . feel to her, something I've never sensed before." A look of reverence clouded his face, but then he abruptly stepped back and shook his head. "We need to get moving."

I eyed the fairy commander who seemed intent on putting more distance between himself and the woman, an unsettled look on his face.

"We'll take her back to headquarters," I ordered. "If she's in our database, the processing bay technicians will be able to identify her."

Major Reichman carefully scooped her up, mindful to keep the sheet covering her. "I'll bring her back."

"Link up!" Bavar shouted after he'd finished handing out the last of the portal keys. "We depart now."

I looked in the distance, waiting for movement or activity from the elf lord and his warlocks. Surely, they would be upon us in seconds since they could conjure transport portals.

But they didn't come.

"Ready?" Bavar asked, holding a portal key out to me.

Those who weren't overly injured helped those who were. Everyone divided into groups of three or four as Bavar had directed, and one by one, they all disappeared into portals.

Two SF members next to me linked their arms through mine. I fisted the key while keeping Avery close to my chest.

Bavar and Major Reichman would be the last to leave. Commanders were always the last to evacuate.

I whispered the spell, activating the key, and the portal winds swallowed us whole.

CHAPTER ELEVEN
WYATT

I sat at Avery's bedside in the healing center. An hour had passed since we'd left the fae lands. It was daytime on earth, evening drawing near, and the autumn sunset shone through the windows.

Nicholas stood near the far wall, having come to the healing center when he heard that we'd returned.

The rest of the squads were in various rooms on the ward. We'd nearly filled the damn place with the extent of our injuries.

Farrah held her hands over Avery, doing another assessment. The scent of the healing witch's magic tickled my nose when she floated her palms up and down my mate's body. She'd tried to treat me, too, but my burns were almost completely recovered—my skin pink and new—so I insisted that she focused on my mate.

"Anything new?"

Farrah frowned. "No, she's just sleeping. Her body is probably healing."

I peered at Nicholas. Once again, his contribution had helped us. If he hadn't remembered that scroll containing the information about the Elixias Mountains . . .

"I owe you a sincere apology."

He cocked his head at me.

"I've been wrong about you. Even though we haven't retrieved the poisoned beverage, I believe you when you say that you didn't compel my mate. And you were right about what you said in the library. About how I've treated you. It hasn't been fair, and I've treated you as a scapegoat. I'm sorry."

The vamp's eyes widened for the merest second, then he dipped his head. "Apology accepted."

"So all is well between us?"

He gave a curt nod. "All is well."

A sharp intake of breath lifted his chest just as Farrah fiddled with the IV in Avery's arm.

Avery's eyelids fluttered open.

Farrah grinned. "Well, hello, Ms. Meyers. It's good to see you joining us again."

Avery blinked, then pushed up on the bed, confusion evident on her features. "Where am I?"

"The SF headquarters." I sat forward more and reached for her just as Nicholas pushed away from the wall.

The urge to touch her, comfort her, and soothe her nearly overwhelmed me, but I stopped an inch short of her hand when I saw the fear in her eyes. "We brought you back here after you moved us all to safety in the Elixias Mountains."

Her lips parted, then her gaze shot to mine. She scanned my face, then my body. "The burns."

"They're healing. I'm okay."

The worry pinching her brow faded even more when she saw Nicholas. "You're alive too."

The vampire nodded, a smile curving his lips. "I am."

"So you didn't kill Nicholas?" she asked me. Her face scrunched up. "My memory is still fuzzy, but I distinctly remember your rage when you entered the Whimsical Room."

My jaw tightened. "No, but I almost did."

Her gaze whipped back to Nicholas.

The vampire shrugged. "He beat me up, but we've had a heart-to-heart since then, and all is now well."

She licked her lips. "What about everyone else? Are they okay? Did they all make it out? I tried to put everyone together, even those who'd—" She inhaled. "Even those who died. Did I forget anyone? And Charlotte?" Tears welled in her eyes. "I didn't see her there, does that mean—"

"Charlotte's fine." I gripped her hand, no longer able to hold myself back.

"And you didn't forget anyone," a male answered from the hallway. Everyone's attention shifted to Wes McCloy as he strolled into the room. He crossed his arms over his chest. "You prevented a lot of bloodshed by what you did, Ms. Meyers. The SF owes many lives to you."

She glanced at me, her eyebrows drawing together.

"This is General Wes McCloy. He's in charge of the entire Supernatural Forces organization." I guessed her confusion was because she didn't remember him.

"It's, uh, nice to meet you," she said haltingly to him.

His expression gave away nothing as he addressed Farrah. "She's still suffering from amnesia?"

"Yes." Farrah clasped her hands. "It appears so. Avery, do you remember me?"

Avery frowned. "Of course. You're the woman who came to see me at the inn in the capital and did those funny scans on me."

"But before that? Do you remember me from before that time?"

"No, I don't."

My jaw locked, and I once again wondered if her memory would ever return.

"At least her memory's stayed intact since the alignment," Farrah murmured to Wes.

He grunted, then pulled out a chair by my side so we both faced Avery.

Nicholas edged toward the door, but before he left, he leaned down and pressed a kiss to the top of Avery's head. "It's good to see you well and safe. As for what happened in that room between us—"

"We don't need to talk about it. I'd rather just forget. It was awful and unfair, and we were both victims."

Her declaration was like a blow to my chest. Nicholas truly *hadn't* lied about being drugged.

"Where's Marnee? Has she been caught?" Avery's winged eyebrows drew together.

"No, not yet," I replied. "We found her SF suit discarded on the shore of the Adriastic sea, but it will most likely be months before we find and apprehend her."

"Will she be punished?"

"Definitely."

Nicholas pulled back, then squeezed Avery's hand. "Don't worry about her. She didn't succeed."

Avery gave him a fleeting smile before the vamp

departed.

Before, I would have lunged at him for even daring to touch her, but now . . .

I saw that his concern was genuine and not based entirely on his vampiric lust, and he hadn't lied. He'd been a victim of Marnee too.

Gods. I've been so wrong about him.

After Nicholas left the room, Wes gave Avery a once-over. "Are you up for answering a few questions?"

My hackles rose, my inner wolf letting out a low warning growl. My mate had just been through a horrific ordeal. Rest, food, and safety were what she needed now. Not an interrogation.

Wes cut me a sharp look. "This is standard procedure, Major Jamison, regardless of whether or not she's your mate."

I took a deep breath and reined my temper in. Wes was right. Questioning victims immediately after an attack was the norm. The sooner we asked, the more likely it was they would remember specific details. If we waited too long, details began to fade, or if the trauma was too great, they never remembered at all.

I gave a curt nod. "Fine. Continue."

Avery shot me a pointed look as Wes's lips quirked up in an amused smile. As if he needed my permission to continue. But as for Avery's annoyance . . . I frowned, remembering what Nicholas had said in the library, about a wolf's protectiveness toward his mate also being his downfall.

Smothering was the word the vampire had used.

Gods, did Avery truly feel that way about me?

"Avery," Wes began quietly. "Did you stop time again to bring the SF members to that safe location they woke up in?"

She pulled the sheets up more, then gave a single nod.

"We all thank you for that."

"It was the least I could do. Everyone was fighting to save me. I know some died."

Wes's eyes grew hooded. "Yes. Three members died there. Their families will be grateful they have bodies to bury. Another thing we can thank you for."

She cast me a wary glance, probably wondering where this was going.

"And I see you also brought an unidentified victim back," Wes continued.

Avery abruptly bolted upright in bed. "The goddess! Where is she? Is she here?" She frantically looked around.

Wes and I shared an incredulous look.

"She's the goddess?" I asked.

Avery nodded frantically. "She's Verasellee, the

Goddess of Time, just like the scrolls said. Lord Godasara lured her to the fae realm two thousand years ago and tried to take her power, but she cursed him and threw her power into the galaxy. It attached to the Safrinite comet and other magical events, like the alignment, and was then given to me. I'm holding her power for her, but it's not mine. It's hers. I need to give it back."

Silence descended on the room so swiftly that the only sound was the slight hum from the air ducts.

"That is more information than the scrolls revealed. How did you learn that?" Wes asked.

"From the goddess and the elf lord."

"You've *spoken* with the goddess?" My eyebrows shot clear to my forehead.

"I . . . not really, but she's come to me in my dreams. She's shown me her memories from the past and tried to warn me about the ritual. She's in a dormant state now, but her mind is still active."

Projecting. So the goddess does that too.

"Okay," Wes said slowly. "How about we start from the beginning. Tell us everything you know, and we'll see if we can get to the bottom of exactly what's happened to you, the goddess, and Lord Godasara."

Avery licked her lips again, some of the panic leaving her face. "Okay, I will, but first I need to see Verasellee, so I can know that she's okay."

CHAPTER TWELVE
AVERY

When I stood from the bed, my body felt like I'd been run over by a bulldozer. Considering I'd carried dozens of full-grown supernaturals over hundreds of miles, I wasn't surprised.

Wes begrudgingly led me from my room and down the hall. I knew that he wanted to question me further, but until I saw the goddess I wouldn't be able to think straight.

Farrah walked on one side of me, Wyatt the other.

Wyatt's hand continually drifted to my lower back. Every brush of his palm made my stomach tighten. I kept reminding myself that he was alive and okay. And I was still amazed that he wasn't scarred. Because seeing those flames engulf him had made me think that if he did survive, he would have lasting damage.

Gods. He'd come so close to death. It had nearly undone me. But he was fine.

Which left room for my other thoughts to creep in . . .

He'd locked me in the Whimsical Room. I'd been drugged against my will and then abducted.

I stiffened and closed my eyes briefly as we continued walking. I didn't know what to think. Relief that Wyatt was safe or annoyance at how he'd treated me.

Or both.

He removed his hand, his Adam's apple bobbing as turbulent emotions stormed in his eyes. I could only imagine the scents I was giving off right now.

Several healing witches watched us when we passed them.

My stomach turned into a bundle of nerves.

Wyatt's nostrils flared.

Yes, I felt things for him, but I also had a problem with being told what to do with no regards for my wishes. Wyatt was an alpha. He was incredibly domi-nant given his nature. That meant he had no problems bossing me around, taking the upper hand, or answering for me as he'd done with Wes earlier.

And while I liked his protective and possessive instincts, they also drove me mad.

If not for them, he never would have guilt-tripped me into the Whimsical Room. So what did that mean? Were we destined to be constantly arguing while he tried to dominate me and I tried to assert my independence?

And then there was the whole mate thing, which just made it more confusing.

Wyatt one hundred percent believed I was his mate, and given how I reacted to him when I thought he was going to die, apparently my body agreed. But did that innate bond mean that I didn't have a choice in our relationship? Was I destined to be with him even if I came to resent how he treated me?

I nibbled my lower lip and shifted my attention back to the hallway. *Ugh.* I didn't have the energy to think about this. I needed to focus on the goddess. The Gods knew *that* would be easier to deal with than *this.*

Wes paused at a doorway at the end of the hall. He waved toward the interior. "As you can see, she's still asleep and alive."

"She's in there?" I hurried past him, and my shoulders slumped in relief when I saw the goddess lying quietly on the bed. A sheet was still draped over her body, but her face was exposed. And as Wes had said, she was breathing.

The power inside me rattled and hummed, swelling to the surface of my skin. Electricity zapped my nerves, and crackling energy filled the room.

It felt as if her power wanted out.

Of course! Maybe I could give her power back to her now. Maybe *that* would wake her up.

I closed my eyes and concentrated on her power. It swirled inside me like a spiraling tornado. *Come on. Just go to her!*

I grabbed and clawed at it, trying to release it, but it only crackled more. It felt as if I was playing tug-of-war with energy-infused mist.

Wrenching my eyes open, I tried harder.

Farrah gasped, and I knew that my irises had turned violet.

"This power is hers," I said quietly. *And I need to return it.*

The goddess's power continued to swell under my skin, but it wouldn't leave me no matter how hard I tried to coax it up and out of me.

I nearly smacked my chest in frustration but managed to refrain myself. But dammit, why couldn't I control it? It was bad enough I couldn't use it at will, but to not even be able to give it back to its rightful owner? *Gods.*

But that didn't mean I would stop trying. However, what I was doing wasn't working. I would have to think of another way.

A fierce protective instinct surged through me. I needed to keep her away from Lord Godasara in the meantime. If their lives were linked, then I needed to protect her until I could find a way to *unlink* them and give her back her rightful power.

"Avery?" Wyatt said quietly.

It wasn't until he said my name that I realized everyone had retreated to the hallway. Sizzling energy skated around me, filling the room.

Damn. I was going to start an electrical storm if I didn't get myself under control.

I took a deep breath and reined the goddess's power back in. Slowly, the current pulsing through the room abated, and those in the hallway exhaled sighs of relief.

"You've grown quite strong," Wes remarked.

"I guess I have, even though I still don't understand how to use her power, but in times of crisis it's worked." I darted another glance at Wyatt.

He was frowning.

"And maybe that's what matters." A tinge of bitter-ness filled my tone. Despite trying to avoid all things complicated, the messy bond Wyatt and I shared resurfaced, eliciting a flare of irritation when I thought again about being locked in that safe room.

Wyatt's eyebrows drew together more, and he made a move to step closer to me but I backed away.

A growl of dissatisfaction rumbled in his chest, but I ignored it.

"We can discuss what happened in the fae lands now," I told Wes. "As long as Verasellee will stay here and be kept safe."

"She will be," the general replied, his attention shifting to the alpha at my side, whose gaze was so heated it could've melted lead.

But I rounded the bed despite knowing Wyatt was starting to wonder what was going on with me. "Then lead the way."

I FOLLOWED Wes through numerous hallways and checkpoints to one of the main SF buildings, while Wyatt prowled just behind me.

And it certainly was a *prowl*. Low rumbles came from Wyatt continuously, and the few times I glanced at him, gold flashed in his eyes.

So he wasn't happy that I was putting distance

between us. Huh, imagine that. Well, that was too damned bad. I was in no mood to get into it now, not after everything I'd been through.

Wes scanned us in to a conference room on the second floor when we reached it. Once inside, he waved toward the chairs surrounding a large board table.

"Have a seat, wherever you wish."

I pulled out a chair across from him, taking in the large, impressively sized room. From what I'd seen of the SF so far, there were numerous training facilities both inside and outside, wide hallways zigzagging through each building, and dozens of wings and command centers stationed throughout.

Everything was made of concrete or steel and seemed to swim in magic. Not to mention there was constant security scans at every doorway. Our movements were perpetually monitored.

It was intense, to say the least, and to think I'd trained here for three months and didn't remember it . . .

That blew my mind.

Wyatt pulled out the chair at my side, the concern on his face giving way to frustration, but I still kept my focus on Wes.

The general settled himself on the chair across from me. "Now, I need you to tell me what happened while you were under Lord Godasara's hold. All of the details. No matter how small they seem, they may be crucial to capturing him."

I folded my hands in my lap. Despite distancing myself from Wyatt, with him at my side, his looming presence drew me in like a magnet. *Damned mate bond.* But I managed to keep myself firmly in my chair, despite my body's irrational desire to shift closer to Wyatt.

"What will you do with him if you catch him?" I asked Wes.

Wes cocked his head. "If we catch him alive, which is unlikely, Lord Godasara will go on trial in the supernatural courts. The same process would happen to him that happens to all criminals apprehended by the SF."

"Why is it unlikely he'll be caught alive?"

"Given how strong he is, and how he has no qualms about killing our squad members—" The general's jaw ground together, and a flash of remorse filled his eyes before he veiled it. "It's unlikely we'll capture him alive. Most likely, he will die in battle if we're able to find him again."

I interlocked my fingers. But if they killed him . . . I'd have to stop that or the goddess would be lost. "And would the supernatural courts execute him too?"

"No," Wes said haltingly. "We don't have capital

punishment, but it's likely his life would be leeched by the gargoyles should his sentence demand that."

"Meaning he *would* die."

"Meaning his life would be cut short." Wes cocked his head. "Where are you going with this, Ms. Meyers?"

I leaned forward, resting my forearms on the table. I knew I had to come clean and be blunt with him. It was the only way. "You can't kill him. He can't be allowed to die."

Wes glanced at Wyatt, a weighted look passing between them.

Wyatt leaned closer to me, his oak and pine scent drifting around me like a comforting cloud. I jerked back. I needed to keep my head on straight and not be persuaded by him. I *needed* to ensure the goddess's safety.

Jaw locked, Wyatt retreated to the center of his chair. With a furrowed brow, he said evenly, "Lord Godasara is responsible for hundreds of deaths, if not *thousands* through the sacrifices he and the warlocks conducted to extend their lives. And you're saying he should be allowed to live? Even knowing that he would have killed you?"

A heavy ache filled my chest. Wyatt's question didn't contain any judgment or derision. It was merely curious sounding. He genuinely wanted to hear why I felt this way.

Damn him. There he went being all perfect again when the reality was that our relationship was far from perfect.

Regardless, my body wanted to soften toward him.

I snapped my spine into place, refusing to let that happen. Seriously, the man was infuriating. It was as if he knew exactly how to make me cave, even if he wasn't doing it on purpose.

Vowing not to let that happen, I replied curtly, "His life is linked to the goddess's. If you kill him, you kill her. I can't allow that to happen."

A moment of silence fell.

"What makes you think that?" Similar to Wyatt, Wes sounded curious.

A tiny part of my guard lowered, and for the merest second, I wondered if I could trust both of them. "Because Lord Godasara told me. The reason Verasellee's body is still here, living and breathing, is because he tried to kill her but then realized that if he did he would die too. It's because of the curse she placed on him. If she dies, he dies. It was how she ensured that she lived, but unfortunately, that curse works both ways. The universe is nothing if not fair, karma or whatever.

So the lord placed her in a dormant state to keep her alive because he's unable to kill her."

Another veiled look passed between Wyatt and Wes, and irritation prickled my skin.

"If you have something to say, just say it," I snapped.

Wes cocked an eyebrow, and a low discontented rumble came from Wyatt.

"We're not hiding anything from you, Avery," Wyatt said calmly. "I think both of us are just surprised at what you're saying."

"Why is it so surprising?"

"Because the man—" Wyatt took a deep breath. His hands curled into fists, the veins on the backs of them standing on end before he said in a clipped tone, "He abducted you, held you prisoner, and was going to *sacrifice you* in whatever ritual we interrupted. Just the thought of him doing any of those things makes me want to rip his head off, yet you, the victim of those atrocious crimes, are trying to save him."

"But it's not because I want him saved. I just don't want her hurt. There's a difference, and I would have killed him if I could have, but since I couldn't I—" I licked my lips as bile rose in my throat. "I incapacitated him so we could escape."

Wyatt frowned. "Incapacitated him how?"

My stomach churned. "I . . . I cut his legs off so he couldn't follow us."

Wes's eyebrows shot clear to his hairline, and surprise filled Wyatt's eyes.

I slapped a hand over my face. "I know that makes me sound like a monster, and I feel sick about it, but I had to stop him. He would have killed all of you, and it was the only way to slow him down while not killing him and getting all of you out."

Wyatt's fingers curled around my hand and gently pulled it down from my face. Gold light rimmed his eyes. "You're one of the bravest women I know. You have nothing to feel guilty about, and if keeping Godasara alive right now is what needs to be done then —" His throat worked a swallow. "We won't kill him."

He held eye contact. And in that moment, I could see that he truly was trying to understand. All of the protective feelings he had for me, all of the possessive mate-driven emotions that had been birthed between us and were begging him to end Godasara's life at the next opportunity were there, yet . . .

He was listening to me.

I turned away from him toward Wes, that flipping feeling starting in my stomach again.

Not what you need to be focusing on right now!

"So do you promise you won't kill him? Or turn him

over to the gargoyles or whatever?" I asked Wes. "Because if you do, she will die. The only way out of this is if we can find a way to unlink them. If their souls are no longer linked, then theoretically, the elf lord could die and Verasellee would still live."

General McCloy studied me for a long moment, then tapped a finger on the table. "But . . . does she need to live?"

My breath sucked in.

"I'm just asking the question. What you're proposing makes this assignment more complicated, and our mission first and foremost is to protect supernaturals here on earth. It's not to protect gods from other realms."

I clasped my hands together as they'd begun shaking. Rattling energy skittered along my nerves. Verasellee's power rumbled and swelled inside me. I took a deep breath, trying to calm myself, but it did no good.

"Yes, she needs to live." My words thundered toward Wes, ringing with Verasellee's power. He leaned back in his chair, as if a rush of air had blasted over him.

I tried to rein my anger back inside. I didn't know why, but I felt incredibly protective of the goddess. Despite choosing me as her heir and fucking up my life, I still wanted to save her.

Maybe that was a byproduct of having her power

inside me, maybe it wasn't. I didn't know, but I wasn't going to sit on the sidelines and let them kill Lord Godasara and destroy Verasellee in the process.

"You feel strongly about this," Wyatt said quietly.

"Very much so."

He and Wes shared another look—those damned looks—before Wes said, "All right. I'll confer with my sorcerers about unlinking them. It seems the least we can do given how much you've helped the SF. However, I can't promise anything. You have to understand that my priority lies with the SF. If Lord Godasara resurfaces and threatens the safety of my squads or innocent bystanders again, we'll take him down without question."

"But—"

He held up his hand. "I can promise that I'll look into whatever connection links Verasellee and Lord Godasara. I'll have Nicholas get on it right away. If we can find a way to unlink them safely, we will."

I sat stiffly since I knew that was the best compromise he was willing to offer. "Okay, then I guess that's the plan moving forward."

CHAPTER THIRTEEN
WYATT

Wes sat forward in his chair after sending a rapid-fire message to Nicholas. "I'll see what the Bulgarian gargoyles are able to find," Wes said, "then I'll meet with my sorcerers tomorrow morning. But right now, I need you to finish telling us exactly what happened to you."

My mate's shoulders relaxed more as she answered his straightforward questions, and with each passing sentence, some of the halting distrust I'd scented in her —that Wes had no doubt scented too—diminished.

Inside, my wolf growled lowly because something was going on with my mate. Not only was she acting skittish, but something else had changed between us.

I could feel it.

And I'd be damned if I didn't get to the bottom of it.

Because all of the softening I'd felt from her during our days at Shrouding Estate seemed to have disappeared.

It was as though she'd experienced something extraordinary and it had altered her. I snorted quietly to myself. Funny how amnesia, an abduction, imprisonment, and a near sacrifice could do that to a person.

Wes cocked his head. "After you finished removing all of the SF members from the battle, what did you do? Wyatt said he awoke to find you unconscious. Do you remember what happened?"

Avery stiffened, her first sign of hesitation since Wes began questioning her an hour ago. She'd already told us everything he wanted to know: what she remembered of the abduction, what had been done to her in the cave systems, who had been involved in her detainment, and what she remembered of the ritual.

Despite all of those grueling memories being dredged up, she'd answered all of his questions willingly and honestly. Her scent couldn't lie, but now—

Something was making her wary, and neither my wolf nor I liked it.

"It's okay." My hand automatically went to her lower back, but I stopped myself and curled my fingers around my chair instead. "Nothing you can say will surprise us."

Violet light intermixed with her natural brown-and-gold irises when she looked at me. Her scent changed, too, that sour odor entering it.

Whoa. Okay, whatever she wasn't telling us was causing her serious concern. A low growl rumbled in my chest, my senses going on high alert at just the inkling that something was making her this fearful.

"I won't let anybody hurt you," I reminded her.

"Not even yourself?" she whispered under her breath.

My head whipped back, an incredulous expression no doubt forming on my face. She honestly felt fearful of me?

Cold hurt slammed into my chest. Did she really not trust me at all?

"Avery, you have my complete assurance that you're safe here," Wes added. "Lord Godasara would never be able to penetrate the protective wards around the SF. We just want to know what happened so we can solve what's going on and get to the bottom of it. That is the main objective with all Supernatural Forces' assignments."

Her eyes flashed violet again when she addressed him, and tingling energy grew around her. "It's not Lord Godasara I'm afraid of right now."

Wes cocked his head. "Then who are you fearful of?"

"The SF."

What? Is that what her earlier comment meant? I leaned closer to her. "Nothing you say will be used against you."

She grimaced. "You promise? You absolutely promise that nothing will be used against me?"

Wes's frown deepened, but he nodded. "You have my word."

She licked her lips, which suddenly looked dry, then took a deep breath. "After I carried all of the SF members to that second location and before I incapacitated the elf, I—" Her hands twisted, and a strong sour scent rose from her again.

A stone sank in my gut. "Did something happen after you went back? Did they—" I swallowed down the rage that was working its way up my throat. "Did they hurt you?"

She gave a short brittle laugh. "No, they didn't hurt me." She fiddled her fingers together and looked down. "It was the opposite actually. I hurt them."

A feeling of such intense relief washed through me that I had to sit back in my chair. I'd been imagining the worst. That she'd gone back to the lord and warlocks, that they'd broken through her power, perhaps beaten her, raped her, or did something else equally atrocious, and that perhaps she'd retaliated. Because the fearful scent coming off her had been so similar to the scent other victims gave when reliving the horrific situations they'd experienced and had fought back against.

"Go on," Wes said quietly.

Her gaze remained lowered. "After I returned to the fire pit, I knew that they would keep coming after me if I didn't end it. I knew that innocent people would die, perhaps hundreds more. So I picked up a sword left by a fallen SF member, and I—" She peeked up, her eyes luminous. "I vowed to kill all of them right there. I was going to kill the elf lord first, since he was the biggest threat."

A small smile curved my lips. *Smart girl.*

"Then I was going to kill all of the warlocks. I know it's wrong to kill someone like that in cold blood." A stench of self-loathing filled her scent. "But I felt like it was my duty to do so. I didn't make that decision lightly. I thought it through, but just when I was about to kill Lord Godasara he told me about his link with Verasellee. He was beginning to break through my hold on time. He was able to move his mouth enough to speak, and he said that if I killed him, I'd kill her." She entwined her hands again. "And the crazy thing is, I don't think he was lying. Initially, I thought he was just trying to stall me, but then if that were the case, why was the goddess still alive? If her power was in me, he had no reason to keep the goddess with him unless he was speaking the truth. So I didn't kill him." Her face abruptly paled. "But that didn't mean I left them all alive."

"You killed the warlocks," Wes said matter-of-factly.

She nodded, her lips beginning to tremble. "I did. I decapitated all of them, one after another, and—" She raised her chin. "As much as it made me sick to do it, I don't regret it. I would do it again to protect innocent people from the sacred circle's vicious rituals. And I know that makes me sound like a cold, heartless bitch, but they were going to kill me and all of you, and they weren't going to stop their human and fairy sacrifices. I knew that moment was my only chance to stop them, so I took it." Her cheeks flushed, her eyes flashing violet light again. "Like I said, I'm not proud of myself for it, even if they were evil to the core. I'll have to live with the knowledge that I took their lives, but I don't regret my actions. So if you have to arrest me for murder, then I suppose you'll have to arrest me."

The breath rushed out of me, then a harsh laugh followed.

Avery's eyes shot to mine. "Is this funny to you?"

"No, it's not, really." But I couldn't stop the immense relief I felt. "I'm just glad this is what was worrying you. Do you actually think we'd arrest you for killing the warlocks who abducted you, hurt you, and were going to *sacrifice* you?"

Her eyebrows drew together in a sharp line. "I killed them in cold blood. I wasn't defending myself, because they couldn't fight back. They were still frozen. I literally—" Her throat worked, a look of shame washing over her features. "I literally *executed* them."

"And the SF thanks you for that," Wes said.

Her gaze whipped to his. "What?"

He leaned forward more, propping his forearms on the table. "Warlocks are dark sorcerers. They practice black magic, which is illegal. One of our objectives in this assignment was to eliminate them using whatever means necessary. And any warlock who would have survived to go to trial would have eventually died from gargoyle leeching. You have nothing to worry about. You haven't done anything illegal."

Her lips parted, her mouth opening in surprise. "I haven't?"

"No. Wes is right." I shook my head, still reeling at the reaction I'd had from thinking the worst.

Wes's tablet buzzed. He read something, then jumped back into the conversation, asking his remaining questions in rapid-fire succession, which meant whatever message he'd received required attention.

"Let's head back to the healing center." Wes stood from his chair after he'd finished the interview. "One of the processing bay technicians will be there to help us verify the woman's lineage, then we'll know for certain if she is the goddess."

Avery cocked her head. "You don't believe me that she's Verasellee?"

Wes headed toward the door. "It has nothing to do with beliefs. We operate on data and facts. We need to verify her lineage to confirm it."

A growl rumbled in my chest again. "All right, but only if it's quick. Avery's hungry and no doubt tired. She needs a break from this."

A knowing glint lit Wes's eyes, probably because he understood the protectiveness I felt toward my mate. He was the same with his wife. "It'll be quick."

Avery gave me a pointed look. "I definitely have time for it even if I am hungry and tired." She made a move to stand, and when I went to pull her chair back, she brushed off my hand.

My brow furrowed, and for what felt like the twentieth time I wondered what had changed between us.

BY THE TIME we left the conference room and were striding down the hallway, it was late evening, which only made my mood sour more. My mate was hungry despite her assurances she could continue. Her stomach had growled repeatedly during the past hour. She also needed to sleep. Dark circles were beginning to smudge the skin beneath her eyes.

But despite my only desire to provide for her and care for her, Avery kept her distance from me. I didn't know how to interpret that, but common sense told me she was angry, and Nicholas's warning kept returning.

Smothering.

Was that truly what I was doing? And could that be the cause of Avery's resistance with me? But I only wanted her cared for. Surely, Avery knew that?

My wolf prowled in my belly, and a feeling of ash coated my throat. Dammit. I was fucking everything up again even though I didn't know for certain what I'd done wrong. What I did know was that only days ago Avery had been looking at me with lust in her eyes and possibly the beginnings of love, but now she was looking at me like—

I resisted the urge to slam my fist into the wall.

I didn't like how she was looking at me.

Wes quirked an eyebrow in my direction as our feet tapped quietly down the hall. I knew I wasn't hiding anything from him. Given he was also a werewolf who could scent emotions, he'd no doubt inhaled my frustration.

Because everything felt worse now, even more than it had after Avery had initially woken up in the healing center. Not only was she *not* allowing me to touch her, she was also putting physical distance between us. She'd opted to walk with Wes in between us.

I raked a hand through my hair as we rounded a corner.

Focus, I berated myself. My mate had been through a lot. She needed food, rest, and a safe place to unwind. That was where my priorities should lie, not worrying about why she was upset with me. I could address that later.

Because once my mate was rested, well fed, and not as surly, then I could sit her down for a much needed chat about *why* she was forcing this sudden distance between us.

Wes checked his tablet again. "The processing bay technician should be there by now, so this shouldn't take long."

I wasn't surprised by Wes's actions. Even though Avery was convinced the unconscious woman we'd brought back was Verasellee, the Goddess of Time, it was possible that she was someone else entirely.

A familiar head of purple hair flashed down the hallway when we stepped onto the healing center's ward. Eliza River stood patiently by the goddess's door, a scanning device in hand.

Of course. Wes had probably purposefully requested Eliza since he knew she'd been friends with Avery. Just one more reminder from before the alignment to hopefully jog Avery's memory.

I subtly glanced at my mate to see if any signs of recognition had sprung across her face, but the closer we got to the room, the less hopeful I became. Nothing changed on Avery's expression. Nothing.

Eliza was a different story. Excited energy danced around the fairy when we reached her. I could tell she was trying to maintain her professionalism, especially since Wes was here, but she kept darting happy looks at Avery.

But from the bewildered energy drifting from my mate, I knew Avery had no idea why.

"Private River." Wes dipped his head. "Thank you for coming."

"Of course, sir." Eliza glanced at Avery again, some of her excitement dimming when Avery merely frowned.

I cleared my throat. "Avery, Eliza and you were in the new recruit program together. You were roommates and friends during your three months here."

Avery's lips parted, and her cheeks flushed. "Oh, of course." She gave a tight smile. "I'm so sorry, but I don't remember—"

"It's all right," Eliza blurted. "Charlotte told me your memory hasn't returned, so of course I'm not upset that you don't recall our friendship, but I'm most pleased to see you again. Char and I have been gravely concerned about you."

Some of the anxiety surrounding Avery lessened. "Charlotte's been amazing to me. Have you seen her lately?"

A cloud drifted over Eliza's face. "Yes, I have."

"Is she okay? I haven't seen her since the castle was attacked."

"She says she's well, but she seems a bit distraught by all that's happened even though she's trying to conceal it. She's been in two skirmishes this week in which someone's died. That is no doubt a toll on one's soul."

Avery's face fell. "Gods, of course, I should go check on her—"

"And you will, *tomorrow*," I cut in.

Avery's lips pursed, but I wasn't budging on that. She was running on fumes. She needed to eat and sleep.

"Shall we get to work?" Wes asked, checking the time on his watch.

Eliza jolted upright, her back going ramrod straight. "Of course, sir. Sorry, sir. How can I be of assistance?"

Wes pointed inside the unidentified woman's room. "I'd like you to scan the woman in there. We need to identify her species."

"Of course, sir. Right away." Eliza kicked into action, her purple hair drifting in loose strands around her face. She proceeded to the bedside, then drew up short when she stood beside the woman. "Wow," she murmured.

Wes cocked his head. "Is everything all right, Private?"

Eliza gazed down at her, a look of wonder growing on her face. "Don't you feel it?"

Avery rushed forward, her lips tilting up. "Do you feel it too? Her presence?"

Eliza nodded quickly. "She's—" She shook her head. "She's magnificent."

Avery grinned. "Yes! I feel that too!"

And just like that, I knew that Avery and Eliza would fall back into an easy friendship, probably just as quickly as it had happened with Charlotte.

A moment of satisfaction filled me. It was good to see my mate connecting with her old friends and forming meaningful female bonds again, but at the same time . . .

Envy stole my breath.

Why couldn't it be that easy for us?

"Private River?" I said gruffly. "Will you please scan her?"

Some of the excitement abated from Eliza's energy. Very carefully, she picked up the woman's forearm and turned it over. She touched her reticently, almost reverently, and I couldn't help but wonder if Avery was right after all. Because Bavar, also a fairy, had acted strangely upon seeing Verasellee for the first time.

Which would make sense, because Verasellee was a goddess in the fae realm. She wasn't a goddess here, in earth's realm. Our supreme beings were different in this universe—there was only one, and while our maker had divine creatures, he was the only supreme ruler.

Yet, in Eliza's realm that wasn't the case. Dozens of gods and goddesses ruled her universe. Perhaps on some deep, innate level, she recognized this woman as a goddess from her realm.

Wes and I shared a curious look, and I had a feeling he'd also come to the same conclusion.

Eliza activated her device, then held it above the woman's inner wrist. An eruption of lasers shot out of it, swathing the woman's brown skin. A symbol appeared.

A symbol we'd only seen once before—the symbol for a divine creature.

"She *is* a goddess," Eliza breathed.

Eliza scanned the woman again, at Wes's assistance, and when the same symbol reappeared we knew without a doubt that Avery had been right.

Verasellee, the Goddess of Time, was currently a patient in the Supernatural Forces' healing center.

CHAPTER FOURTEEN
AVERY

By the time everyone's amazement had died down over the fact that I'd been right—that a living, breathing *goddess* currently lay in a bed on the healing center's ward—Wes whipped into action.

Twenty-four-seven security was placed on the room, and half a dozen of the SF's top guards would be on duty at all times. Now that the SF believed me about her, they weren't taking any chances, even if their perimeter wards were fail-safe.

Because it wasn't just me Lord Godasara would be after now. It would be Verasellee too.

An hour later, all security measures were activated, so I finally felt comfortable leaving the goddess. Eliza had stayed to keep me company, and of course, Wyatt hadn't budged from my side.

Eliza pulled me into an unexpected hug as she stood to leave. "It's most wonderful to see you again. We shall have to visit soon."

I hugged her back, her hair tickling my cheek. "I'd like that. Me, you, and Charlotte should all get together."

"We will." She said her goodbye, and I waved farewell.

I was sad to see her go, because it'd felt good to have someone around who understood as innately as I did who lay on the healing center's bed. That and Eliza provoked good feelings in me, similar to how Charlotte had.

I frowned. Even though I didn't specifically remember them, it was almost as though a part of me recognized them. Just like a part of me had recognized something in Wyatt even though I didn't remember our history either.

When the room finally cleared, minus the guards, some of the adrenaline I'd been running on faded. I leaned against the wall. Bone-deep weariness seeped through me. I brought a hand to my forehead. Damn. I was *so* tired.

"We should turn in. It's getting late," Wyatt said gruffly.

I jolted upright, his abrupt demand erasing all of the

fuzzy feelings that Eliza's presence had evoked.
"Excuse me?"

A look of confusion fell over his face. "I said it's
getting late. I'm taking you back to my apartment, so
you can sleep and get something to eat." His brow
furrowed more. "I don't understand. Aren't you tired?"

I crossed my arms, my frown returning. "Yes, but
don't I have my own apartment here? Can't I go back
there?"

The muscle in his jaw tightened. "You used to, but
not anymore. Your new recruit program is over, which
means that your former apartment is now being lived in
by other new recruits."

"Oh." My frown deepened. I hadn't realized that. But
I figured there had to be guest quarters somewhere on
the grounds. I was about to ask if I could go there, but
Wyatt continued.

"Furthermore, as was the case at Shrouding Estate,
it's my job to ensure your safety, so you'll be staying
with *me*." He watched me intently, probably waiting for
me to fight back as I had when he'd initially demanded
it, but as irritating as it was, I also knew there was no
point fighting.

I wouldn't win, just like I hadn't won when the battle
hit the estate, which was why I'd ended up in the Whimsical Room.

A snag of bitterness filled my chest. He was so damned authoritative, and the more I thought about it, the more I realized that I was still majorly pissed at him. If he hadn't locked me away in that damned room, it was possible I never would have been abducted, abused, and nearly killed.

I was mad at him for that, damned mad, even though the abduction had ultimately led me to the goddess.

Finding Verasellee was the only good thing that had come out of it. Well, that and I'd killed all of the warlocks . . .

Still, what was going to happen when there was another fight between us? Because I had no doubt there would be. So what then? Would he still be the alpha in all situations? Would he keep demanding that I obeyed him?

Wyatt's expression turned more wary the longer I looked up at him without saying anything.

"Avery?" he finally said, breaking the silence.

I tightened my arms across my chest. "So is this like the estate then? I have no say in anything?"

"It's for your *safety.*"

I rolled my eyes clear to the top of my head. "Right. Everything is for my *safety.* Of course, how could I forget?"

"Is that what all of this is about?" he asked gently.

I didn't fully understand what he was asking, but I was in no mood for a lengthy discussion, so I didn't reply. Besides, as much as it irked me, he was right. I was tired and hungry. So I merely gave a tight smile and waved toward the door. "Lead the way, Commander. I'll follow you."

His eyes narrowed, but he turned toward the door without commenting further.

I followed him down the hall. On our way out of the healing center, we passed the station the witches sat at. One of them, a pretty redhead watched Wyatt from beneath her lashes. When our gazes met, envy filled her expression, and with a start I realized she was envious that I was leaving with Wyatt.

My stomach tightened, and I glanced over at the commander.

Wyatt strode beside me, his large presence dominating the hall. The width of his shoulders stretched his shirt, the cut of his jaw made him sexy in a deadly sort of way, and the sheer physical strength of him would make any female look twice.

Because dammit, he was hot. Damn hot. Even I could admit that despite being pissed at him.

When we neared the door, I glanced over my shoulder.

The redhead snatched her gaze away.

So she *had* been watching him.

A pang of jealousy flowed hotly through me, which made no sense whatsoever. Wasn't I mad at Wyatt and unsure if I wanted to be with him long-term? Besides, Wyatt believed I was his mate, therefore he would be faithful to me. Right?

He'd said as much, but that didn't mean the redhead hadn't been with him. Had they ever dated? Or hooked up? Had he once dated her and me at the same time? I still didn't fully know what had caused such a rift between us. Was that it?

An unbidden image scorched my mind. It was of the redhead and Wyatt wrapped up in one another's arms, her head lolling back, her eyes closed, as he did all of the delicious things to her that he'd done to me.

Intense rage raced through me, nearly making me stumble.

Avery, WTF!

But I couldn't stop myself from thinking of the two of them together, or having such an intense reaction.

Which only made how I was feeling worse, because it reinforced the fact that Wyatt was still a stranger to me since I couldn't remember our history, but he was also a stranger who I had a *damned fucking mate bond* with, so my body was literally crazy for him.

A dark storm cloud drifted through my thoughts.

With each step I took, energy crackled inside me. It didn't help that I was so tired. I'd barely slept while trapped in the caves and using so much of the goddess's power had zapped me of all of my strength, so much so that I'd passed out.

I was crabby, irritable, and looking for a fight. Despite knowing all of that, it didn't stop the anger building inside me.

By the time we reached the exterior doors on the first floor, I wouldn't have been surprised if my eyes were glowing violet.

Wyatt pushed open the door, then held it for me. He tracked my every move, that wary and confused expression still in place. With curled fingers, he held the door rigidly. I was probably wrong, but I could have sworn he was leaving dents in the metal.

Keeping my gaze down, I ducked past him, careful not to let our bodies touch.

He sucked in a breath, and the door banged closed when he finally let it go.

Once on the sidewalk, neither of us said a thing as he led the way to his barracks, but I continually glanced around, searching for something, *anything* that felt or looked familiar.

But the fields that surrounded us, the dark rolling hills in the distance, and the huge concrete buildings that sprawled everywhere, looked as foreign to me as Mars.

"We had our first date right over there," Wyatt said, pointing to one of the fields. "We ate a sponge cake you baked while you told me about Greek philosophers."

I frowned. *Greek philosophers?* If I really tried, I could probably wrack my brain and come up with a few Greek philosophers' names, since I seemed to know about *things* just nothing about *me*. But why would I have mentioned Greek philosophers?

"I'll have to take your word on that," I replied tersely.

He sighed again, the sound heavy, and I could have sworn that he was about to pinch the bridge of his nose but stopped himself.

We carried on down the sidewalk until we reached the last building. "This is me."

He scanned us in, then opened the door. I stepped inside, searching the entryway of his building for anything that tickled a memory or a sense of déjà vu.

But as was becoming the norm—nope, *nada*.

"Bavar's apartment is there." Wyatt pointed to the first door on the right. "If he convinces you to make him more cookies, which he inevitably will, that's where you can drop them off."

"Did I drop off a lot of baked items to him?"

"Not as many as I'm sure he would have liked."

His tone was teasing, and given the hopeful look in his eyes, I guessed he was waiting for a comeback quip from me, but I merely quirked an eyebrow. "And you? Did I drop off cookies at your door too?"

A veiled look descended over his features. He remained silent, and I didn't think he was going to answer me, but then he said, "You tried to once, but I didn't accept them."

It felt as if the wind got punched out of me. Why? What had happened between us to make him reject me?

But that was a loaded question that I didn't have the energy for, so I settled with, "Oh. I'm guessing that had to do with whatever problems we had?"

"It did." He waved toward the stairs. "I'm on the top floor."

We trudged up the stairway, then down a hall. He stopped at the second door on the left and placed his finger pad against a holographic lock. His door clicked open, and I hesitantly followed him inside.

He flipped a wall switch, and standing lamps clicked on. Soft light bathed his apartment in a muted glow. His home was small and clean. On the left, a counter with stools overlooked an open kitchen. The kitchen wasn't big, but it held all of the necessities. For the most part, it looked like a normal kitchen devoid of any magical devices.

The rest of his apartment had a masculine feel. The entire color scheme was grays and dark greens. On the right, a living room held a leather couch and a recliner—both steel-gray. Several metal end tables sported lamps but no personal items. Only one picture was hung on the wall, a beautiful mountainous landscape of forested hills covered in snow.

"Not many knickknacks," I commented.

He kicked his shoes off. "I don't really like stuff, if you know what I mean."

I nodded absentmindedly. I searched for photos and spotted a few on a table near the TV. After slipping my shoes off, I went to them.

"Is this your family?" The photo showed him with two other men, a young woman, and a middle-aged couple. They all had similar colored hair and builds.

I felt him approach me from behind. It was as though the energy in the room shifted to accommodate his immense magic. "It is. Those are my brothers Lance and William, my dad, Walter—the Alpha of the British Columbia pack—my mom, Lisa, and my sister Lassa. You've met all of them."

My fingers tightened around the frame. So this was Lassa, the woman Nicholas had told me about in the Whimsical Room. And I'd met these people. Just like I'd 'met' my parents, Eliza, Charlotte, Wes, Wyatt, and probably dozens of others that I'd passed in the hallways of the SF and didn't recognize.

Despite knowing that my memory loss wasn't my fault, it didn't stop the growing frustration that all of this was embarrassing. It made me feel like a forgetful child, and hearing that everyone in his family were people I'd once met and interacted with made that twisting sensation start in my stomach again. Why couldn't any of this be easy? *Why?*

I hastily set the photo down. "Do you mind if I take a shower and go to bed?"

He stilled, his presence still looming behind me. "If that's what you want. Or I could make you something to eat while you're showering. I know you're hungry."

My stomach rumbled again as if on cue. "Yeah, fine, that works too." I knew my words were short, but I couldn't help it.

He slammed a hand through his hair when I turned to face him, and the energy off him soared. "I'll grab you a towel. Your belongings should be in my room. Wes moved all of your stuff out of your old apartment when you finished training and stored it here. The clothing that survived the battle at the estate was also shipped here, so you should have plenty to choose from."

"Oh," I replied in surprise. They'd thought of every-thing, which was probably good. Funny how I hadn't even thought about not having a toothbrush. All I'd been thinking about was escaping this suffocating feeling of not remembering anything or anyone. It was doing my head in.

He remained a yard away, his expression impossible to read, but the weight of his gaze let me know he was anything but calm. "Do you like sandwiches?"

Gods. This was intense.

But then I realized that he was asking me about food. "You don't know if I like them?"

He tugged a hand through his hair again. "Honestly, no, I'm not sure."

"Yet we were together as a couple?" The worry in his eyes increased at my question, and he opened his mouth to reply, but since I was in no mood to dive into that subject either, I added, "Sure, whatever you want to make is fine. I'm not picky." At least, I didn't think I was. "Oh, but no carrots. My mom was right about that one."

I darted away before our awkward conversation could get any worse.

Since his apartment was small, it wasn't hard to find the bathroom and his bedroom. They were literally the only two rooms down the short hall.

I didn't linger in his room. The king-sized bed dominated the small space and reminded me of the nights we'd shared at Shrouding Estate, but that was then and this was now. At that time, he'd literally been a stranger to me that my body craved.

Now, I was beginning to get to know him and I wasn't so sure about us being a couple. Yes, I enjoyed sleeping with him, *really* enjoyed it. But since the Whimsical Room, I'd seen a side of him that I hadn't during our hot encounters at the estate. He was controlling. Demanding. And often spoke over my wishes.

Shaking my head, I grabbed a pair of cotton pajama pants and a T-shirt out of one of the boxes piled by the wall. Neither were sexy, which was exactly what I wanted. The last thing I needed was for Wyatt to use his sex-mojo on me and have me panting like a bitch in heat beneath him.

After grabbing what I needed, including toiletries, which *surprise surprise*, I didn't recognize either—but figured they were mine since they were feminine products—I ducked into the shower and made quick work of it.

I tried not to think about the intimacy of showering in Wyatt's bathroom by ignoring the brand of shampoo he used and how he liked for his toilet paper to hang over in front of the roll and not behind, but it was impossible not to notice some of the details.

Like the fact that he kept his towels folded on the rack versus left on the floor, and how his trash can was lined with a plastic bag versus just the bare can. Or how his razor and extra blades were stacked neatly on the counter's corner.

So I learned something else about him. He liked cleanliness and tidiness.

But just as quickly as that thought came, so did a heady dousing of frustration. Was that because the SF required order and discipline, or was that truly how *Wyatt* was?

I didn't know.

Because I didn't *know* him.

Ugh.

Once dressed, I combed through my damp hair and padded back to the kitchen. Gods, I was tired, and my brain was asking too many questions again.

Wyatt stood at the kitchen counter, piling meat and cheese onto bread slathered with mayo. He glanced up, his gaze raking up and down my body. A glow lit his irises.

I wondered what he'd found so appealing. Nothing about how I looked screamed sex kitten.

Maybe it was the intimacy of hanging out with me in my pajamas that he liked?

But then I reminded myself that he'd seen me before and after showers at Shrouding Estate so this was nothing new. And there was nothing that intimate about this. For goodness' sake, I was wearing a *baggy T-shirt and cotton pants*—not exactly lingerie—but one would never have guessed it given the frequent side-eyes Wyatt was sending my way.

He picked up two plates loaded with food. "The sandwiches are ready."

"Okay. Thanks." With stiff movements, I walked to the counter and pulled out a barstool.

Wyatt came around the corner and joined me, pulling out the stool at my side.

I tried not to shift when our arms brushed, but as had been the case every other time we'd had physical contact, a bolt of pleasure shot up my limbs and my breath quickened.

Dammit! Why do I have to be so attracted to him?

I dug into the sandwich, focusing on eating it quickly and getting to bed pronto. Given the constant glances Wyatt gave me as I shoveled food into my mouth, I had a feeling he'd noticed.

Once finished, he took the dishes to the sink. "Should we go to bed?"

My mouth went dry. Wait, we? He said *we*.

"What?" I somehow managed.

He brought a washcloth over and cleaned up the crumbs from the counter, and my traitorous eyes watched his large hand and muscled forearm swipe back and forth across the surface. Seriously, how could *that* be sexy? But it was.

"You look tired, and I imagine you didn't sleep much after he"—his jaw locked—"after Lord Godasara took you, so I figured you'd want to go to bed now."

"Together?"

His movements stopped. That glow lit his eyes again, and the muscle in his jaw twitched. "Yeah, I'd assumed together."

Since he didn't offer to sleep on the floor, and since this wasn't my apartment, I replied, "I'll stay on the couch."

A heavy scowl formed on his face. "You're not sleeping on the couch."

"Watch me."

"Avery." He sighed and tore a hand through his hair. A moment passed. And then another. The entire time his gaze stayed locked on mine, and even though his expression had smoothed, his emerald eyes held a stormy torrent.

With a muscle still ticking in his jaw, he straightened, the dish rag in his hand forgotten. "I'll sleep on the couch if that makes you more comfortable." Even though he said it in an even tone, the glow around his eyes increased.

I huffed. "Well, yeah, actually that would make me

more comfortable, because you know, I didn't realize we were officially a couple now who slept together every night."

Wyatt picked up the dish rag and folded it slowly, his movements precise. "We certainly seemed like a couple back at Shrouding Estate."

"Why? Because we fucked a few times?"

He threw the dish rag in the sink. So much for folding it.

"Is that what it was to you? Just *fucking?*"

"Well, yeah, isn't that exactly what it was? That's usually what it can be classified as when two people sleep together who don't really know each other. Or are we officially committed now?"

His lips thinned more, but I didn't stop.

"You know, silly me, but speaking of committed relationships, I thought *equality* existed between well-suited couples. But as I've come to learn with you, equality doesn't exist. You're the alpha, I'm your supposed mate, therefore I do as I'm told. Right? Isn't that why I was banished to the Whimsical Room in which I was drugged and then abducted? Poor helpless me. Good thing I have someone big and strong like you to protect me. Oh no wait, you didn't, because I was *abducted.*"

His lips parted, and pain shot through his eyes. "Is that what this is all about? The fact that I didn't protect you? That I wanted you to go to that room in the hope you'd be safer?"

My stomach quivered. I knew he'd tried to prevent my abduction. I *knew* it haunted him that I'd been taken. And despite what he'd just said, he had protected me. Because of him, the ritual had been stopped. If he hadn't intercepted, I'd be dead at this very moment.

But he'd still taken away my choice when the battle hit Shrouding Estate. He'd robbed me of it by guilt-tripping me into doing what he thought was best.

And it *hadn't* been best.

Still, the pained looked in his eyes was making me feel like the biggest bitch.

I looked down, his guilt eating away at me. "I . . . uh . . . I'm going to bed." I hopped off the stool and rushed to his bedroom.

As angry as I was with him, I still felt awful for delivering such a low blow. Inside his dark room, I made myself grab one of the pillows off the bed along with a blanket and place them outside in the hallway.

Guilt still ate at me, but I didn't hear Wyatt approaching, so maybe it was for the best that we both went to bed. Separately.

So with that, I closed the door.

CHAPTER FIFTEEN
WYATT

What the fuck just happened?

I stood at the kitchen counter, my breaths still coming too fast. So Nicholas had been right? He'd told me my overprotectiveness could come between Avery and me.

Dammit.

But before I could get over my shock and round the corner to talk to my mate about why I'd asked her to go to the Whimsical Room, she had already disappeared into my bedroom and closed the door.

I didn't think she was even aware of how fast she'd moved. She'd sped from her barstool as fast as a vamp, the goddess's power shining in her eyes.

With soft steps, I prowled to my bedroom and

stopped outside of it. Disbelief filled me when I saw the pillow and blanket on the floor.

She'd actually kicked me out. She was really gonna make me sleep on the couch. *Fucking A.*

Okay, so she was pissed. Really pissed. But my mate and I were going to talk about this whether she liked it or not. But if she wanted me on the couch tonight, then fine. I would sleep on the damned couch.

But come tomorrow morning, she and I were talking.

With a huff, I collected the pillow and blanket.

My wolf snarled inside me. His growls and irritation weren't helping. What I needed was a run. A long, pounding run under the moon with nothing but his paws thundering on the ground to make me forget how much I was fucking everything up.

But that didn't mean I couldn't fix it.

Still, I resisted the urge to bang my head against the wall.

Growling, I stormed back to the living room and threw the pillow and blanket on the sofa. I paced a few times, but as much as I needed a run, I couldn't leave her. Because if I did, then Avery would be here alone after I'd insisted that she had to come here with me so I could protect her.

I scoffed. What a crock of shit. It was more like *she*

was protecting *me*. Twice she'd saved me from Lord Godasara. Twice she'd gotten the SF out of situations we couldn't handle. And twice she'd done it all on her own.

The reality was that I hadn't done anything to protect her, because she was more than capable of taking care of herself.

And I was only just realizing that.

Nicholas was completely right. I constantly underestimated her.

I tore a hand through my hair when the door cracked open behind me. The scent of lilacs carried with it.

I stilled, my back to the room.

"Wyatt?"

Blood thundered in my ears at her soft tone. "I'm sorry if I disturbed you," I said stiffly over my shoulder.

My voice stayed even despite the frustration riding high inside me. I expected her to close the door again, or maybe retreat to the bathroom to relieve herself before she fell asleep, but what I didn't expect was the soft pad of her footsteps on the carpet.

She paused at my back.

Her lilac scent called to me. What I really wanted to do was lift her against the wall and fuck her anger right out of her, but I wouldn't exert my will on her. I knew now that forcing my dominance over her led to nothing but problems, and dammit, I would figure out how to suppress my urges.

"I'll wake you in the morning and take you to the command center," I said gruffly, still refusing to face her. "If you would rather have your own accommodation, I can arrange that—"

"Wyatt, look at me."

The sharpness in her tone made my heart thump. I turned to face her, the movement slow and precise. When I finally did, my breath caught.

Wild violet light danced in her irises, swirling and blending with the natural brownish-gold that I loved so much. Damn, I loved her fire.

"I didn't mean what I said earlier. I'm sorry. I never should have said that."

Her apology had my jaw dropping. She was apologizing to *me?*

Shame crept into her vivid irises, and she took a step forward. "I was mad at you. So mad, and I lashed out in anger, but that doesn't excuse—"

"No. Don't apologize. You don't need to feel bad. You were right to tell me off like that. I haven't protected you. I've totally and completely failed at protecting you ever since—"

"I didn't mean it!" she said vehemently. "It was cruel

to say that, and I don't want to be cruel. I've just been angry with you. So angry because—"

"Because I've been an ass, I know—"

"No, that's not why!" She blew a strand of hair from her face, zapping energy radiating off of her. "Just listen to me, dammit. You're not an ass. Well, sometimes you are, but I'm mad at you for what you did at the estate. I didn't want to go into the Whimsical Room, but you basically forced me into it, and it's made me resentful. I feel like you keep trying to control my life, and it's driving me crazy. *I* get to make my decisions. Not you."

I opened my mouth to reply, but she continued.

"Initially, I blamed my capture entirely on you because I was drugged in the Whimsical Room. Even though I can't remember all of the details, I do know that I did things with Nicholas, which left me feeling violated in an entirely different way from what the sacred circle did. I also know that if I hadn't been drugged when Lord Godasara grabbed me then I would have been able to fight back.

"I blamed you for all of that when I was in those caves, but just now when I was sitting in your room hearing you outside the door, it finally dawned on me that my anger was misplaced. *You* didn't drug me. Marnee did. I see that now. And you didn't physically force me into the Whimsical Room—guilt-tripped me, yes—but not physically forced. I chose to go to appease you when I should have chosen to fight. Basically, I've been blaming you for Marnee's and my actions and I shouldn't have. It's not fair to you, and I'm sorry for doing that, although you do need to stop answering for me and trying to make my decisions. I don't care if you're an alpha. *I* make my decisions, not you."

The breath rushed out of me. Avery was legit apologizing. This incredible, vibrant, strong, beautiful woman was apologizing to *me.*

"No." I shook my head. "You do *not* need to be sorry." I wanted so desperately to gather her in my arms but stopped myself. I needed to look her in the eyes so she wouldn't feel these misguided emotions. "You have every right to be furious with me. I'm the one who fucked up, not you. You were right to be angry with me for asking you to go in that room. I shouldn't have. I should have let you fight. I shouldn't have locked you away. I should have *listened* to you, but I let my wolf instincts take over. And even if I didn't put that drug in your drink, I'm still to blame. I'm a commander. I might not have been Marnee's direct commander, but both Bavar and I were distracted, yet we knew she posed a threat and we didn't do anything about it. It's our job—*my* job—to see things like that and make the right call. I didn't. So, you're right to think that if it wasn't for me, you never would have been in that room in the first place, and you never would have been drugged."

She shook her head, her long hair falling over her shoulders. "You can't be expected to know everything and make the right calls every time. And even if you believe you're to blame for Marnee, you're not. She's one hundred percent responsible for her actions, and I see now that she was determined to cause problems between us."

A low growl rumbled in my chest. "That she was."

"And it worked." She raised her hands in exasperation. "Look at what she accomplished by drugging me. I blamed you, not her. Unknowingly, we've both played right into her hands."

My jaw dropped. Avery was right. Marnee had gotten exactly what she wanted. She was causing problems between me and my mate.

"Shit," I whispered.

Avery shook her head again. "Do you think she's still in the sea?"

"Probably. She was due for a soak. She was supposed to take leave a few months ago for one, but things got rather busy. Bavar and I think that's why she acted how she did."

"So she wasn't always that crazy?"

I scoffed. "No, not at all. She was normally level-headed."

"What will happen to her?"

"It depends if she returns to the SF on her own or not. After a soak, her mental state will improve and she should revert back to her former self. If she turns herself in, her punishment will be more lenient. If she makes the SF hunt her down, that's another story."

"Well, she must have had it really bad for you to do what she did."

I pressed my lips into a thin line. "Marnee's actions are entirely unforgiveable, even if she did have a crush on me."

A clouded look filled her eyes, and her upper body stiffened.

I immediately went on edge. "What?"

"It's just I feel like I'm coming to know you bit by bit, and one thing that's becoming quite apparent to me is that women notice you. No, more than that, they're *attracted* to you and want you."

"Just because one siren went a bit crazy over a brief one-night stand—"

"There was that redhead at the healing center too." Avery's eyes gave away nothing, but I still caught the slight tightening around her mouth. "I'm guessing you hooked up with her at some point?"

"The redhead?" I stroked my chin, frowning. "Are you talking about Sally?"

She stiffened even more. "Is that her name?"

"If you're referring to the red-headed witch at the healing center, yes, her name is Sally, and no, nothing's ever happened between us. I never dated her. I never slept with her, but she's shown me signs on a few occasions that she would be open to the possibility."

"Oh." She made a move to cross her arms, but I stopped her and closed the distance between us.

"This reminds me of something," I whispered, leaning down to her.

She grew rigid. "What's that?"

"You were jealous of Sally, too, before the alignment."

Her head whipped back. "I'm not jealous!"

My lips twitched. "Are you sure about that?"

She rolled her eyes, but a reluctant smile tugged at her lips. "I was jealous of her before as well?"

I nodded, a smile streaking across my face which I couldn't stop. "I think I like it."

"You like that I'm jealous?" She slugged me in the arm. Hard.

Damn. Okay, maybe that wasn't the right thing to admit, but fucking hell, I could feel my mate's fire rising and it was turning me on.

"Yeah," I whispered, brushing my lips near her ear.

She shivered. "I like it. It means you have feelings for me, even if you don't want to admit it."

Her breath quickened, growing shallower as my lips danced over her skin. "Well, I for one don't like it at all."

"It's not just you, you know," I said, kissing her softly below her ear.

A shiver wracked her body.

"It's me too. I get jealous any time another man looks at you. And the thought of some other guy touching you . . ." My fingers curled into her clothing. "That I can't handle."

"But no men ever look at me, not like women do at you."

I whipped my head back. "Is that what you think?" I asked incredulously, then dipped my hands lower until I was softly kneading the muscles in her lower back. Another shiver raced through her. "I'm pretty sure Nicholas has a permanent boner around you. Not to mention the dozens of SF members who give you second looks when they pass you on the sidewalk. Or how Bavar is obsessed with your cookies—"

She slugged me again, except playfully this time. "Just because Bavar likes my cookies doesn't mean he likes me that way."

I chuckled, loving the teasing light dancing in her eyes. "Maybe he hasn't overtly flirted with you, but that's probably only because he knows I'd rip his head off if he did."

A smile curved her lips. "Hardly. Nicholas's head is still intact even though you claim he has a—how did you put it so eloquently? A permanent boner for me?"

My mood darkened. "I almost ripped his head off when I found him on top of you in the Whimsical Room. If Bishop hadn't been there, I would have."

Horror lit her eyes. "You found him on top of me?"

"He was feeding on your neck, and you were—" I cleared my throat. "Enjoying it."

Her face paled. "Oh Gods." She twisted her hands. "Were we doing . . . anything else?"

"No, thankfully. You still had your clothes on, and while he was shirtless, he did have his pants zipped." I plowed a hand through my hair. Just thinking of that moment made my wolf snarl, and fury lit my blood on fire. "Your embrace was rather passionate, but that was all that happened. I would have scented it if it'd gone further."

A flush filled her cheeks. "And you walked in on that? Oh Gods, Wyatt, I'm so sorry."

I cradled her face in my palms, her tone cutting through the agony that moment had born. "You have nothing to be sorry about. You were drugged against your will with a powerful aphrodisiac. Anybody would have responded as you and Nicholas did. I'm just glad that I interrupted before it went any further."

Her eyes widened even more. "I still haven't fully remembered what happened after we drank that poison. It's still all a blur, but I'm glad it didn't go past an embrace." She shuddered. "If I ever walked in on you doing that—"

"You never will." I tilted her face up, my gaze drawn to her plump lips that—fucking hell—I wanted to kiss so desperately. "Because I'm yours. Forever. I said it before, and I'll say it again. You're my mate, which means you're the only woman I'll ever want now. That I'll ever"—I swallowed down the thickness in my throat—"love. And I know that's a lot to take in and ask of you considering you don't remember who I am, but it's the truth."

"But what if we're not actually compatible?" Her winged eyebrows knit together. "What if this bond is the only reason we're together? What if we stay together and learn that we don't even really *like* each other?"

I shook my head. "I already know I like you. For years I liked you before it became anything." I cradled her face more. "You're smart, Avery, and so strong, and you care about others. You help people when they need it. And you're so damned resilient. You stand up again and again even when you're knocked down. I saw that daily in your training. Your magic may have been weak, but your soul is strong. I *saw* who you really are then and back in Ridgeback, and I love that woman. I love *you*." I kissed her jaw, her ear, the tender skin on her neck.

She shivered.

"And I know you don't remember me, but at one time in your life, you liked me too. And I'm okay with that. I'm okay with you needing to get to know me again before committing. You can bet your damnedest, though, that I'm going to do everything I can to make you fall for me all over again. But to answer your question, no, it's not just the mating bond that attracts us to one another. Yes, that contributes to my insatiable need for you and why I can get it up again and again, even if I've fucked you fifty shades since Sunday, but it isn't why I love you. I love you for you, not because of the—"

She was on her tiptoes, closing the remaining distance between us before I could utter another word. Her lips pressed to mine, and I couldn't hold back.

I gripped her to me, the savage need to claim her so strong I nearly ripped her clothes off.

Her lips opened, her tongue sliding out to dance with mine. She threaded her fingers through my hair, a low moan escaping her.

Fuck, she tasted good. I tore my mouth from hers, knowing that if I didn't get this off my chest now, I never would. I was two seconds away from wrapping her legs around my waist and fucking her against the wall.

"Avery, you need to know something."

Her glazed eyes stared up at me, her rapid breaths making my dick strain against my pants even more. "What?"

"I'm a werewolf, Avery. You need to understand what that means. Every instinct in my body *demands* that I protect you. Do you understand what that entails? My wolf, my inner being, orders me to protect you from everything and everyone that could harm you. It's why I so desperately wanted you in the Whimsical Room. I thought it was the safest option. I didn't want you to fight even though you could have probably ended Lord Godasara right there."

She nodded, some of the lust fading from her eyes. "Okay. I understand."

"But do you? That's instinct, Avery. I *can't* overcome instinct. It's the essence of who I am. I'm always going to want to fight for you, protect you, cherish you, save you, even if I've been shit at saving you lately."

She laughed softly.

My grip on her tightened. I didn't want to say the next bit, but I knew I had to. I would never rest easy if I didn't. "But I've also seen the hesitancy in you. That maybe you want something different than me. And you deserve someone who doesn't force you into rooms to hide. You deserve a man who will proudly march into battle with you by his side—"

She pressed a finger against my lips. "Okay, first off, I don't plan to make it a habit of going into battles. And secondly, even though your overbearing dominant nature is *infuriating* at times, I'm capable of saying no to you, which I plan to do from now on. And I don't mind your dominance all the time. In fact—" A rosy blush filled her cheeks. "I kind of like it, in other ways." A scent rose from her. A rich, musky scent, tinged with heady lilacs that told me exactly what kind of *other ways* she was referring to.

A jolt of lust shot through me. Fucking hell. So she liked a bit of dominance in the sack. And fuck if that didn't make my dick just go as hard as iron.

She threaded her fingers through my hair, the sensation utterly distracting and arousing. "I just don't like when I feel I don't have a choice. At the estate, I felt like I couldn't say no to you. And yes, I know your reasoning for me going in that room made sense—we still didn't know if the goddess's power inside me could be trusted to work—but I still felt like you undervalued me. And for the record, it's been *twice* now that I've been able to fight when it was needed, so I think I've proven that I'm not a complete weakling. I can be trusted to hold my own."

"You've never been a weakling," I groaned. I crushed her to me, no longer able to hold back.

Her breath came out in a sharp exhale.

I cradled her to me, then leaned down to bury my nose in her neck and inhale. "I'm sorry," I whispered. "I'm so fucking sorry for doing that, but you have to understand that sometimes my instincts rule me. I can't stop them, but I *can* learn to control them better. Fuck, Little Flower, if you give me a second chance, I will spend the rest of my life working to control my instincts each and every day."

She tenderly brushed a lock of hair from my forehead. "You don't need to control them *that* much, but I do ask that if I want to do something that you don't try to stop me. Even if your instincts want to cover me in bubble wrap, please don't guilt-trip me again into doing what you think is best when *I* don't want to do it."

"I won't." I shook my head. "I mean, I probably will do that again, but point it out to me when I do, and I'll stop. I don't want you to feel suffocated or grow to resent me. I want you to stay as you are and keep fighting me when I'm being pigheaded and unreasonable."

She ran a finger along my chest.

My erection grew even stiffer.

"I can do that," she said coyly.

I kneaded her hips, drawing her even closer to me until she felt my stiff length. Her breath hitched.

"Does that mean you're going to give me a second chance?"

She laughed. "I didn't realize we were already done with the first chance."

"I thought you weren't sure if you wanted to be with me."

Her eyes flashed violet, the shade mixing with her natural hue. "You're right. I'll be honest, I was having second thoughts. But the truth is that I'm as drawn to you as you're drawn to me. I don't think I could walk away from you."

"So that means we'll always figure things out? That you won't ever run from me?" I rubbed her against me more, and the musky scent in her lilacs grew. *Fuuuuuuck.*

"Well, I can't promise I'll never run from you. I have a feeling that if I did make you chase me, the sex when you finally caught up would be worth it."

I groaned. "If that's the kind of chasing you want, babe, I'll chase you all damn night."

"In that case—" She abruptly tore from my arms and sprinted from the living room.

The next thing I knew, my apartment door was open, the scent of lilacs growing fainter.

She did not just do that.

For a moment, I stood there, shock filling me. But then my wolf rumbled in excitement. He was right. She *did* just do that.

That's right, buddy, I said to him, tearing my shirt off and exploding into my wolf form in a glimmer of magic. If my mate wanted a chase, I was more than happy to appease her.

Game on, Avery. Game on.

CHAPTER SIXTEEN
AVERY

Night wind caressed my cheeks as the goddess's power infused speed into me. I raced across a training field, the world a blur around me. Behind me, a wolf howled, the sound long and filled with impatience for the hunt.

A shiver danced down my spine, because the thought of Wyatt chasing me and then pinning me . . . it made me so hot with anticipation.

I sped across another field, my loose pants making it easy to jump and leap over training equipment and brush. The forest's dark trees waited ahead. Within seconds, I was in the woods.

I didn't hear his wolf's howl again, but I knew that Wyatt pursued me. An ache had already formed in my core, throbbing with need for the man chasing at my heels, and the feel of the cool night wind flowing across my skin only made me burn hotter.

Dark branches forked out of the trees like spindly fingertips. I dipped and swayed around them, calling upon the goddess's power as I sprinted among the trees.

The scent of dry leaves and mineral-laden soil filled my senses. Goosebumps pimpled my skin, and anticipation heated my blood.

I had no idea how long it would take Wyatt to catch me, but I knew he would.

The terrain grew steeper, but I didn't feel the exertion. Power flowed through my veins, little jolts of electricity zinging along my nerves. The goddess's power hummed in my chest and gave me strength that I'd never known I had.

I leapt over logs and ducked under branches as I ran up the hill. My speed didn't slow despite the strenuous climb.

Reaching out, I was about to grab onto a tree branch and launch myself farther up the hill, when something nipped at my heels.

My breath rushed out of me in a squeal of surprise. I stumbled forward about to fall onto the dry soil when a large wolf suddenly appeared right in front of me.

He broke my fall, so I landed on him. I giggled when I got a face full of fur.

Wyatt in his wolf form whined and licked me, his tail wagging as eagerly as a puppy's.

I laughed again and threaded my fingers through his soft fur as he licked my face again.

Panting from breathlessness, I took in his beautiful coat. Moonlight outlined his silver, white, and black colors. He was an absolutely *beautiful* wolf.

"Aren't you a handsome boy?" I said, laughing again when he eagerly licked my cheek.

He whined and wiggled beneath me, but just as I was about to compliment him further, an explosion of heat erupted beneath my palms, and then Wyatt's naked body was beneath me.

"Oh!" I exclaimed.

He chuckled, not missing a beat. His hands went to my hips, pinning me to him. "Got you!"

His eyes glowed in the night, teasing and full of fun, as his fingers dug into my flesh like an anchor. All of the breath rushed out of me as an entirely new excitement grew inside me.

"Something tells me you liked that," he said huskily. He leaned up and nipped at my neck. The feel of his lips on my skin made lust shoot to my core.

I somehow managed to swallow my moan, even though he'd started doing the most delicious things with his tongue. "Maybe," I replied coquettishly. "Maybe not."

His chuckle deepened, the sound rumbling in his chest. "You can lie all you want, Little Flower, but your scent tells me something else entirely." He ran his hands around my ass, then cupped the globes.

I pouted, pretending to be put out. "You know, I was enjoying getting to know your wolf a little more. Did you have to spoil our fun?"

His lips curved up. "You can play with him some other time. Right now, I want to be in control."

I quirked an eyebrow. "In control for what?" I asked innocently.

His pupils dilated as his hand kneaded my ass through the thin pants. "Did I ever tell you that you have the sweetest ass I've ever seen?" He dug his fingers into the flesh, and my core tightened. "I should take you from behind. Pound into you until you're screaming my name."

My eyes fluttered, my legs automatically parting. "I suppose I could let you do that."

He pulled me flush against him, then pressed kisses down my neck. "Although if you're going to make me chase you every time I want to smack this ass—" As if to get his point across, he smacked me lightly and damn if my core didn't turn molten. "Then I think I should be rewarded, don't you agree?"

"Hmm?" I replied, his lips distracting me again as he

kissed under my ear. But then my foggy brain honed in on the word *reward*. "You want a reward?"

His tongue darted out, making a shiver curl my toes. "Don't you think I deserve one? You just made me chase you several miles across fields and woods. I think that warrants a reward, don't you?"

A breathy moan escaped me when his fingers dipped lower, between my legs, so close to the aching juncture between my thighs. "Maybe, but . . . what kind of reward . . ."—I managed between pants—" . . . did you want?"

His lips moved down to my collarbone while his fingers continued to tease and taunt.

He brushed my baggy shirt aside, using his teeth to drag it along my skin, and then his tongue was trailing across my collarbone, nipping and biting as he went.

A delicious shiver made liquid heat slicken my folds.

"I'm thinking my reward should be a little taste."

"A taste . . . where?" I somehow managed when his erection rubbed against my stomach.

His hands slipped around my ass to in between my thighs. He swirled them along my swollen sex, my pants growing damp from the contact, and the movement making me moan in pleasure.

"How about here?" he asked, then tapped the bundle of nerves.

For a moment, I couldn't speak. My body lit on fire. "I suppose," I finally whispered, "I could accommodate that."

"Well, that's good to hear. I would hate to force a reward on you that you weren't wanting in return."

"Oh, no," I said quickly. "I really don't mind."

His deep chuckle filled the quiet woods around us, and I suddenly became aware that we were outside in the middle of a forest without any privacy whatsoever. "Do you think anybody will know what we're doing out here?"

He shrugged, not looking the least bit bothered by our clandestine activities. "The sorcerers' wards keep anybody out who shouldn't be here, and I don't scent any other SF members around at the moment. If that changes, I'll tell you."

Before I could say anything further, my loose pants were ripped off me, and cool night wind washed over my naked sex.

I moaned when his thick fingers met my bare flesh. He fiddled them against my core again, light swirls and soft caresses that instantly had me straddling him and grinding against his length.

He groaned. "Now, now, someone's getting a bit too eager." In a swift move, he rolled me over and pinned me beneath him.

KRISTA STREET

The dry forest soil and crunching leaves pressed into my back as he spread my thighs and inched my shirt up higher.

His nostrils flared as he took a deep inhale. "You smell like a bouquet of the sexiest lilacs I've ever encountered. Did you know that, Little Flower?"

I giggled. "Sexy lilacs? I don't think I've ever smelled flowers quite like that."

"That's because you're one of a kind." He dipped down to cup my breast through my shirt before sucking my taut nipple through the cotton.

I completely forgot what we were talking about as I arched beneath him.

"I can tell you . . ." He pulled back, and the damp material rubbed over my breast, making my nipple ache with need. "That nobody else in the world smells like you do."

His head dipped again, and before I could muster a reply, he was kneeling between my legs and kissing my inner thighs.

A rush of anticipation flowed through me when he nipped and bit softly near my core, the tastes teasing and quick, designed for nothing more than to drive me mad.

I cried out, and ran my heels down his back, urging him closer to my swollen mound.

210

"Someone's a little eager," he commented.

"More than eager," I moaned.

Chuckling deeply, he nestled himself on the forest floor and kissed closer to my clit.

I curved off the ground, wanting so badly for him to lick me that I was willing to beg for it. "Please, Wyatt, I want you."

"Is this what you want?" His tongue slid out and lapped against me, the movement making my toes curl and a breathy moan escape my throat.

"Yes." I pushed down until my swollen sex met his face. "That's what I want."

He growled, the sound deep and low. "Then I suppose I must oblige."

And then he *devoured* me.

My arms jerked out, my fingers digging into the soil, when his tongue became unleashed. He sucked and licked me to the point of combustion, lapping and teasing me until I was writhing beneath him.

The man was truly a magician with his tongue. Within seconds, I was on the verge of coming as he ate me out like a starving man.

I cried out again when his tongue swirled over my clit, because I wanted more, I needed *more*.

He seemed to sense it, because he abruptly stopped

and crawled up my body, leaving my sex wet and open in the cool night.

"Wyatt?" I whispered imploringly.

"Yes, Little Flower?" His eyes were like two shining gold stars, lust and desire glowing in them. "You taste like the sweetest honey." He dipped down and kissed me, just as his rigid length prodded my entrance.

I bucked, then tilted my hips to guide him inside me.

I expected him to tease me, probably wanting to torture me as he'd done continually at Shrouding Estate, but his need seemed to rival mine, because he readily allowed me to position him at my entrance before he slid into me in one giant thrust.

I cried out as the feel and width of him made me scream in ecstasy. His erection was so big that he stretched me to capacity, but my body was hot and ready, and he felt so good.

"Yes," I moaned. I gripped his ass harder as he began to move inside me.

"Gods, you feel like heaven." He shifted one arm underneath my neck to hold me tightly. With his other hand, he gripped my hip, holding me in place as he began to thrust deeply, wielding his erection like a battering ram.

I threaded my fingers into the hair at his nape,

curling them around his neck before gripping his shoulders.

The feel of him sliding in and out of me, his thick length curving and rubbing on that spot deep inside of me, made my desire for him rocket as the waves began to build.

He picked up his tempo. It wasn't long before I was on the verge of coming, and I knew that he was right there with me.

"Oh Gods, Avery, I don't think I can wait much longer," he groaned. "You feel so fucking good. So tight. So hot."

"Don't stop," I panted.

I held on to him as he pounded into me, each slap against my hips like a burst of fire licking my core. The waves built higher, then even higher, threatening to slip me over the edge at any moment.

"I'm going to come, babe. I'm too close," he groaned.

"Yes." Seeing the tightening of his face and the veins in his neck stand on end careened me over the edge.

I screamed as an explosive orgasm rocked through me.

Wyatt's shout came a second later. He slammed into me one final time before taking us both home.

Gripping his shoulders, I bucked and arched beneath him as my climax shattered my core. His entire body shuddered above me, his groans deep and low as his seed shot into me.

We lay like that for a moment, our bodies slick and joined as the aftereffects of our lovemaking settled on our skin.

It felt like minutes before I could catch my breath, and when I finally did, I opened my eyes to see him staring down at me.

He smiled tenderly, and brushed a leaf from my hair. The loving look on his face took my breath away.

"Have I ever told you that you're the most amazing woman I've ever met?" He fingered a lock of hair behind my ear.

"I don't know," I replied, my lips tilting into a teasing smile. "Have you?"

He chuckled. "Gods, I certainly hope so. But if I haven't, I'm telling you now, you are the most *incredible* woman I've ever met. No one's ever made me feel the way you do."

My stomach dipped, the emotion in his eyes making everything inside me melt. "Good, because I would hate it if you felt this for anyone else."

He grinned, then nuzzled my neck and gathered me closer in his arms.

When another gust of wind flowed across my limbs, I suddenly became aware that we were nearly naked and we were miles away from his apartment. Alarm shot through me.

"Are you going to walk back like that?" I asked. "As naked as the day you were born?"

He shrugged. "I suppose I'll have to."

"You don't want to run in your wolf form?"

Another teasing smile lightened his expression. "Do you want to get to know my wolf a little bit better?"

I shrugged. "He is rather gorgeous, and I wouldn't mind petting him again." My eyes widened. "Or would he not like that? I mean, is that like demeaning or something, since he's really you or whatever?"

Wyatt barked out a laugh. "No, it wouldn't be demeaning, and if you want to pet him, I'm sure he'd eat it up. And just so you know, I'm pretty sure you can do whatever you want with him, and he'll like it. He would probably even play fetch with you."

I laughed but rolled my eyes. "I don't think I'll be doing anything as demeaning as that, thank you very much."

He chuckled again, the sound deep and filled with delight. "Just saying. I don't want you to hold back, 'cause when it comes to you, he'll do anything."

His statement was filled with mirth but also complete truth. It made my breath hitch. "How did I ever get so lucky to meet you?" I asked quietly.

He sobered, that tender look filling his eyes again. "I'm just glad we met again at all. Before, I wished that it had been two years from now, so my commitment with the SF would be done, but now, I thank the Gods that I found you when I did, because if I hadn't, maybe the Safrinite comet would have killed you."

I cocked my head, wishing I knew more about what he was talking about, but my mind was still a blank canvas of nothingness for everything before waking up in that field outside the capital.

"Then I'll count myself fortunate that I came here," I replied. "Because Safrinite comet or not, I feel so lucky that we met."

Cool autumn air swirled around us. When I gave a shiver, Wyatt rolled me to my side until his body covered me more and his heat warmed me.

"We should head back," he said, giving me a quick peck on the nose. "As much as I'm enjoying this, I know you're tired and need to sleep."

I yawned as if on cue. "Yeah, you're probably right. Do you think it's a long walk?" I had no idea how far I'd run before he'd caught me.

He shrugged. "No idea, but I can get us back in no time if I carry you."

Before I could protest, Wyatt dressed me, and then I was off the ground and swept up in his arms. Wind suddenly streamed across my face and flowed through my hair as he sprinted downhill through the trees with me cradled to his chest.

I squealed in surprise, which only elicited a deep laugh from Wyatt as he ran harder.

A few minutes later, we were back at the front door of his barracks, coming to a sudden stop.

His chest rose, deep breaths filling him, and I gasped in surprise. "How did you get here so quickly?"

He shrugged, not letting me down. "I can run fast when I want to."

I looked down. His rather impressive dick, even when soft, dangled between his legs. I arched an eyebrow. "Is that how you run in public normally?"

He opened the front door, not seeming the least bit perturbed by his nudity, and stepped into the entryway. "Only when I don't have any clothes."

Before I knew what was happening, he was bounding up the stairs two at a time and suddenly, we were in front of his apartment door—a door that was still wide open.

I slapped a hand over my mouth when a laugh bubbled up. "I wonder how much time actually passed between me running out of here, you catching me, and us, *you know*, before getting back here." I glanced at the clock, not even sure what time I'd initially left. "Do you think fifteen minutes sounds about right?"

He arched a teasing eyebrow before kicking the door shut behind us. "Actually, it was fourteen minutes. For a moment there, I thought you were saying I was slow."

I laughed as he carried me into his bedroom.

Green fire smoldered in his eyes when he set me on the mattress. The room was dark and cool. Moonlight streamed in through the open curtain.

I rubbed my legs together, an aching pulse already starting low in my belly. From the growing rigid length between his legs, I had a feeling that he was up for round two as well.

Mate.

My thighs automatically parted, my blood singing with need for him.

His nostrils flared as he moved on top of me, his stiff erection prodding my entrance before he sank into me.

I gasped at the feel of his hard length buried inside me. Gods, I would never get enough of this.

He groaned when I tilted my hips, forcing him to move. "Something tells me, Little Flower, that we're not going to be getting much sleep after all."

CHAPTER SEVENTEEN
AVERY

T he sound of a crackling fire filled the air, yet the fire pit was nowhere to be seen.

I hovered in space, a spectral form in the night. A pair of dark, all-seeing eyes watched me from the distance.

I was in a small room with a lone window. But wait, where was the forest?

A woman lay below me on a bed, covered in a sheet. A machine hummed beside her, and another woman dressed in a long robe stood nearby, doing something on a tablet. Armed guards stood in each corner of the room.

My breath sucked in as I recognized the surroundings. The healing center.

Oh Gods! I'm projecting!

"Goddess Verasellee?" The healer had moved to her side,

completely oblivious to me also being in the room. "Can you open your eyes?"

The goddess didn't move, didn't respond. Her chest rose once, then twice, but her complexion . . .

I peered closer. Something wasn't right about her skin. She looked sickly.

A deep ominous growl rose in the distance. I whipped around, searching for the source of that sound. I didn't see anybody, yet I knew it was him.

"She's dying in your realm, you little fool," Lord Godasara called out. "You can't keep her there. You must bring her back to me, or you both shall perish."

A bolt of terror zinged through my nerves. He knew. Lord Godasara knew where we were because all of our souls were *messily linked to one another in that sick ritual he'd done thousands of years ago.*

"Hurry," he called. "You don't have much time."

I JOLTED UPRIGHT IN BED, my soul slamming back into my body like a blast of Arctic wind. A scream crawled up my throat as I gasped and gulped for air, but I managed to swallow my scream down.

I'd projected to Verasellee, and Lord Godasara had just projected to me while I was on *earth*. But I thought that wasn't possible? That he couldn't project across realms?

But he was so much stronger than anybody else. Perhaps he could project through his sheer power, just like the goddess could.

Whatever the case, his dire warning haunted me. Verasellee couldn't survive in this realm. She needed to return to the fae lands. We would never be safe from him.

"Oh Gods, no," I whimpered.

Wyatt stirred beside me, as early morning light streamed into his bedroom. His hand automatically went to my lower back as his eyes looked foggy and glazed, his hair disheveled. "Avery, what's wrong?"

Terror slid through my veins like ice water. "Lord Godasara knows we've returned to the SF headquarters, and he knows the goddess isn't well. She can't stay in this realm. She doesn't belong here. I have to go to her."

I scrambled off the bed, needing to see her *now*. Her power hummed and zapped inside me, electrifying my nerves.

Somehow, I managed to get out of bed without tumbling to the floor.

In a blink, Wyatt was standing beside me. "I don't understand. What happened?"

His naked, gorgeous body momentarily snagged my

attention. Chiseled abs, rounded shoulders, and pecs that begged for my touch were only inches away.

But I jerked my gaze to the floor and searched for my cotton pajama pants and T-shirt from the night before, because even Wyatt in all of his beautiful nakedness couldn't lure me back to bed.

Not after what I'd learned.

"I had another dream." I yanked my pants on, then slid my arms through the shirt. "I saw her—the goddess—and I saw him. Lord Godasara knows we're here, and he knows that we took the goddess from the fae lands. He said that she'll die if she stays here. And he's right. I saw her in my dream. She's sickly. I need to help her."

Wyatt's hands shot out, grasping my upper arms. His warm palms closed around me, and a fraction of my soul calmed. "Projectors can't cross realms, and he probably knows that you and Verasellee are here because common sense says this is where we would have taken you. It's the safest place on earth for you to be. He would know that."

His touch soothed some of the panic that was sliding through my veins, but he was wrong about common sense being the reason. "Maybe other supernaturals with projecting abilities can't cross realms, but that's not the case for him. He's so strong, Wyatt. He *can* project across realms. I'm sure of it. Now, I have to go. I have to see Verasellee."

His grip tightened. "Please, let's just take a minute. Can you tell me more about the dream, about what happened."

"But Verasellee—"

"Is okay. We would've been notified if she was unwell. Now, start from the beginning and tell me what's going on." He guided me toward the bed until I sat down.

His calm and soothing demeanor helped quell some of the fear quaking in my chest, until I realized what he was doing. Anger exploded in me, electrifying my nerves. "You're doing it again!"

His head snapped back.

"Stop trying to control me and prevent me from doing what I want!"

His face turned ashen, then smoldering light filled his eyes. "Shit. You're right. I'm sorry." He ran his hands over his cheeks, then slapped them. "You're distraught, and my gut's telling me to soothe you. Dammit. It's instinct. I'm fighting instinct, and I promise that I'll keep fighting it. I didn't mean to try and control you."

Desperation lined his words, and his eyes turned so pleading that my stomach flipped. Still, I didn't have time for this. "I have to go."

He didn't try to stop me a second time, but he followed me to the door. The sharp emotions rolling off him were as prickly as a desert cactus, and his brow was so heavy with worry its weight filled the room.

"Can I come with you?" he asked when I paused to slam my feet into flip flops.

I grasped the door handle. Wyatt had just asked for my permission to tag along. Back at Shrouding Estate, he wouldn't have.

His throat worked a swallow. "I'll stay here if you'd rather go alone, but I—" Another swallow. "I'd like to come with you if you'll let me."

I took a deep breath, the air stuttering out of me. "Okay. Let's go."

THE HEALING CENTER was only minutes away, yet neither of us spoke on my mad dash there.

Wyatt followed just behind me, his presence like a looming shadow as the early morning sky glowed overhead.

The glowing green sign for the healing center came into view, but before I reached it, Wyatt asked, "Can you tell me more about your dream? If you're willing?"

His request was so quiet and halting. I knew my

explosion back in his apartment had cut him deeply, because the great Wyatt Jamison wasn't infallible. Even he fucked up.

But he was trying. I could admit that despite all that was going on.

I explained the dream to him in detail, telling him about how I'd been in Verasellee's room at the healing center and how Lord Godasara had been watching. "We're all linked because of the ritual he conducted thousands of years ago, and the prophecy the goddess set in motion. All of us must be able to project to one another."

"Projecting takes so much magic."

"Well, he certainly has enough." I yanked open the door and stepped into the healing center.

As we climbed the stairs, some distant part of my brain latched onto the history of the elf lords and their immense power. A millennia ago, they'd grown extinct, not through natural selection but through genocide. They'd once ruled the fae lands with an iron fist, ruthlessly powerful and disarmingly magical.

It was only through centuries of battles that they'd been taken down one by one, until the fae realm was allowed to exist under lesser-magical but multiple rulers.

The Nolus fae ruled the land around the capital. The

Silten fae governed the continent across the Adriastic sea. Solis fae ruled the frozen north, and Lochen fae controlled the vast oceans and seas.

Before, none of those fae had ruled. They'd all been slaves to the elves, the elf lords being the most powerful of them all.

But now, separate governments controlled the fae lands. Those governments stretched far and wide, across vast seas and frozen tundra.

Even though the elf lords were long dead, the fae lands wasn't without its problems. Skirmishes still occurred. Diplomatic alliances at times were tenuous at best. But the realm hadn't seen dark times since the reign of the elf lords.

And now one elf lord remained.

Lord Godasara, dormant for thousands of years, who was just as ruthless as his predecessors, strove to retrieve his great power, his iron fist, his wrathful rule. And with the goddess's power he would be guaranteed complete control. The fae lands would descend into a world of death and carnage if he wasn't stopped.

Wyatt and I reached the top of the stairs and walked toward the ward's doors. "It's why I've been having these dreams. The goddess has been projecting to me, trying to warn me. She was trying to tell me what Lord Godasara wanted to do when we were back at

Shrouding Estate, but I didn't understand at the time. Now I do. She and Lord Godasara called me to her room just now. Something's wrong with her. I know it."

Wyatt nodded, his moss-green eyes bright. "Okay, then we'll fix it."

The clock read seven in the morning when we pushed through the healing center's doors. My eyes felt gritty even though my mind had sharpened to an arrow's point.

We passed the witches' station and neared the end of the hall. When we reached Verasellee's door, the guards made room for us to enter but an older woman emerged and nearly collided with us before we could.

She drew up short, her eyebrows pinched together. "Oh my, I didn't see you there." She gave us a once-over, her gaze lingering on my pajamas and flip flops. "Good morning, Ms. Meyers and Major Jamison." The woman dipped her head, her jowls jiggling. The nameplate on her robe read *Cora.*

"Morning, Cora." Wyatt gave a curt nod. "How is the goddess doing?"

Cora's brow creased together so tightly I could have popped off a bottle top on it. "We were just discussing her. A few of her numbers have changed. We were going to call in Farrah and Douglas so they could do an assessment on her—"

My stomach seized, and I dashed into the goddess's room.

The interior guards came to attention when I raced inside, but I ignored them. The goddess's power hummed and swirled inside me when I ground to a halt at her side. My stomach twisted as I gazed down at her unconscious form. She looked sickly.

My dream was right!

"We need to go back to the fae lands!" I whirled around to face Wyatt and Cora. *Gods. What if we're too late?* I pointed at Verasellee's exposed upper arm. "Look at her skin. She's paler. And look at her complexion. She looks sick. She needs to return to her realm."

Nervous energy clouded around Cora, and a frown creased Wyatt's expression.

I knew I was acting like a bit of a lunatic, but they didn't have an inner connection to the goddess. They didn't feel what I felt.

Something about the goddess felt *off*, like an oily substance had coated her essence.

To the marrow of my bones I knew that if I didn't act soon, she would die.

"I don't know if Wes will allow that." Cora twisted her hands.

"It doesn't matter if he will or won't. I'm taking her back." Because even though Lord Godasara was an evil elf, his warning in my dream had been right. He hadn't been trying to trick me, although I knew when we returned to the fae lands that would change. I was under no illusion that he'd simply leave us alone.

He wanted Verasellee, and he wanted me, and despite me taking out his sacred circle I knew that he wasn't going to stop.

"Don't you feel it?" I gestured toward the goddess. "She's *dying.*"

Cora gave Wyatt an apprehensive glance.

But instead of giving me a pacifying comment, Wyatt crossed his arms and leveled me with a solid stare. "You can feel that she's deteriorating?"

"Yes. I *know* that she is."

"Speaking of being affected by our return to earth, how are you feeling?"

His question took me by surprise. "Fine. Why?"

"We've been concerned about how your health would fare here on earth."

I waved my hand in annoyance. "Well, you shouldn't be. I'm from this realm. I'm totally fine."

Cora still grabbed some probes and slapped them under my shirt before scanning me as I stood there. "She's right. Her magic and life force are strong."

I crossed my arms, irritation making me as prickly as a hungry grizzly bear rising from a long hibernation.

"Like I said, I'm fine. Now, can we concentrate on the goddess? She's who matters."

Wyatt nodded curtly, while Cora continued to look frazzled.

"I'm not understanding," the healing witch said. "How can you know how she's doing? You don't have any scanning devices and you're not a healing witch with natural-born assessment skills."

"Their souls are linked," Wyatt explained to the healing witch. "Avery can sense things from Verasellee that none of us can." Wyatt whipped out his tablet. "I'll let Wes know. We'll see what he says about returning to the fae lands."

I lifted Verasellee's sheets and threaded my fingers through hers. Her skin felt cool, smooth, and *different*. There was something about her that quite simply felt otherworldly.

Her power inside me hummed and flowed, some of the panic in my chest easing. "I know you're not doing well. I'll get you out of here," I whispered to her.

She didn't respond, not one twitch or flutter of movement, but I could have sworn that the power inside me responded for the barest moment, an electric spark coursing through me.

Twenty minutes later, I was still holding her hand when Wes and Bavar walked through the door.

The SF general wore the same uniform as the rest of the squad members. Despite his age, he looked trim and fit. "Ms. Meyers," he said by way of greeting. "Major Jamison has told me you're concerned about Goddess Verasellee."

Behind him, Bavar hung near the door. He casually crossed his arms as the dagger strapped to his waist flashed in the morning sunlight.

I nodded a hello to him, then turned to General McCloy.

"I had a dream about her," I said simply, knowing that going into details would take too long. "She and I are linked, our souls are connected. I can feel that she's dying, and Lord Godasara warned me of the same thing in my dream. He said that if I don't get her out of earth's realm and back to the fae lands soon, that she would die."

Wes raised an eyebrow. "Lord Godasara?"

"We're all linked," I said in a hurry. "Like I told you yesterday. It's why the elf lord can't die while that link still remains. It's hard to explain, but he did come to warn me, and yes, I know we can't trust him, but I also know that without Verasellee alive nothing he's planned can come true. He needs me and her for whatever ritual he tried to do."

"You don't think this is merely a trick? That he's trying to lure you back to the fae lands?"

"It's not a trick. He's right. She's dying. But I understand your concern. If I couldn't feel her, I probably would think it's a trap, but I *can* feel her, so I know he's right. Verasellee's not well. I think it's because she doesn't belong in this universe. She's not one of our gods. She needs to return to where she belongs—the fae lands realm."

"Speaking of the link you all share . . ." Wes placed his hands on his hips. "I've spoken with my sorcerers, and with help from Nicholas and the Bulgarian library gargoyles, I think they might have a spell that will work to unlink all of you."

My eyes widened. "Really?"

"Yes, but I don't know for sure yet. They're still looking into it."

Wyatt stepped forward. "I can take Avery and the goddess back to the fae lands."

A flash of gratitude jolted through me. I knew how hard that declaration must have been for him. Lord Godasara was waiting for me there. No doubt, Wyatt's instincts were begging him to keep me here.

But he wasn't going to act on them. He was going to do what I'd asked.

I remembered what he'd said last night, about

promising to no longer exert his dominance over me and being willing to listen to me when he slipped and fucked up.

He'd fucked up this morning but had been quick to acknowledge and remedy it.

He's really trying to change. And in that moment, I knew that he would. It didn't mean he'd never fuck up again. Of course, he would, but the most important aspect was that he was now accepting there was a problem and working to correct it.

Just as he had now. He knew how important protecting the goddess was to me, and despite the dangers of returning to the fae lands, he wasn't demanding that I stay here at the SF where I was safe from Lord Godasara.

Wes's fingers tapped against his hip bones. "That will be fine, although you can't take her back quite yet. We're not prepared for that. We'll need several squads ready to go so we can finish this once and for all. It'll take some time to arrange that."

I shook my head. "She doesn't have time to wait. I can *feel* her dying. She needs to go back. Now."

Wes opened his mouth, and I knew he was going to argue, but Bavar pushed against the door and trailed to Wyatt's side. "My squad's ready to go. I know it's not ideal since we took a big hit, but we're all rested, and quite frankly Bishop, Heidi, Terry, and Charlotte are looking for blood. We have a fallen member to avenge. Squad Three can accompany Wyatt, Avery, and the goddess to the fae lands this morning. I'll need an hour to alert my team and mobilize them."

"Fallen squad member?" I asked.

Bavar's face clouded. "Lex died at the battle at Shrouding Estate."

I gasped. "I didn't know. I'm so sorry."

Bavar dipped his head again. "Thank you. We look forward to avenging his death."

Wes looked between the three of us, his brow pinching together. "I don't like it, but if you're confident that you can keep this assignment under control, I'll allow it. I know how much a fallen member can impact a squad, and sometimes getting back into the fight right away is the best course of action. You're still down a man and woman though," he said tersely, his expression souring when he referred to Marnee. "So I'll arrange for a few other squad members to join you. And I'll have additional squads mobilize and meet you all later today in the fae lands. Until those additional squads arrive, you're to lay low. Understood?"

Wyatt and Bavar both nodded curtly.

"Now, where do you plan on going?" Wes asked.

Bavar rested his palm on his dagger's hilt. "I'll touch

base with the king and queen. There are a number of family homes that would offer reasonable protection until we can work out a plan which ensures we capture Lord Godasara. We'll just need to stay well away from any homes surrounded by forest."

Wes nodded. "Assuming I can have your replacements fulfilled quickly, you can all plan on leaving this morning."

I knew my eyes flashed violet when the goddess's power rumbled inside me. "Perhaps we can do the unlinking process while we're waiting in the fae lands for the other squads to arrive?"

Wes nodded briskly. "I'll speak with the sorcerers again. With any luck, we can begin the unlinking process today as well."

CHAPTER EIGHTEEN
WYATT

I knew Avery wanted to head to the fae lands immediately, but Bavar needed an hour to mobilize his squad, and she hadn't eaten since the sandwich I'd prepared for her last night. Not to mention, she still wore her pajamas.

After Wes left to confer with the sorcerers, assign additional members to Squad Three, and arrange for more squads to join us later today, I inched toward my mate and put an arm around her shoulders.

Energy sparked from her, sharp and vibrant. I didn't think she was aware of it.

The guards in the room watched us, but I didn't care. Avery was my mate, and if they didn't like that I was constantly touching her to settle my inner wolf, then that was their problem.

I massaged her stiff shoulder muscles, then leaned down and whispered into her ear, "Why don't we return to my apartment, get dressed, and have something to eat? Squad Three won't be ready for an hour. We have time."

I nuzzled her neck, inhaling her scent.

She shivered, her eyes closing. When they opened, violet light swirled in her irises. "Do you think she'll still be okay in an hour? She's dying."

"I know, and no, I don't know what she'll be like in an hour, but I'm hoping she's strong enough to survive. Besides, I think you need to wear proper footwear before heading back to the fae lands." I nodded down. "Don't you?"

She shuffled in her flip flops and sighed. "You're probably right, but I feel so scared for her."

I pulled her closer, her lilac sent wafting up. My wolf rumbled in contentment at having her so near. "I know. And we'll go soon, but let's get properly dressed before we do."

I didn't force her from the room, though. Instead, I waited for her to make her own decision, thinking again about her explosive reaction this morning when I'd accidentally exerted my dominance over her.

Thankfully, she seemed to come to the same conclusion as me. "You're probably right. We have time to dress properly and grab a quick meal."

Avery reluctantly let go of the goddess's hand and I gently propelled her toward the hall. Once in the hallway, she whizzed into action.

I marveled at her speed, which once again I wasn't sure she was entirely aware of, as I followed her back to my barracks. She moved as fast as a vampire, turning into a blur on the sidewalk.

Once inside my apartment, she hurried to my bedroom, then whipped her shirt off over her head and scrounged around in her boxes.

For a moment, all I could do was stare. Her breasts were on full display, the lacy bra she wore doing little to hide her dusky peaks and protruding nipples.

Unable to stop my reaction, my length hardened. Damn, all I had to do was glance at my mate and I had a boner rivaling the Sears Tower.

She nibbled on her lip, peering into her boxes of packed clothes, completely oblivious to the effect she was having on me. "Is it always like this at the SF? It seems like it's one crisis after another and you're always dashing from one place to the next in the hope of saving whoever's in harm's way."

The corner of my mouth kicked up. She wasn't wrong. It was actually more accurate than she probably realized. "Sometimes, yes. Other times, there are periods of peace and we can focus more on training and keeping our skills sharp. But you're right, there have been plenty of times in the SF's history when we've been stretched thin and we've had to jump from one crisis to—"

She slipped her pants off.

Fuck, she has nice legs.

She cocked her head. "What were you saying about a crisis?"

I cleared my throat. "Um . . . one crisis to—"

She unclasped her bra, and her breasts sprung free.

Gods. How the hell was I supposed to carry on a conversation after seeing that?

She seemed to finally understand why my tongue was tied. With a coy smile, she turned fully toward me, her breasts bobbing, and only those damned lacy panties covering her.

She knew that drove me crazy.

"Like what you see, Commander?"

I couldn't help myself. I crossed the distance between us in a blur and locked my hands on her hips, yanking her toward me. "Fuck, yes." My hands came up to cup her breasts, my thumbs flicking over her erect nipples.

She shuddered but placed her hands on my chest and pushed back. "We really should be getting ready to go."

I made a non-committal sound. "You're right, we

should be." I stepped closer, my hands leaving her tits to curve around her waist. I slipped my fingers around her panties' thin waistband.

"We're supposed to be getting dressed and not undressed," she added, when I tugged her panties southward, but her voice had turned breathless, and a hint of musk entered her scent.

"Perhaps, but given how fast you move now, I have no concerns that we won't be able to redress quickly." Her panties fell to the floor, and I ran my fingers near her core. "Besides . . ." I glanced at my watch. "We have forty-five minutes. It doesn't take that long to dress."

She gasped when my finger dipped inside her, her warm heat clamping around me.

"This could be quick too," I continued, my voice turning husky. I slipped my finger out and then back in, pumping the digit. Her channel clamped tightly, getting a growl out of me.

She tilted her head back and moaned when I pumped into her again.

"All I'd have to do is bend you over the mattress, slide my dick in, and I could have you coming in seconds. We have time for that, don't you think?"

Her eyes fluttered when I leaned down and kissed her neck. I drifted lower and sucked her tit into my mouth.

A soft cry parted her lips, and with a spin, she positioned herself over the bed, her tits hanging on the sheets, and her ass pointing my way.

Her sex was already swollen and ready. My nostrils flared when I caught the scent of her arousal.

Damn . . .

She eyed me over her shoulder, her eyes clouded with lust. "Don't waste any time now. I have a goddess to protect."

In less than a second, I was naked and positioned behind her.

She cried out when I penetrated her in one swift thrust.

True to my promise, and as demanded by my mate, I didn't waste any time. Her body tightened and coiled around me as I dipped my other hand to the front of her, finding that nubbin of nerves which guaranteed her pleasure.

She moaned, the sound lighting my blood on fire.

My tempo increased. "Damn, I love the hot, slick feel of you."

She pushed back against me, grinding her ass into my groin, burying me deeper inside her.

I hissed. Already, her body was gripping me so tightly—just like it did before she came. Her aroused scent grew, and my cock throbbed. I swirled my fingers over her clit some more.

"Come for me, babe." I leaned over her back and nipped her ear.

Her fingers curled into the bed sheets, and I rubbed her nubbin harder. Her inner walls enveloped me like a glove, so hot and wet. Fuck, *so* wet.

My erection grew even thicker.

Her moans increased, and I knew she was close. I rubbed her harder, and it was enough to send her over the edge.

She cried out when an orgasm ripped through her.

Thrusting one final time, I came hard and roared my release as her cries continued to fill the room.

Breathing hard, she collapsed on the bed, a small smile on her face as her hair covered her eyes. "That was—"

"Quick? As promised?" I panted.

She pushed a lock of hair from her eyes and laughed. "That too, but it was also—" She sighed. "Gods, that was good. I think I needed that. I was feeling so stressed about the goddess, and now I feel like jelly."

I chuckled and bent over her back again, biting her playfully on the neck. "I aim to please."

"Well, you certainly know how to do that, Commander. You make me come so easily."

I growled, pleasure rumbling through me. "That's because you're my mate." I kissed the soft skin at her nape. I was still inside her, and she wiggled, getting a groan out of me. "I was made to pleasure you."

"Well, you certainly do that."

I chuckled, then groaned when she wiggled again. Already, my dick was hardening for round two. "I hope so, 'cause as long as I'm pleasing you, then I'm hoping you'll let me fuck you every chance I get."

She laughed, the sound making me grin. "Since that round was so quick, maybe we have time for another? How much time do we have?"

I glanced at my tablet. "Thirty-nine minutes. Plenty of time to pleasure you again, shower, dress, and eat."

"In that order?"

"Yes, ma'am."

She giggled and pressed against me again, her tight sheath gripping me. "Then what are you waiting for?"

Growling, I grasped her hips, my erection hardening until I grew thick inside her once more.

Fucking hell. No woman had ever turned me on enough to make me ready again that fast, but all I had to do was look at Avery and my dick was a rod of concrete.

"Your wish is my command." I slowly pulled out before pumping back into her.

Her back arched as a deep moan parted her lips. That

musky aroma coated her lilac scent again as her fingers curled into the bedsheets. "Do that again," she commanded.

I was more than happy to oblige.

As promised to my mate, our morning quickies didn't make us late. We were showered, dressed, fed, and my mate thoroughly pleasured, by the time we entered the main SF building.

My wolf purred since the stress lines that'd been marring Avery's mouth were gone. I knew she was still worried about Verasellee, but the anxious panic that had tinged her scent an hour ago had given way to one of contentment.

It was a scent I would love to smell on her for the rest of my life.

When we stepped into the command center with its benches lined with advanced magical machinery and holographs, Avery saw Eliza and grinned.

The fairy skirted around the control panel, obviously on duty for the day. Her purple hair was pulled back in a low ponytail, which highlighted her pointed ears.

"Good morning, friend!" She pulled Avery into a hug

as a shimmer of fairy magic pulsed from her. "I've been informed that you are departing shortly for the fae lands." Eliza pulled back but kept her hands on Avery's shoulders. "Charlotte told me that she shall be joining you, too, and I wish you a most uneventful journey and many blessings as you strive to correct all wrongs."

I bit my cheek to stop the smile that wanted to form. Considering Eliza was from one of the older villages in the fae lands, she still spoke in the old ways: formal and stiff.

But Avery had either already gotten used to it, or didn't realize that it was unusual for a fairy to speak as Eliza did in the earthly realm, because she just shrugged casually. "Thank you. I'm sorry we're leaving so soon. I was hoping that you, Charlotte, and I would have time to get together today, but—"

Worry etched across my mate's face again when she glanced behind us to the goddess.

Verasellee was already in the command center. She'd been transported on a hovering stretcher which was magically enchanted to keep her supine and warm while the device drifted a few feet above the floor.

Eliza nodded in understanding. "It is nothing to be concerned about. After this situation has come to a conclusion, I will be delighted to see you again, and then you, Charlotte, and I shall join together in a merry cele-bration."

Avery grinned. "I'd like that."

The sound of footsteps came from the outside hall. A second later, Bavar, Heidi, Terry, Bishop, and Charlotte appeared in the doorway.

And just behind them waited Reese, Avery's sorcerer trainer during her new recruit program, along with Nick Baker, another new recruit from Avery's former squad.

My eyes widened when I spotted the young sorcerer. Nick was tall and somewhat lanky, with brown hair and a calm demeanor. He kept glancing toward Charlotte.

Nick was still in magical training, but as a naturally talented sorcerer who was incredibly powerful, I wasn't surprised Wes had chosen him.

Considering Nick's potential, I wasn't surprised to see Reese either. Reese was often chosen to teach our gifted recruits. I had a feeling those two had been hand-picked for this assignment because of how powerful Nick inherently was, regardless of the fact that he was still fairly new to the SF.

Scratching my chin, I opened my mouth to asked Wes if Nick possessed the specific magical strengths that would be needed to unlink the goddess, Avery, and Lord

Godasara, when another supernatural appeared behind the group.

A grin streaked across my face when Dee Armund strode into the room.

CHAPTER NINETEEN

AVERY

Wyatt's smile was so bright as he watched the approaching woman that jealousy pinched me. They greeted each other warmly, fist bumping. I told myself I was being asinine, but I'd never seen him so happy to see another woman before.

"Wes told me you guys needed backup," the woman said. She stood around six foot and was so toned her muscles looked like rocks. Her full lips parted on her dark-brown, blemish-free face.

The woman was beautiful.

Which wasn't helping my ridiculous reaction.

"That we do," Wyatt replied, still smiling. "Have to say, I'm glad you've got my six for this."

The woman shrugged. "I couldn't let a fellow

KISSED BY SHADOWLIGHT

commander down, and besides, I hear my former
protégé has turned into something to be reckoned
with. I wanted to see for myself." Her gaze skirted
my way.

I stiffened, but Wyatt waved me over. "Avery, this is
Major Dee Armund. She's the woman you trained under
for three months."

All jealousy left me. This woman was the reason I
knew how to fight?

I squeezed Eliza's hand goodbye as the fairy twirled
back to her station before I joined Wyatt and Major
Armund. Charlotte nodded at me as she stood in the
corner with her squad, waiting for direction from Bavar.
I couldn't help but notice the lanky young man with
brown hair who kept looking at her. Charlotte's attention also kept shifting his way.

Hmm, something was *definitely* going on there, but I
didn't know what.

But that would have to wait for another time.

"Nice to see you again, Avery, even though I'm
guessing you don't remember me," Major Armund said.

"I'm sorry, but I don't."

Dee shrugged, her eyes glittering. "I've been told you
took down a dozen warlocks on your own."

"I did," I replied evenly, then suppressed a yawn as a
sudden sense of sleepiness overtook me.

"Damn. That's impressive. Maybe you won't need the moves I taught you after all."

"Actually, I did need them." I remembered how I'd fought the warlocks in the cave system, how some part of my brain and body had known what to do, dipping and swaying, kicking and jabbing. "In fact, I think I have you to thank for being alive. If I hadn't fought back in the caves, Lord Godasara would have been able to conduct the ritual earlier, before Wyatt and the SF found me. I'd probably be dead at this very moment."

Wyatt stiffened. He already knew that detail from the debriefing I'd given Wes, but I imagined hearing it again wasn't easy for a mated werewolf male.

Dee's eyes lit up. "Is that so? Did something happen where you had to fight?"

I gave a small laugh even though my time in the caves had been anything but funny. "There was."

"Then I'm all ears."

I suppressed another yawn, and then divulged the details to Dee, which she seemed more than eager to hear.

Around us, Squad Three got busy preparing to go, strapping weapons to their suits, while Wyatt and Bavar discussed last-minute plans with Wes.

When I finished telling Dee about the caves, she cocked her head. "You were always a good student and so much tougher than the magic you had inside you. It's good to see your magic now rivals your inherent strength."

"Except it's not my magic. It's hers." I pointed at Verasellee, who was still floating on the enchanted stretcher. Another wave of sleepiness overtook me, but I brushed it off. "I have to give it back to her, but I don't know how."

Dee crossed her arms, a contemplative look on her face. "Word on the street is that Corporal Baker and Reese have a plan."

"Already?" I replied with a grin.

"That we do," a tall man with crystalline blue eyes replied. He was walking toward us, evidently having overheard his name. "I'm Reese. We've met, but I've been told you have amnesia."

"You trained with both Reese and me," Dee added. "Reese helped you with your spells."

I smiled awkwardly. "Um, nice to meet you . . . again."

Unlike Squad Three, Reese and the young lanky man —the one who looked to be enamored with Charlotte— didn't carry any weapons. I figured they were sorcerers who were powerful enough that they didn't need them.

Reese inclined his head toward Verasellee. "With the help of a few ancient texts, I'm confident I know what to do. We'll begin the unlinking process as soon as we're in the fae lands. We need their stronger magical environment to conduct the ritual."

My blood chilled at the word *ritual* just as another roll of fatigue overtook me. This time, I couldn't stop my yawn. "What's the ritual like?"

Reese grinned. "You'll see."

WE USED portal keys to transport back to the fae lands, except this time instead of hiding in a sequestered castle in an enchanted forest, we stayed well away from all trees. The portal dropped us smack in front of a huge palace in a bustling city.

"Where are we?" I asked, my eyes drooping. Seriously, I needed a nap. I shifted closer to the goddess, who lay beside us on the magical hovering stretcher.

Her power crackled and burst inside me as if responding to her presence.

"The capital," Bavar replied. "We'll be staying in the king and queen's residence. It's one of the most heavily guarded palaces in the lands. And as you can see, there are very few trees for the elf lord to call upon." His arm swept out to the cobblestone lanes and busy streets zigzagging below.

"But what if he comes here and hurts innocent people in the city?" I asked.

"He's a lone elf now," Wyatt reminded me. "Without his warlocks, he's not as strong as he once was, and I don't think he's a fool. If he came here alone, our numbers would overpower him. We'll keep you and the goddess safe."

I bit my lip. The goddess's power hummed again inside me, and another yawn overtook me.

Wyatt eyed me, concern lighting his eyes. "Are you feeling okay? Do you think your sickness is returning?"

I knew he was referring to how sick I'd become after the Safrinite comet. Despite the positive results of the scan Cora had performed on me, he still seemed worried.

I shook my head. "I don't feel differently or worse. I'm fine, really. Just a bit tired." I turned my back to him, so he wouldn't see my next yawn, and in doing so, I got a rather impressive view of the capital.

I pretended to admire it as I fought the fatigue sweeping through me.

The palace rested on the top of a small mountain, and the sprawling city swept out below. The hustle of it was apparent as fairies meandered the lanes, peddlers sold their wares on street corners, and music spilled from one area.

To those living here, it was just another normal day.

Yet for me, it was anything but. *Damn, why am I so tired?* I smothered yet another yawn.

"Squad Three, come with me," Bavar called. His orange hair flashed in the sun, while his jeweled dagger glittered on his waist. "I'll get you up to speed on the palace while we work out a plan to capture the elf lord. The sooner he's dead the better."

My heart rate picked up. I'd overheard a bit of Wes, Wyatt, and Bavar's conversation at the command center. The SF was still adamant they had to stop the elf lord by killing him, and if the unlinking ritual worked then they could.

But if it didn't work . . .

"See you soon," Charlotte whispered to me as she departed with Bavar, Heidi, Bishop, Terry, and Dee.

I gave her a tight-lipped smile, wishing I could have spoken with her more, but everything had happened so fast since we'd met in the command center.

The sorcerer everyone called Nick, along with Reese and Wyatt, hung back with me.

"We need to set a few things up before we begin the unlinking ritual," Reese explained, "but we should be ready shortly."

"Do you really know how to unlink our souls?" I shifted my weight as I stood by the goddess. As it had on earth, her body lay quietly, but already I could feel her strength returning. She didn't feel as distant and as weak as she had in earth's realm. At least bringing her back to the fae lands had been the right move.

"I believe so," Reese replied. "Corporal Baker comes from a rare line of sorcerers. If we combine our magic, I think we may succeed. But it's not an easy ritual. We'll need to prepare for it. We'll call you when we're ready."

Behind us, the sentries standing at the palace doors watched us with blank expressions. When we walked toward them, they extended their spears until an X formed, blocking us. A clang of magic reverberated through me, the goddess's power humming in response.

The sorcerers and Wyatt stopped, letting the sentries do their monitoring. Since they were so good at detecting ill intentions, sentries guarded many entries and exits in this realm.

I jolted. *How do I know that?* Once again, it was apparent that I remembered *things* just not *me*.

The sentries' eyes shifted to silver, swirling like mercury pools as they studied us closely.

The goddess's power fizzled inside me, zapping in response to their magic as they scanned us.

One of them cocked his head at me, his expression never faltering. A moment passed, then another, before he finally relaxed his stance and moved to the side. "Proceed."

The four of us entered the palace with the goddess hovering behind us. Her stretcher was spelled to follow as commanded, but I still made sure to keep close to her side.

The main gates deposited us into a huge foyer, but even though the palace's decadent architecture was impressive to say the least, I couldn't have cared less about the vast stone floors, soaring domed entryway that reached up to the third floor, numerous stairways and balconies perched above, or the luxurious tapestries that hung from the walls.

All I could think about was the churning anxiety in my stomach. I knew the SF wanted Lord Godasara dead, and I knew that I had to be unlinked from the goddess at some point, but what if their spells failed? Worse, what if they didn't unlink the goddess from the elf? Then she would still be tethered to him, and she would *die* if the SF killed him.

"I think I need to lie down." I came to a stop near the stairwell.

Nick and Reese were still peering around at the grand display, their eyes wide with excitement. I figured it was their first time in the palace.

Wyatt's brow furrowed as his hand went to my lower

back. "Avery, what's going on? I can tell something's the matter. Are you sure you're not sick?"

"Yes, I'm sure." My lips parted when his warm palm settled on me. His touch soothed the roiling in my stomach, but it didn't fully quell it. I wanted to tell him that something didn't feel right about unlinking the three of us, even though I had no rational explanation for that, but damn, I was just *so* tired. I couldn't think straight enough at the moment to voice it.

"I think I just need a nap. So much has happened lately. Do you mind if I lie down for a bit?"

Worry flashed in his eyes, and he waved at a passing servant, summoning them over. "Will you please show Ms. Meyers to an empty bed chambers? She needs to rest."

The servant bobbed her head. "Of course, my lord."

"I'm not a lord. Sir or Wyatt will do."

The servant blushed. "Apologies, sir. Of course, sir."

The servant beckoned me to her side, but I glanced toward Verasellee. "Can she come with me? I feel better when she's near."

The concern in Wyatt's eyes grew, but he nodded. "I suppose, but only if you promise to tell me if something is actually the matter. Are you sure it's just fatigue?"

I hesitated, my weight shifting between my feet, but then I forced a tight smile. I figured I wasn't lying, just withholding information for the time being. I would tell him everything after I'd taken a nap and didn't feel this bone-weary exhaustion anymore. "Yeah. I'm just tired."

"You have time," Reese called. "The king and queen still haven't approved the ritual, but we're expecting a response by this afternoon at the latest. We'll collect you when we're ready. Rest up."

The other sorcerer—Nick, the one that had googly eyes for Charlotte—gave me an encouraging smile before shifting his attention back to Reese.

The two sorcerers were now in an intense discussion, obviously shifting their focus to the ritual.

Wyatt gave me a kiss just below my ear. As always, having him so near and feeling one of his soft kisses pressed to my skin made tingling start deep in my belly.

"Take the time you need. I'll hold these two off if need be."

I brushed my lips over his before he pulled back. A contented growl came as his response.

"Thank you," I whispered.

He squeezed my hand, and then I followed the servant who scurried ahead of me down one of the long stone corridors.

I kept a tight hold on the magical stretcher as royal guards followed, some of the power inside me relaxing with the goddess so near, but it didn't stop my persistent fatigue.

I smothered another yawn.

The servant guided me to an opulent room on the second floor. It was probably bigger than those in most homes, and reminded me of the bed chambers at Shrouding Estate.

One thing I was quickly learning about this realm was that the king and queen had more money than they apparently knew what to do with.

"Thank you," I said to the servant.

She curtsied before closing the door as the guards stood watch outside.

Alone in the room, I gently moved the goddess closer to the bed, until she was hovering beside the large mattress. I didn't bother shutting the thick velvet curtains even though bright daylight streamed in through the narrow windows shaped like icicles. Instead, I could barely keep my eyes open as I climbed onto the huge bed.

The second my head hit the pillow, I was fast asleep.

I WAS FLOATING in a sea of nothingness, warmth and tingling energy surrounding me. It was soothing and tranquil here, and it felt as if I could exist in this moment for eternity.

"Avery," a voice whispered.

Rousing, I opened my eyes to a world of swirling violet light, wispy fuchsia clouds, and glittering distant stars. I hovered amidst it all, my body weightless, my soul content.

Wow. It felt as if I were in another dimension, a beautiful, otherworldly space of nothing and everything, of endless time and eternal grace.

I tried to sit up, but it was as though I didn't have a body. I simply floated. Existed. Yet instead of feeling panicked, I felt nothing but calm.

"Avery." That soft whisper carried through my senses again, and I swiveled left and right, taking in the vastness around me.

I didn't see anything at first, just the same awe-inspiring, endless beauty I'd been looking at since opening my eyes, but when I turned fully around, I gasped.

A glowing figure of a woman hovered behind me. She bobbed in spectral form, her black hair flowing down her shoulders and her smooth brown skin glowing faintly.

"We don't have much time," she said urgently. "Once the ritual is complete, we won't be able to find him."

My lips parted. "Verasellee?"

She dipped her head.

Stunned, for a moment all I could do was stare at her. She was so beautiful, so enchanting, and I soaked up every moment of her presence. My form tingled, my nerves electrifying. I'd never been in the presence of a goddess before, and the effect was absolutely intoxicating.

"Avery, we must find him," she said, breaking the spell.

I jerked, forcing myself out of the trance I'd been falling into. "Find who?"

"Lord Godasara. With our souls linked, he's able to find us, but it's a mutual bond. We can also find him.*"*

With a start, I realized why I'd felt so tired. The goddess had wanted to communicate with me, and the only way to do that was when we were projecting.

Except, unlike my other dreams, this one felt as though it'd transported me to another dimension, a plane between this realm and the others. That innate instinct, the one that occasionally guided me, told me that Verasellee was able to speak with me so clearly because of how physically close our bodies were.

Of course. *Her stretcher was hovering right next to my bed in the palace.*

That had never happened before because we'd always been so far away from one another, except in the caves—

The memory slammed back into me of the dream I'd had in the cave. Of the crystal clear memory Verasellee had shown me of the ritual two thousand years ago. That *was how she'd* shown me her memory. *Because we'd been in close proximity to one another.*

I shook my head in wonder. "How is this possible—"

"We don't have much time," the goddess interrupted. "I need to show you something." She shifted and waved a glowing arm. The purple mist parted to reveal a scene in the fae lands.

A forest appeared below us, as if we hovered a mile above it. The thick swamp of trees looked nearly impossible to penetrate.

We zoomed toward it, careening toward the ground like a comet barreling toward earth.

I yelped in surprise when we crashed through the trees, even though I didn't feel or hear anything. Our movements abruptly stopped and I found that we were now hovering just above the ground.

I gasped. A man who I didn't recognize at first was crouching on the forest floor, but then his hood tipped back.

Huge pointed ears rose alongside his head. A pale-green hand rested on one of his knees, the skin taut and shiny. He was bent over, the skin on his lower legs similar to his newly regrown hand.

Lord Godasara. *He'd regrown all of his appendages, and he was scribbling runes frantically into the soil.*

A chill made me shiver. "He regrew his limbs?"

"Yes, but that's not all he's done. He's still in the Derian Forest, except now he's conjuring new spirits. If we don't stop him, he will raise a vast army that will march on the capital. Your friends think that he's been weakened, but he hasn't been. Even though he lost his warlocks, he's not weak. He carries such immense power, and when he's with the trees, that power only increases. If he comes here, he will destroy the city. You can't let that happen."

My eyes snapped to the goddess's. Fear was etched into her ethereal features. "But what do I do? How do I stop him?"

"You must first unlink me from him, so that he may be killed, but you cannot unlink the two of us. I need my tether to you. If we are unlinked, my soul will be lost. I will no longer exist. You are who ties me to the fae lands, to my body. You cannot return to earth until he is dead, and until then, we cannot be unlinked. You have to stop the sorcerers from doing that."

It struck me then why I'd felt such an urgent need to sleep. If I hadn't taken a nap, Verasellee never would have been able to tell me all of this before Reese and Nick conducted the ritual. Her soul would have been lost.

"But how is any of this even possible?" I asked, shaking my head. "How am I linked to you and Lord Godasara? How did I get your power? How did we even end up in this situation thousands of years after you came to this realm? I know you showed me the scene when you shot your power into the galaxy, but why did it come to me? Why was I chosen?"

She gave me a sad smile, the violet light around her

flexing and flowing as if disturbed by a breeze. "You ask many questions, and we don't have much time."

Annoyance flared through me. "Your power killed me. I lost all of my magic. My entire life was turned inside out and upside down because of you. I think the least I deserve is an explanation for why I was used to do your bidding even if it takes a few minutes."

Violet light flared in her eyes. "Careful, child. Remember to whom you speak."

A burst of her power flowed over me, scorching me in its intensity, and it was enough to remind me that her being was so much greater than mine.

Still . . .

"Please. All I want is an explanation."

"Very well." She began speaking rapidly. "Thousands of years ago, the elf lord tricked me. I thought my lost love was in this fae realm, but he wasn't. But by the time I got here, it was too late. Lord Godasara and the warlocks were ready and they captured me. Using their immense magic, they took my power. I tried my best to show you that in a dream. I showed you what they did to me and how I fought back.

"Flinging my power into the galaxy was the only thing I could think of in the short time I had, so I wove a spell around my power. My power would only go to an heir of a starlight-fated couple. I wanted the heir to be born of love—real love—and grow in a happy family so she could be strong and whole.

But I also spelled it so the heir had to be strong. She would have to be strong enough to complete my task."

Her eyes glowed violet. "It took two thousand years before my prophecy came to light. You are the heir of the starlight couple, and you have the strength to right what's been wronged."

I shook my head. "But I'm not strong. I never have been. I've been told that my magic was weak before the Safrinite comet, and now I don't even have my magic anymore."

"No, you don't. My spell had to kill your magic and body before my power could reside inside you. My power is so great. It's not meant for a human or supernatural body. It had to burn away all of the magic inside you and unlink your soul from your body before you could endure the physical feat of accepting my power inside of you."

Shock rippled through me. "That's why my magic was destroyed and why I was killed by the Safrinite comet."

"Yes, and once that part of the prophecy was complete, the alignment birthed my power inside you. You were born again when the alignment glowed as bright as a moon. Except with that birth, you now had the power of a goddess even though you were still in your human form."

My mouth opened as understanding slammed into me. "And Lord Godasara knew that. He knew you had flung your power into the galaxy and it was only a matter of time before it returned to fulfill your prophecy."

"Yes, which is why he also went into a dormant sleep. He stayed alive by feeding off the warlocks, using their dark magic conjured by human and fae sacrifices." Rage erupted in the goddess's eyes, making them glimmer like purple diamonds. "Thousands died to keep them alive, all in the elf lord's attempts to take and wield my power. For that, he will pay."

She looked down, her fury-filled eyes dripping with vengeance. "But you have my power now, Avery. It's up to you to stop him and save me and this realm. If Lord Godasara succeeds, he will capture the both of us; he will take my power from you, and you will die.

"But it's not just your life that will suffer. Everyone in this realm will suffer. If he ensnares the Power of Time—the power you currently have—he controls everything. Do you understand? If you control time, you control the world. You can stop it as you wish. You can go back in time if you desire. You can go forward in time if you make a leap.

"With that kind of power, you control the planet. All you would need to do is pause the realm, kill your enemies, and take their riches. He would have absolute and complete control of the fae lands. You cannot let him succeed."

My lips parted. "But I don't know how to wield your power. The few times I've used it, it just happened without me doing anything. And the times I've tried to consciously stop time, it didn't work."

She hovered closer to me, her glittery form bobbing and swaying. "Let me show you." She placed a hand on my spectral body, and then memories slammed into me.

The power of the action was so great that my mouth opened in a silent scream.

Millions of memories coursed through me. Hers. The realm's. The universe's.

Her eternal knowledge consumed me, filling me, devouring me.

Only seconds had passed, yet it felt as if years, and then a millennium, had been lived through me. The goddess removed her hand. "Do you see now?"

"I . . ." My mouth opened and closed like a fish. The knowledge of how to use her power was suddenly there. *"Yes. I see now."*

"You have my power and its strength." She drifted back just enough to disperse her crackling energy. "And you are worthy. It is why you were chosen. You have inherent strength, Avery, and now you know how to use my power. Do not doubt yourself."

My heart hammered as something came back to me that Wyatt had said. Your magic may have been weak, but your soul is strong.

Was he right? I didn't know, because I couldn't remember.

"Why can't I remember anything?" I asked, my eyes pleading. "Why don't I know who I am?"

Her gaze turned apologetic, the first truly remorseful expression I'd seen her wear. "For the same reason you had to die to birth my power. It killed all of you, including the connection to your memories. Your memories are still there, but the pathways to access them are gone. It's possible some of those pathways will return, some probably already have, or they may never. For that I am sorry, but we don't have time for more questions. You need to wake, and you need to act."

I took a deep breath, my thoughts whirling, but she was right. Now wasn't the time to answer all of my burning questions, or mourn the loss of my memories, not if Lord Godasara was building an army as we spoke. "What do I need to do?"

The increasing urgency in her voice when she spoke next let me know that time was still ticking. The irony of it made a bitter laugh bubble up in my throat. Because of one sick elf lord, the Goddess of Time was unable to fully control time.

"First, you need to stop the sorcerers from unlinking us. Convince them to unlink me and the elf lord, but that's it. And then once I am free of the lord, you must go after him."

"But what if they don't agree? What if I can't make the sorcerers do as I ask?"

"You must. That is all I can say. You have to find a way to succeed."

"And then I have to kill the elf lord?"

"Yes. After the link he and I share is broken, go to the Derian Forest and kill him."

"But he's so strong. He's the only one who's been able to break through your power inside me." Fear flashed through me when I remembered how he'd watched me at the inn, and how he'd spoken to me at the mountain when I'd stopped time.

Verasellee drifted closer, urgency flaming in her eyes. "Do not doubt yourself, Avery. You have my power. You have a soul of steel. You are strong. You can defeat him, but you must hurry. The more time that passes, the stronger he grows. If you wait too long, he will have an army at his fingertips. The warlocks were merely a gateway to the ritual to ensnare my power. He knows that. He knows he'll need to create new warlocks to finish the ritual to harvest my power, but he doesn't have time for that now.

"But he's smart. He knows what's most important right now is to capture you and me. If he does, he will bind you again, and all will be lost. And remember, Godasara will go to any lengths to make that happen. That's why he's using the forest right now to create an army. Because if he has an army, he can destroy the capital. The capital will fall, and all will be his. Then time won't matter. He can re-create his warlocks if he has us ensnared."

She drifted closer to me, her eyes alive with violet light. "You have to wake now, Avery. Unlink him and me, and then finish him once and for all. The fate of this realm depends on you."

"So I go to him with the SF? We fight him before he can finish his army?"

"No! Aren't you listening? He's almost done building his army, and once he is, he'll be unstoppable. You must go to him now. You cannot wait for the Supernatural Forces from the earthly realm. By the time they arrive, it will be too late. His army will have risen and this realm will be in peril. You must go now, Avery. Unlink my soul from his and stop him!"

Her voice thundered in my ears as a rush of energy barreled into me. Violet light. Crackling power. Her command careened into my soul with the strength and magic of a godly entity. That sense of fractured time cut into my spectral form, as if everything had stopped and then was joltingly restarted.

I bolted upright in bed, gasping for breath. Bright sunlight drifted around the bed chambers as my thoughts whirred with everything the goddess had just revealed.

I frantically sought for her physical form.

She lay on the enchanted stretcher, her figure still, her expression serene. Until she and the lord were unlinked, she was vulnerable to his power.

My eyes widened at everything Verasellee had revealed. I didn't have much time. I had to act *now* if I wanted to stop Lord Godasara. Because if I failed, this entire realm would perish.

Throwing the covers off me, I shot out of bed.

CHAPTER TWENTY
WYATT

*S*omething is going on with Avery. I paced in one of the palace's large open rooms used for entertaining guests, as Nick and Reese prepared themselves for the ritual.

A niggling feeling ate away at the back of my mind. Avery had been tired since we'd arrived in the fae lands. I knew she'd been through a lot in the past few days, but I had a feeling that something else explained her tiredness.

But what exactly that was, I didn't know.

I paused, my feet coming to a stop on the stone floor. *If only Avery would talk to me.*

I'd checked on her after she'd retired to the bed chambers. She'd been fast asleep, but twenty minutes had already passed since. If she was only taking a cat nap, it was likely she would wake soon, and I needed to lay my eyes on her. I needed to know that she was okay, and most importantly, I wanted to know exactly what was going on as soon as she woke up.

I'd demand . . . no, scratch that. I'd *request* that she speak with me and tell me what was bothering her.

Fucking A. It was hard to fight my instinct to dominate and demand submission, but I'd learned my lesson. No forcing my mate.

I was two steps away from the door just as Nick and Reese were finishing the last of their preparations for the unlinking ritual, when Avery careened around the corner and barreled right into me.

I fell back, my foot automatically planting behind me on the stone to stop us from falling. I caught her, my arms closing around her. She'd been moving so fast, even faster than a vamp. Gods, she'd grown so powerful.

"Whoa," I managed. I held her to me, peering down at her frantic expression. "Looks like you're awake."

Her eyes flashed to mine, violet light swirling in them. *Shit, what the hell is going on?*

"Where are Nick and Reese?" she blurted out, but then her eyes widened when she saw them behind me.

"They've been preparing for the ritual. I believe they're almost—"

She broke free from my arms and raced toward the

sorcerers. That churning feeling in my stomach increased as I took in her manic energy.

She blurred to a stop, Nick doing a double take when she suddenly reappeared. "Are you ready? To do the unlinking ritual?" she asked.

Nick and Reese had been in deep discussion, but both stopped short.

I prowled closer to them, my gut clenching. I didn't fully understand how they would conduct the ritual, but I knew it was complicated. Not many sorcerers were capable of what they were about to attempt.

"Yes, I believe we're ready," Reese replied evenly. "It's not a simple ritual, though. We must get everything precisely right, or it could result in more harm than good."

Avery grasped his hands, violet light bleeding through her irises again. "You need to unlink Verasellee and the elf lord *now*. We cannot wait any longer."

Nick and Reese glanced at one another warily, then at me.

When I reached Avery's side, energy wafted around her. It was so strong, even my dominant energy wanted to submit. Fuck, she was powerful.

As if feeling similar, Reese took a cautious step back. "What's most important right now is that we save you, Avery," he replied calmly. "We need to unlink your soul from theirs so that the elf lord can no longer track you."

"No!" she exclaimed, and the force of her command thundered through my ears, rose the hair along my arms, and made me want to drop to my knees. The goddess shone in her eyes, and the power of the Gods demanded that we do her bidding.

Nick and Reese responded, too, both lowering, bowing, as if intrinsically aware that we must do as she desired.

My breath caught in my throat. *Gods. What is happening?*

"You must unlink Verasellee and Lord Godasara only," she continued. "Do *not* unlink me and the goddess. Please. I know what I'm doing."

I shifted to stand behind my mate. Some of her power eased, releasing the chokehold she had on all of us. My hands automatically lifted, coming to rest on her shoulders as the urge to touch and comfort her nearly overwhelmed me. She was still *my* mate. Mine to protect. Even if she wielded enough power to command an army.

She jumped at the sudden contact.

"Avery," I said softly, gently turning her to face me. My heart stopped. That anxious feeling again coated my stomach at the frantic swirling violet light in her eyes. "What are you not telling us?"

She took a step closer, her expression yearning, until her hands settled on my hips. Squeezing, she said, "Please, just trust me. You trust me, don't you?"

"With my life."

"Then believe me when I tell you that this is how it has to be."

My jaw locked, as warring emotions battled inside me. On the one hand, I knew that she was in full panic mode. And rarely did a panicked decision result in a good outcome.

But on the other hand, she'd proven me wrong, time and time again.

Before, I hadn't listened to her. I hadn't let her make her own decisions. I'd forced my will and dominance on her, and each time it had ended disastrously.

I took a deep breath, forcing myself to submit to her. "What do you need us to do?"

CHAPTER TWENTY-ONE

AVERY

A relieved smile curved my lips as a fierce glow lit Wyatt's eyes. *Mate.* He was my mate. How could I have ever doubted that?

"Thank you," I whispered. I stood on my tiptoes and pressed a soft, quick kiss to his lips. His oak and pine scent clouded around me. More than anything, I wished I remembered him from before, but I didn't. That was the price I had to pay for fulfilling the prophecy that Verasellee had birthed two thousand years ago.

But even though I may never remember the shared history that Wyatt and I had, what I'd come to learn in the short time I'd known him, was that he was willing to compromise. He would meet me halfway and treat me as an equal, even if his instincts demanded that he shield me.

And I loved that about him.

A sharp pang of lust, wanting, and need shot through me. *Gods, this man.* I would give anything to fight for what we had.

"Just tell us what you need, and I'll make it happen," Wyatt repeated softly. "I'm the senior officer here. Nick and Reese are under my command. They'll do as I order."

Nick and Reese shuffled their feet behind me, clearly uneasy.

I kissed Wyatt again, my fingers entwining through the hair resting on the nape of his neck. A low growl rumbled in his chest. His tongue danced with mine, his mouth opening as his arms crushed me to him.

I didn't know what was to come of me when I confronted the elf lord. Even though I carried the power of a goddess inside me, the elf lord wasn't without resources.

It was possible that this was the last moment I would ever be able to feel or touch Wyatt. I wanted to savor it even though I knew time was running out.

"I love you," I whispered.

His grip tightened. "I love you, too, more than you could ever know, and I meant what I said last night. I won't force you anymore. You can trust me, as I trust you. I've got your back, Little Flower."

My heart snagged in my chest, my throat tightening. How was it possible to love somebody this much? "Thank you."

I clung to him. I had no idea what lay ahead for me, but I knew on some deep, instinctual level that the goddess was right. If we waited for the remaining squads to arrive, if we didn't act *now*, this would end disastrously.

I knew I could tell this to Wyatt, explain that we didn't have time to wait, but then I remembered the battle at the mountain. Three SF members had died. Three. And Wyatt had almost died too. And that was when we'd only been battling the lord and a small group of warlocks. Now, Lord Godasara potentially had an army.

Squad Three would most likely all die if I took them with me. My friends. My mate. Their lives would be sacrificed if I let them join me.

I wouldn't do that.

Verasellee's command rang through my mind. *Do not doubt yourself. You have my power. You have a soul of steel. You are strong. You can defeat him.*

With the goddess's power, I could freeze time. But that power only extended to me. I couldn't freeze time for Squad Three.

Using Verasellee's power, I could keep myself safe,

but I couldn't shield my friends and Wyatt from the elf lord, so I had to go alone.

I wouldn't let Verasellee down, and I wouldn't let Lord Godasara capture this realm—even if something happened to me in the process.

I released Wyatt, and his eyes glittered like fiery emeralds. Thick tension strummed from him in steady waves, and his fingers dug into my waist.

I knew he didn't want to let me go. I knew he was battling his instincts at this very second.

And I fiercely loved him for it.

With a final squeeze, I twirled around to face the two powerful sorcerers. "We don't have much time, so you need to listen."

THE GODDESS HOVERED on the stretcher in the center of the room, Nick on one side, Reese on the other. Wyatt and I stayed back near the closed door, as I anxiously watched on.

"Are you sure?" Nick asked, glancing over his shoulder. "We still haven't received permission from the king and queen to conduct the ritual. Are you absolutely certain you want us to continue?"

"Yes," Wyatt replied with a brusque nod. "Unlink

Verasellee and Lord Godasara only. Do *not* touch the bond that she and Avery share."

"All right," Reese said reluctantly. "But you do also realize that leaves Avery vulnerable. If she's still linked to the goddess, and the goddess wakes up and wants her power back, Avery could die. Given the debrief I got, it sounds like the goddess's life and power are what's fueling Avery, because Avery *died*. I just want to make sure you understand what you're asking us to do. I can't guarantee Avery's safety if we do this."

My heart tripped. I knew the risk was there. I had no idea what would happen to me when Verasellee wanted her power back, but it was hers, not mine. All I could do was hope that I didn't die in the process and that some sliver of myself remained inside of me, so I didn't die again.

The muscle in the corner of Wyatt's jaw ticked. He balled his hands into fists, the skin stretched taut across his knuckles. He cast a pained look my way.

"Please," I whispered, my heart breaking at what I was asking of him, but it was the only way.

Wyatt closed his eyes, his breath shuddering out of him. When he opened them, liquid pools of gold swirled in his irises, but he nodded curtly.

He addressed Reese again. "Do as my mate wants.

Unlink the goddess and elf lord. Now. I'll deal with the repercussions from the king and queen."

Reese gave a final reluctant nod, then turned back to Nick. Their gazes locked.

"Begin," Reese said quietly.

In perfect synchronicity, the sorcerers' hands rose, their fingers slipping through the air as their arms dipped and swirled in a magical dance. Their movements perfectly mirrored one another's as each began to whisper in low tones.

A burst of power swept through the room, like a north wind had blasted through the walls as a chill that promised snow bit into my cheeks.

The candlelit sconces flamed out, smoke rising from the wicks.

Outside, daylight dimmed as if the sun had fallen into shadows.

The sheet over the goddess fluttered.

My eyes widened as an ancient magical force awakened around us.

Wyatt stepped closer to my side, as day turned to night outside. The sun completely disappeared behind thick clouds, and the hum of the city that had drifted through the open windows fell to a hush.

The hairs on my arms stood on end, as my heart picked up a rapid staccato beat.

All the while, the two sorcerers never faltered. Their bodies stayed rigid, yet their arms became as fluid as snakes, dancing as one as they swirled immense magic between them.

A blue cloud formed over the goddess, sparks skating along its surface. The goddess's body lifted from the stretcher, hovering in mid-air as the power inside me rattled.

I clutched my abdomen, as Verasellee's power responded to the ancient force. It crackled and flowed, demanding that it be returned to its rightful owner.

More than anything, it wanted out. It wanted to go to Verasellee, but I needed to stay bound with her. This ritual wouldn't wake her from the dormant sleep. Until the elf lord was killed, that spell would stay in effect, so I needed to keep her power inside me in order to kill him once and for all.

I shoved the crackling power down, but it still vibrated to my toes, the power of an army rippling through my veins.

Nick and Reese continued with the ritual, their voices growing louder, deeper, as they became lost to the immense magic.

Startled cries rose from the city below. I had no doubt that the fairies enjoying their day had come to a sudden stop. The sun was completely gone now, as if an unknown eclipse had descended on the land.

Rapid footsteps came from the hallway. The king and queen must have been alerted to the magical force being wielded in their palace. Shouts came next, then the clang of swords being unsheathed.

"Hurry," I whispered. "Hurry, we can't let them stop us."

Wyatt stayed at my side, his jaw muscles ticking as he fought to stay true to his promise. I knew how hard this was for him. I'd known how much I'd asked of him, especially since we still hadn't heard back from the king and queen about conducting this ritual. No wonder the guards were mobilizing.

I threaded my fingers through Wyatt's, forcing his fist to loosen.

He squeezed, his large palm engulfing mine, as Nick and Reese continued to chant and wield their spell.

Their chanting grew louder, stronger, and even more in-tune with one another, until it sounded as if only one sharp voice rose between the two of them.

The magic whirled and spun around the goddess, growing and growing until it felt as though gusts of wind high in the atmosphere were pummeling us.

A bang came from outside the room as one of the

guards tried to barrel his way through the door. "Open this now! By order of the king!"

My gaze shot to Wyatt's. "We can't let them inside!"

Reese and Nick continued their chanting, oblivious to the threat at the door, their magic tied together as they cast the ancient spell over the goddess's form.

In a flash, Wyatt was at the door, shouldering himself against it. I joined him, placing my hands against the solid wood surface as more shouts and bangs came from behind the door.

The power continued to build in the room behind us, ripping around the goddess like a tornado. The violent winds threatened to pick me up, but I used the goddess's power to give me strength and stay grounded.

Energy crackled around me. Purple sparks rose from my skin. I extended her magic to Wyatt, locking him into place as another giant heave came from the door.

Wyatt groaned, straining and flexing against the onslaught of magic and solar-force winds that rushed around us.

"They're almost done. Hold the door!" I cried.

Another bang came from the other side, and then the sound of an ax. A jolt ran through me when the ax struck again, a heavy thud reverberating through the solid door.

Holy shit, they're going to hack the door down!

Reese's and Nick's voices rose higher, chanting faster and faster as the winds turned into a hurricane.

The goddess spun in the center of the room, a void of time and power swirling around her as the ritual flowed from the sorcerers' lips.

The door under our palms heaved, then opened an inch.

"By order of the king, *open this door!*" the guard bellowed again. Another sharp jolt. A sliver of an ax splintered the wood.

"Hurry!" I yelled to the sorcerers.

The power in the room *exploded* as the goddess spun so fast she turned into a blur.

Pain cleaved my insides, threatening to split me in two, but I held on to her power with everything I had, knowing that if I lost my connection to her, she would never wake.

Another heave came from the door, and then the ax burst through it just as a colossal rush of wind slammed around the room.

Wyatt and I were knocked off our feet. My head cracked against the wall. A large grunt spilled from his lips. The door ripped open, guards at the threshold.

But the next thing I knew, all was quiet.

The goddess lay on the floor in the center of the room between Reese and Nick. Her eyes were still closed and her body immobile, but a small smile curved her lips.

Each sorcerer panted, as if they'd just run a hundred miles. Sweat dripped from their foreheads, their expressions weary.

I frantically felt inside me for the goddess's power just as a dozen guards flowed in through the open door like water through a destroyed dam.

Verasellee's power crackled and sizzled in my chest. Still there. Still intact. Our link was not broken.

The guards encircled us, their swords drawn, wrathful expressions on their faces, but they were too late.

The sun returned to shining outside. The solar-force winds had disappeared.

The ritual was complete.

I turned to Wyatt, rushing toward him until I grasped his hands in mine. He pulled me to him and snarled menacingly at one of the guards when a sword was pointed at me.

I looked at my mate imploringly. "I'm sorry, but I have to do this. If I don't kill Lord Godasara before he creates his army in the Derian Forest, this entire realm will fall."

Stark terror entered Wyatt's eyes and his mouth opened, but before he could speak, I whispered, "Trust me. Please trust me. I love you." I slammed my lips into his, in one desperate last kiss.

And when I pulled back, as his bewildered, fearful eyes met mine, I called upon the goddess's power until it sparkled and electrified inside me like lightning ready to strike.

And then I froze time.

CHAPTER TWENTY-TWO
AVERY

The world was a frozen sea of unmoving fairies and supernaturals, stilled and suspended objects, and lifeless wind as I flew over the fae lands' countryside.

I'd left the goddess's body at the palace. I couldn't take her with me, not for this. She'd shown me where Lord Godasara was. I knew I had to get to him *now*.

His forest army was being created as we'd spoken in my dream, an army of twisting limbs, thick tree roots, and endless power.

Nothing would stop him. Nothing *could* stop an army made and controlled by an elf lord, which meant that I couldn't let him grow any stronger.

Verasellee's power pulsed inside me, the strength of the goddess infusing speed into me as I raced across the fae lands, aiming to cover the journey in a few short hours.

The forest Verasellee had shown me in the dream that the elf lord was hiding in, was the same as the deep, dark forest that surrounded the Elixias Mountains where I'd been held prisoner and where three SF members had lost their lives.

But while he had the forest at his beck and call, and an army being constructed from the vast trees, I had the power of a goddess inside me. It would be me against thousands, but only one of them needed to be killed.

If I could defeat Lord Godasara, his army would fall and this realm would be safe.

As long as I was able to keep time frozen, I would win. The elf lord's head would roll just like his warlocks' had done.

And then all would be well.

SWEAT TRAILED past my ear as I moved like the wind. I covered the hundreds of miles in a blurred sprint as fields, forests, and villages whizzed by me at dizzying speeds.

It took hours, though, to reach the Elixias Mountains. I didn't have access to any portal keys, otherwise I would have transported that way before I'd stopped time, but I wasn't like Bavar. I didn't have wealth and riches at my fingertips. I knew I could have asked him for one, but what if he'd tried to stop me?

I couldn't take that risk.

Despite having the power of the goddess humming through my soul, my legs were aching.

Because I *wasn't* a goddess.

I was barely more than human. Even though Verasellee's power flowed through my veins, my human body wasn't used to such taxing demands. Blisters flared on my feet and my muscles screamed in agony. Having Verasellee's knowledge on how to control her power meant I could keep time frozen, but only as long as I could withstand it.

You have to keep going. Push past the pain. Don't stop.

I told myself over and over again that failure wasn't an option. I buried the pain, pulling strength from deep inside me to withstand the wrenching demands I was requesting of my body, because I had to reach the elf lord.

A dark sky and three full moons bathed the northern land in silver light when I reached it. I followed an instinct as old as time. While I knew the elf lord was in the Derian Forest, I didn't know precisely where he was hiding.

So, I called upon the goddess to guide me. Even though I wasn't dreaming, I still felt her presence. She hummed in my body, through my mind, and entwined with my soul.

She and I were one, a living, breathing entity, and together we would right the wrongs that Lord Godasara had committed.

I realized the second I reached the Derian Forest that it was possible I was too late. I came to a careening halt, my muscles screaming in protest.

Because the once lush, vibrant northern woods that stretched for miles upon miles in this remote area in the fae lands, were now mostly barren and empty. Only in the distance did any trees still stand.

It looked as if a giant had swept his hand across the majority of the land, gripping trees and yanking them from the earth, his vengeful fists inflicting the temper and the power of a god.

My mouth gaped when I took in the devastation. The elf lord had taken *everything*. He'd taken it all.

Bare dirt. Giant holes. Raped land. That was all that remained. The once flourishing, ethereal Derian Forest was all but destroyed.

I have to find him.

I dashed into a sprint again, although my legs weren't as fast this time, and my heart was beating so fiercely that it felt as if I could faint. Sweat slid out of every pore of my body, and exhaustion made my limbs numb.

But I wouldn't stop.

The world continued to stay frozen. My grip on the goddess's power hadn't failed, yet I knew my body was weakening.

I was so tired. So ungodly *tired*, but I only had to hold on for a little bit longer.

A great screeching and creaking sound came from the west. Shock rippled through me, and I slammed to a stop, chest heaving and lungs aching. Had that been real?

The sound came again.

But how? How had I heard that? Time was frozen. There should be no sounds.

I paused, still breathing heavily, as I turned toward where the sound had come from.

It came again, that sickening crunch of cracking and splintering wood.

There.

Movement from the northwest caught my attention. *Movement? Shit.*

I watched as a giant tree was ripped from the ground in a part of the forest that was still intact, before it was twisted and gnarled into figures that resembled demons from another realm. My jaw dropped. Thousands upon thousands of branch-like soldiers stood waiting nearby, ready.

"Good gods," I whispered.

Lord Godasara was nearly finished, and he was strong enough that he was *moving* in frozen time. His power was growing.

Only a few trees remained planted as the elf lord himself walked slowly toward them, his arms swishing through the air as if in slow motion, before he dropped to his knees and scribbled more runes in the earth.

His knees.

My heart pounded even more when I gaped at his reformed legs and arms. As I'd seen in my dream, he'd already healed. Shiny, taut green skin covered his new limbs. I stayed out of sight, clouded in the goddess's power and breathing hard as I tried to form a plan of the best way to attack him.

If he saw me, I would be at a disadvantage. I'd been counting on him being completely frozen, even if he could still talk or watch me. The fact that he was *moving* changed everything.

With a sluggish wave of his hand, the trees responded—uprooting and forming into new soldiers. Lord Godasara was moving faster, even though his movements were still slow. But he was still able to mobilize his army.

My lips parted, the breath rushing out of me, as a wave of fear coated my insides.

Lord Godasara's power had always amazed me. When everyone else had been *completely* frozen both physically and mentally, he'd still been able to watch me. At times, he'd even been able to speak to me. It defied all odds that any creature was allowed to wield the power he had.

As if he had the power of the gods himself.

I didn't know who the elf lords descended from. Nobody did. But given what I was seeing, he had to have blood from the gods in his veins.

I now understood why all of the other fairies in this realm had sought to destroy the elf lords. They were too strong. Their power was too great. With power that rivaled the gods', they had absolute control.

And that power had never been used for good.

The difference between the elf lords and the gods and goddesses of the fae universe, was that the *real* gods, the true gods, did not want to rule over the fairies.

But the elf lords did. They commanded their power like a weapon, slicing and hacking apart anything that dared defy them.

Shock rippled through me as I carefully crept closer to where he worked. For the first time since leaving the palace, I wondered if I'd made the right choice. Maybe I should have asked Wyatt and Squad Three to join me. Maybe we all should have traveled here using portal keys. Maybe we should have fought this battle together.

But then I remembered the three SF members that had died for me at the base of the mountain just south of here. And the SF members and Fae Guard who had died at Shrouding Estate. And the innocent fairies who had died at the Hog's Head Inn when the elf lord made his first attack.

So much bloodshed had been spilled to save me. And for what? Who was I to demand that kind of sacrifice? Why should anyone give their lives when I was capable of ending this on my own?

No. I knew I could do this. I wouldn't regret my decision. Even if I died here, right now, fighting to save this realm, it would be worth it if Lord Godasara was destroyed.

My soul twisted when I thought of Wyatt, of leaving him here without me.

Mate.

I'm sorry, I whispered to him internally. *I will try to get back to you, but I'm so sorry if I can't. Please forgive me if it comes to that.*

I took a deep breath, then moved in a blur until I was closer, directly behind Lord Godasara. He still wasn't aware of me. I'd been careful to stay out of sight.

Rage trembled through my limbs as I watched him create another batch of his army.

Gods, he was strong.

Even though my hold on time was intact, he still moved so much faster than he should've been able to.

I crept behind him, moving as quietly as a mouse. Raising my hand, I reached for the sword strapped to my back that I'd taken from one of the royal guards back at the palace. One clean swipe through the neck would kill the elf lord. I only had to reach him.

I slipped the blade free. The movement sent a ripple through time.

Lord Godasara's head whipped up, and he spun around.

I froze.

No. He'd done that *so* fast, so quickly. How could he be moving that fast?

He grinned, his lips pulling up in a slow-motion saccharine smile. "You've certainly made this easy on me." His words were spoken haltingly as if they too were being said in slow motion. "I thought I would have to hunt you down, but instead you came to me."

He glanced over my shoulder, a scowl forming on his ugly face. "Where is the goddess? Where have you put her?"

"You will *not* have her. Just like you will not have me."

I tightened my grip on the sword, looking for an opening.

He laughed. "Who do you think you are to try to wield her power? Only those as great as the gods can do it."

"So you think you're a god?" I stepped closer, hoping that our conversation would distract him enough that I could cleave his head in one swift blow.

A dark laugh erupted from his lips. "I *will* be a god after I sacrifice you for the power inside you. I will rule this entire realm. It will be as it was when my kind had control of these lands with an iron fist. Except now there is only me, so I will command *all* of it."

"Not if I have any say in it." I tightened my grip on the sword. Only a few more feet. Just a few steps and I would be within striking distance. I inched toward him more, my feet sliding along the dirt.

He smirked. "What do you think you're going to do with—"

I lunged toward him.

His eyes widened, and he stumbled back.

My sword hit the earth, but I whipped it back up, my movements as fast as lightning. I circled him again, prowling around him, waiting for my next opportunity to strike.

"Do you really think you're going to kill me?" He

laughed, his words no longer sounding like they were uttered in slow motion. "I don't know why the goddess picked you. What are you? A human? A barely passable witch? You're not strong enough to command her power, but *I* am. And everybody will see that after I take it from you."

"Has anyone ever told you that you talk too much?" I struck again, springing toward him with the sword raised, bringing it down toward his neck in one swift arch.

He sidestepped at the last moment, but barely, and hissed when my sword grazed his shoulder.

Dammit!

I retreated, circling again, my heart pounding so hard it felt like a bass drum.

"Stupid girl," he whispered. The skin on his arm knitted back together, sewing up like an invisible needle and thread had carved through his flesh.

He glanced at the wound, and it was enough time for me to strike again, but a blow came from behind me, sending me to my knees. I pitched forward, my grip on the sword nearly loosening. I rolled at the last second and turned horrified eyes behind me.

A branch-like soldier stood, its limbs moving sluggishly, but they were still moving.

Lord Godasara was growing even stronger. He was able to move his trees.

No!

The rest of the forest army were moving inch by inch, sluggishly and nearly still, but they'd moved far enough that one of them had reached me from behind without me seeing it coming.

Another dark laugh came from the elf lord. "What was I saying about you being a stupid girl?"

I jumped to my feet and shot a blast of the goddess's power at the tree.

The tree exploded. Bits of tree fell slowly toward the earth as if moving through water.

The smile on the elf lord's face died.

"What were you saying about me being a stupid girl?" I swung my sword, moving it high and fast.

A flash flew from his fingertips.

I gasped, my sword arcing toward him. At the last moment, I ducked, rolling out of the way as his spell shot past me. I landed hard, the sword clattering out of my hand.

His spell hit the soil, sizzling into the ground. It carried with it a hint of sulfur. *Oh Gods.* It was the same spell that had bound the goddess's power inside me.

I somersaulted to the balls of my feet, my legs aching in protest, but I managed to grab the sword again.

He lobbed more spells at me, throwing them out one after another.

I dodged. Leaped. Jumped. Rolled.

With each paralyzing spell the elf lord threw, his movements became faster, his power growing, almost as if the longer he commanded his power the greater its strength became.

With horror firing through my veins, I realized it would only take a whisper of his spell hitting me to render me weak and powerless again. If his spell landed on me, it would release my hold on time.

And then he would win.

I sprang to my feet and called upon the last reserves of my strength. I had to strike him *now* and end this. I summoned the training that my body had apparently once learned.

With a forceful surge, I lunged and swung, coming at him faster and faster. Every spell he threw, I dodged. Every tree he called upon couldn't move fast enough to reach me.

The triumph in his eyes dimmed, hatred taking its place. "You can't win this."

"I believe I am." But sweat was pouring from my face. With each swipe of my arm, every slide of my feet, I'd grown more tired. The goddess's power sparkled inside me, steady and strong, but my human body was failing.

No. End this!

I pulled power from deep inside me, the last wells of my inner strength. Lightning swam through my veins, and energy coursed through my limbs. I was a walking goddess, a living, breathing incarnation of Verasellee, and I would not fail.

My sword arced toward his neck again, the movement sure and strong.

The lord's eyes widened. "Did you know my army has already entered the city? As you fight here, I'm taking the capital, and with it, your mate. He'll be dead even if you beat me."

His declaration sizzled through me, the shock of it making me fumble. My sword missed.

His face split into a grin just before a spell shot from his fingertips. The scent of sulfur rushed past my face, tickling my cheek, like a breeze had caressed my skin.

No!

My hold on Verasellee's power snapped, and the world abruptly began turning again. His spell tingled against my cheek, not fully penetrating me, but seizing my immediate attempts to stop time again.

I struck forward in one last desperate attempt to kill the elf lord.

He sidestepped my strike, laughing the entire time. The sound was so dark and deep.

And then the army came alive around him. The trees groaning and creaking as they formed into thousands of rows of twisted creatures, bent wood, and snarled splinters. They moved steadily and with strength, no longer encumbered by my hold on time.

And the army was ready to do his bidding.

A grin streaked across the elf lord's face, his eyes glowing with malice, as my stomach turned to ice.

CHAPTER TWENTY-THREE
WYATT

I jolted forward, intent on stopping Avery before she carried out whatever plan she'd devised, but when I tried to grab her, all I reached for was air.

"Avery!" I howled.

Around me, the royal guards blinked, as if coming out of a trance.

"Avery!" I roared again, even though I knew it was in vain.

She'd stopped time again.

My mate was gone.

But then I remembered what she'd whispered to me.

"I'm sorry, but I have to do this. If I don't kill Lord Godasara before he creates his army in the Derian Forest, this entire realm will fall."

The Elixias Mountains. The Derian Forest. She was going after the elf lord. By herself.

"No!" I bellowed. What was she thinking? How could she even consider doing something like that, just her against Lord Godasara? Because even though she was immensely powerful, so was he.

The guards surged forward and tried to seize me, but with a vicious snarl I lashed out. I managed to keep the three off that were trying to detain me.

"We need to get to Bavar!" I yelled at Nick and Reese. "Now! Avery's in danger. Stop the guards!"

Nick and Reese snapped into action.

A burst of vicious disabling spells exploded from them, knocking out the surrounding guards one by one.

When it was just the three of us left standing, I jerked my chin toward the door. "Come on, let's go. We need to mobilize Squad Three and portal transport to the Derian Forest. Avery's gone after Lord Godasara by herself."

Nick's eyes widened.

Reese whispered, "Fuck."

We raced out of the room, down the hall, and past a dozen opulent rooms. Thankfully, I knew the palace well enough during my time spent here while searching through their archives, that I knew where to go.

We skidded to a stop outside one of the training

rooms. Squad Three was inside, doing coordinated training exercises.

I burst through the door. "Bavar! Avery's in the Derian Forest with Lord Godasara. We need to mobilize immediately."

The fairy commander swirled around, a confused expression on his face. "Come again, Major?"

I forced myself to take a steadying breath even though rage rippled along my skin as my wolf threatened to unleash.

"Avery stopped time again. She went after the elf lord by herself. She's in the Derian Forest, possibly right now as we speak. The fact that I'm telling you this means that time has started moving again." My lungs seized. I didn't want to think about what that signified. It either meant she'd beaten the elf lord or—

She was dead.

Gods. My claws lengthened, my wolf straining to shift.

No. She was strong. I couldn't think that way. I would completely lose it if I did.

Bavar gave a curt nod. "Squad Three. We move now."

They whipped into action, already suited up since we'd all anticipated an onslaught of problems once we arrived here.

"What about the three squads we're waiting for?" Dee double checked the blades strapped to her legs.

"No time," I told her.

"Copy that."

Bavar reached into his pocket before tossing out portal keys. "You know the drill. Link up. Destination, the Derian Forest at the base of the Elixias Mountains. We go now."

Bishop, Heidi, and Charlotte joined hands. I joined with Nick and Reese, while Bavar grabbed Dee and Terry.

We all whispered the spell-activating words, the portals opening instantaneously.

The portal winds swept around us, the floor disappearing beneath our soles. We cleaved through time and space, snapping and bending as immeasurable magic propelled us to another place.

Cold air greeted us when the portals spit us out.

I took in the evening sky. This far north, the sun had already set. Three moons shone down on us, but it was the sudden scream from my right that caught my attention.

My eyes widened in horror when, not even a hundred yards away, I saw Lord Godasara whipping his arm back, a spell forming in his hand. Behind him, thousands of immobile humanoid tree-like figures waited.

Avery knelt in front of the elf, screaming, as two humanoid trees held her down.

Intense rage slammed into me. "Attack now!" I commanded.

The entire squad dove into action. I shifted mid-run, my wolf breaking into a sprint faster than the wind as my clothes shredded at my back.

Just as the evil elf muttered the last word of his spell, I crashed into him. We went down in a tangle of fur, fangs, and limbs.

Avery screamed again as my wolf clamped down onto the lord's arm. I bit viciously, sinking into his flesh, the taste of his blood making me want to tear him apart.

He cried out, my attack obviously catching him by surprise.

And then the entire squad was there. Charlotte rushed to Avery, hacking her from the trees, as the others encircled me and Lord Godasara.

The elf threw me off him, but I landed on my four paws, sliding to a stop just as he raised his hand and gave a command, all while Reese and Nick threw spells at him and Dee let a throwing star fly.

A shielding spell erupted around the lord, deflecting our blows as the forest army sprang to life.

Thousands of humanoid tree-like figures moved as if commanded by some grotesque puppet master.

In less than a second, we were surrounded, their wicked arms made of whittled branches as sharp and strong as swords.

We didn't slow. Dee, Terry, and Bavar hacked at their limbs. Nick and Reese threw explosive spells in never-ending succession. Bishop and I snapped limbs from the trees as our jaws cut through them. Charlotte dropped her bow and switched to her blade to cleave the wooden limbs in two, while Heidi conjured winds to knock the trees from their rooted feet.

Avery still stood in the middle of us, looking so haggard and exhausted that my wolf's fury strengthened to a cataclysmic reaction. Each tree he pounced upon was destroyed in seconds.

But it wasn't enough.

The trees came at us too fast. There were so many. They were closing in on our group, and we couldn't fend them off.

Because it was ten of us against thousands of them. Not even the entirety of the SF could stop this.

We didn't stand a chance.

Lord Godasara laughed. "Did you really think you could beat me? She thought so too." He cast a scathing glance at Avery. "But none of you are strong enough to take me on. I am the ruler of this land, the *rightful* ruler."

My wolf snarled, rage making him crave bloodlust.

He lunged for the elf lord again, but at the last moment Lord Godasara whispered a spell and my wolf fell to the ground, our ribs cracking under the force of it.

"No!" Avery screamed.

The rest of the forest army was already tearing into Squad Three.

Charlotte screamed. Nick yelled. Dee took a hit to the leg.

The forest descended on us.

Terry managed to fend off another tree, slashing and fighting every single one that came at her, but then a branch shot out, encircling her ankle. She went down in a howl of fury.

My wolf pushed off from the ground, loping again toward the elf lord despite the pain that cleaved my chest. I struggled to breathe, knowing my broken ribs had punctured a lung.

I just needed to get to the lord—to stop him before we all ended.

"Wyatt," Avery called to me. She was on her feet again, but she looked so pale.

I struck at the lord, fangs flashing.

But he was ready this time. He grasped my scruff between his hands. My wolf snarled and fought, claws extending into deadly weapons. They thrashed at the elf lord's abdomen, tearing it open.

But Lord Godasara continued to stand, his skin sewing closed in seconds. His hold around my wolf's neck tightened. He squeezed harder, crushing my wolf's windpipe.

Behind the elf, the trees advanced on Avery, going for her and pinning her down again. Her eyes were still on me. Terror filled her gaze, and then it flashed violet.

I attempted to snarl again trying to break free, but no air could move through my windpipe, and I knew we were too late.

A mournful whine vibrated in my chest and something shattered inside me when a tree picked Avery up like a ragdoll.

I knew we weren't going to survive.

We had failed, and the realm was lost.

CHAPTER TWENTY-FOUR

AVERY

The tree lifted me from the ground despite my attempts to break free. I panted and screamed as panic skittered along my limbs, and my lungs seized.

Lord Godasara had Wyatt's wolf between his two hands, a murderous look in his eyes as he tried to squeeze the life right out of my mate. I knew the only thing keeping Wyatt alive was his dwindling alpha strength.

Around me, the rest of Squad Three was being ravaged by the trees, an entire forested army doing their maker's bidding.

Squad Three didn't stand a chance against the elf lord. With power so great, they couldn't beat him.

But what if I still could? The goddess's power

whirled inside me, crackling and skittering along my nerves, but the whisper of the lord's binding spell had rendered it untouchable.

Unless I could fight off his spell and stop time again.

I closed my eyes as the forest branches encircled me, pinning me to them and holding me tight. The elf lord needed me alive. He wouldn't let the trees kill me. But he would kill my mate and my friends.

Please work. Please, please work! I pleaded with the goddess's power.

Panic consumed me, and I knew this was our last chance. If I couldn't stop time now and reach a sword, not only were all my friends dead, but this entire realm would fall.

A crack formed in my chest, the goddess's power sizzling to life. I called upon it with everything I had, reaching deep within me as I tried to access it and break the lord's spell.

My heart beat at an alarmingly fast speed, but Verasellee's power was there, just at my fingertips.

I called upon her power with everything I had, clawing at the electricity that hummed and flowed through my veins. It gathered as one, into a giant bolt in the center of my chest.

Yes! Just a little bit more.

I reached and pulled again, and a whisper of mist broke through the lord's spell.

Grab it!

Her power caressed my inner self.

Yes!

Heart beating so fast I could barely breathe, I concentrated on that funnel of power. I would get one shot at this. Only one strike. I couldn't miss.

A scream tore from my throat when I called upon the sizzling energy swirling inside me. My eyes locked with Wyatt's.

His life was fading. His eyes were dull. The lord was killing him, and I only had seconds until he was dead.

"No!" I shot the goddess's power from my chest, and a bolt of lightning burst toward Lord Godasara as a ripple of time shot through the realm.

The trees stilled. Screams stopped. The flash of lightning collided with the elf just as a momentary lapse in time unfolded.

I scrambled from the trees' grasp, hacking and cleaving my way through them. Lord Godasara turned, his head still moving. He still managed to move through my ancient power.

I limped toward a sword.

The elf still had his hands around Wyatt. I focused on that. I focused on the life being drained from my mate's eyes. If I didn't stop Lord Godasara, Wyatt would die.

My hand enclosed around the sword that had fallen from Terry's grasp. I raised it above my head.

The elf lord turned, his grip on my mate loosening, as a spell began to form on his lips. It was the spell that would bind me again. If it managed to hit me square in the chest this time, it would bind me completely.

And if that happened, all would be lost.

With movements that felt as if they were done in slow motion, I ran toward the elf, leaping at the last second with the sword raised.

The spell left his lips, traveling toward me at a speed I could physically see. Blue sparks flowed from his body, about to collide with mine.

The sword came down on the bottom of his neck, the feel of metal colliding with flesh reverberating through my grip.

I didn't stop.

I didn't let go.

The sword cut through Lord Godasara's neck just as his spell collided with my body.

I screamed and fell to the ground, paralyzed, as time snapped back into action, the world jolting to a start.

The elf lord's head rolled to the ground at my side.

Then everything went black.

CHAPTER TWENTY-FIVE
WYATT

I sat beside my mate's bed in the palace's healing ward. She'd been unconscious since we'd brought her back from the Derian Forest yesterday. I stayed by her side, though, never once leaving.

But my mood was surly, my temper foul. It didn't help that we were stuck in the fae lands. Due to the stunt we'd pulled with the unbinding ritual, the king and queen weren't allowing us to leave until they'd finished their "investigation" into the matter. But at least they'd allowed several of the SF's top healing witches to join us.

In the other rooms on the ward, every single member of Squad Three was being treated. We hadn't lost anyone, but it had been close. So fucking close.

I cradled my arm to my side, wincing. My ribs were

only halfway healed since broken bones always took the longest to mend, but my collapsed lung was fully recovered as were the numerous cuts and gashes. By tomorrow, I would be back to normal.

Farrah had been tending to Avery ever since we'd returned, insisting that she stay at her side, and since I refused to leave my mate, Farrah had been tending to me, too, even though she hadn't slept in eighteen hours.

"When will she wake up?" I asked Farrah as the witch did another assessment on Avery.

Panic gripped me, making my knee jostle as I sat like a bundle of nerves at my mate's side.

Magic flowed from Farrah's fingertips, settling over Avery like a cloud. Her lips tightened, and she forced a smile. "Give her time, Wyatt. She's been through a lot, more than any of us have ever experienced."

But worry puckered her mouth. Avery wasn't responding to anything the healing witch did. Her heart still beat, and her lungs still breathed, but it was as though she'd fallen into such a deep coma that nothing could wake her.

I was about to ask Farrah another question, when Bavar appeared in the doorway. He held onto a cane, limping, and his mood looked as pitiful as his twisted ankle.

As a fairy, he didn't heal as fast as a werewolf, but in

a week's time he would be as good as new. Still, none of us took well to being incapacitated, commanders especially, as was apparent from the constant sounds of arguing coming from Dee down the hall as she continually insisted that she was fine, even though one of the trees had stabbed her in the abdomen.

"Wyatt?" Bavar said, his eyes wide. He looked as if he'd seen a ghost.

I frowned, concern lacing through me. "What happened?"

He shook his head. "Nothing bad, I don't think. It's, um, just that somebody's here who wants to see Avery."

I expected it to be Avery's parents again—Danielle and Bryce. They'd been here all morning, their pale faces streaked with tears, but Farrah had finally convinced them to take a break and grab some lunch.

I knew that between Avery's anxious parents and my surly mood, Farrah had her hands full. But the healing witch didn't complain even though nothing she was doing was improving my mate's condition.

Bavar's gaze shifted to whoever stood in the hall, a look of reverence descending over the fairy commander's features.

My brows folded together, then rose in surprise when a figure appeared beside Bavar.

"Verasellee?"

She appeared in the doorway, awake and walking toward me. Bavar bowed deeply from behind her.

An ethereal quality surrounded the goddess. Her skin held a subtle, otherworldly glow, and the innate need to bow and submit nearly overtook me.

"You're awake?" I whispered. Last I'd heard, she'd been in the same state as Avery—a deep coma that didn't seem curable.

"Yes, with the help of several SF sorcerers, the spell that had been cast over me is broken. I thought the death of Lord Godasara"—her mouth tightened, and I saw her barely controlled rage when mentioning the elf —"would be enough, but it wasn't. I still needed your sorcerers' assistance to come out of the dormant sleep."

She drifted to my side, her presence again making me want to fold and bend. I barely managed to keep my chin up as she stopped at Avery's bed.

A small smile curved the goddess's lips, and she gently grasped Avery's hand. "This one is *so* brave. So defiant. A worthy soul to wield my power."

A soul of steel. My mouth went dry. It was often how I thought of my mate. She was so strong, innately resilient, even though her natural magic had been weak.

Verasellee reached out, and placed a hand on Avery's chest. She closed her eyes, breathing deeply as violet light began to flow out of Avery and around her hand.

My mate's entire body began shining with purple light as it flowed over her like a cloud, drifting and rising as if in a breeze.

My eyes widened as I realized what the goddess was doing.

Verasellee was taking back her power.

I bolted to a stand, a snarl rising in my throat when I remembered Reese's warning that by returning the goddess's power, Avery's life could end.

But Verasellee gave me a sharp look, an ancient command cutting through her lips. *"Sit."*

My knees bent. I fell back onto my chair. I couldn't have stayed standing if my life depended on it.

"I am not harming your mate, wolf. I would never do that to her after what she's done for me."

The purple light continued to stream out of Avery's body while Farrah stood mutely in the corner, and Bavar remained in shocked silence at the door.

Verasellee opened her mouth, and with a sharp inhale, breathed all of the violet light inside her. Waves and waves of clouded magic flowed from Avery into the goddess. With each moment that passed, Avery appeared to grow weaker and weaker.

My wolf growled. The urge to slam into Verasellee was so strong that the heavens be damned even if she was a goddess. But then I remembered what Avery had asked of me.

To trust her.

She'd trusted the goddess with her life, which meant I needed to as well.

Veins popped in my fisted hands, but I stayed where I was.

A moment passed, and then another. The purple light trickled out of my mate in wispy ribbons, and when the last of it flowed into the goddess, Verasellee tipped her head back, an expression of rapture forming upon her face.

Her skin glowed even brighter, and when she opened her eyes, even stormier violet light gleamed in her irises, and the power that reverberated through her shook the walls of the palace.

It was enough to wield the power of a thousand realms—it was a *galaxy* of power.

"Bless the queen," Bavar whispered.

Farrah looked in a similar state, her face completely white.

Verasellee stepped closer to Avery, who now lay so still and pale that my heart threatened to stop.

The goddess placed her hand directly on my mate's chest and said in that commanding voice again,

"Breathe. Live. Rise." And then, almost as an afterthought, she added, "Remember."

Avery's eyes flew open, her chest rising with a deep breath, as her body arched off the bed.

She bolted upright, eyes wild, as violet light flashed within her irises.

Wait, violet light?

A moment passed, and I frantically flew to her side, but she stared straight ahead, unseeing. The violet light faded and her natural brown-flecked-with-gold irises returned.

"Avery?" I choked out.

It seemed to take another minute, before she became aware of her surroundings. Her head whipped around, going to me, then Bavar standing frozen in the doorway, then Farrah, and at last to the goddess.

Avery reached for my hands, squeezing them, but her gaze stayed on the goddess. A grin streaked across her face. "Verasellee."

"Yes."

"You're awake."

"Yes, your sorcerers were quite helpful in that respect. I was wrong about the elf lord. His death alone didn't guarantee my awakening. But I'm fully awake now, and thanks to you, I have my power back inside me. I have back what is mine."

Despite wanting to crush Avery to me, I stayed at her side, clutching her hand tightly in my palms. She felt warm, *alive*, and the lilac scent that tickled my senses made my heart feel ready to burst.

But Avery and the goddess continued to regard each other. Verasellee was gazing upon my mate with a look of reverence, and I realized that it wasn't just gratitude she felt for Avery, it was also respect.

"Thank you for everything that you've done," the goddess said, breaking the quiet. "I won't forget you, and I won't forget what you sacrificed. That's why I've left you with a parting gift. I know it's not much, but it's enough that you'll be able to continue your life as you had planned. I'm sorry if this journey was unpleasant, but it was a necessary evil to right what had been wronged. I hope that with time, you'll come to remember me fondly, and not be angry about my prophecy casting you as the chosen one."

Avery frowned, a perplexed look growing on her face, but then she looked down, and her free hand shot to her chest. Her lips parted, surprise filling her eyes. "You left me with some of your power."

Verasellee gave her a coy smile, the look entirely humanlike, before she nodded. "Yes, a small bit. It's not enough that it will hinder me in any way, but it is enough for you to be magical again."

Avery grinned, then laughed, the sound as sweet and high as tinkling bells. It was filled with so much warmth and happiness that I could have died right there a happy man.

"Thank you," Avery breathed when her laughter finally died down.

"No. Thank *you*," the goddess replied. "And goodbye for now. You never know, one day I may see you again."

She leaned down and placed a soft kiss on Avery's cheek. As soon as she pulled back, the world began to spin, as if everything had paused and jolted out of time.

The next thing I knew, I was standing at Avery's side alone.

The goddess was gone.

"What just happened?" Farrah asked quietly.

Bavar shook his head, his orange hair glinting in the overhead lights. "I think we were just in the presence of a goddess who reclaimed her power and returned to her otherworldly realm. But I could be wrong, since, you know, I've never experienced that before, but that's what it felt like."

I sank to my knees and cupped Avery's cheeks between my palms.

Tears filled her eyes when she focused on me. I could tell a part of her was overwhelmed by Verasellee's departure, but also touched beyond measure by the goddess's parting gift.

"Are you okay?" I whispered. My gaze skittered along her features, down her length, over her frame. My mate looked whole and healthy. But I didn't know how she felt inside.

Tears poured down her cheeks, and she threw her arms around me. "Yes, yes, I'm okay. And I remember! I remember everything about me, about *us*, Wyatt. She didn't just give me some of her power. She gave me back my memories too." She squeezed me harder. "Gods, Wyatt, I wish you could feel what I do."

I pulled back, my head cocking as my chest felt so tight I thought it would burst.

Avery threaded her fingers through the hair resting at my nape, and for the briefest moment, her irises flashed violet.

My breath sucked in.

"She left me with some of her power, Wyatt. It's still inside me. I don't think it's strong enough to stop time, but I could probably slow it, which means I'm not weak anymore. I'm no longer the weak witch that I was born as. That means that I can still be a part of the community. I can still join the Supernatural Ambassador Institute, just like I always dreamed of. I'll have to go through new recruit training again and pass my final test, but this time—" She laughed, the sound so happy and full of merriment that it was impossible for me not to join in. "This time I *know* I'll pass!"

My grip tightened around her. Gods, but I wanted to strip her naked and feel *all* of her around me. We still, however, needed to sort out one detail. Now that her life was back on track, reality had rejoined us.

"But I still need to stay at the SF." I brushed a lock of hair tenderly behind her ear. "I can't break my promise to Marcus. I need to train Elijah."

Her lips curved into a smile. "I know, and I would never ask you to break that promise. Your sense of honor and duty are two of the things I love so much about you, and yes, I *remember* what you promised Marcus, so we'll compromise. I still have to go through my new recruit training again, right? And in the meantime . . ." She quirked an eyebrow, a cheeky grin forming on her face.

I laughed, because the new recruit program for her didn't start until next year. "Does that mean you'll live with me in the meantime?"

She laughed, a deep joyous laugh which made my toes curl. "Why, Major Jamison, is that an invitation?"

EPILOGUE
AVERY - SIX MONTHS LATER

I pulled a batch of cookies out of the industrial-sized oven, their sugary and floury scent rising around me and filling the bakery with doughy goodness.

I'd been working at the bakery for several months while waiting for my new recruit training program to start. It was crazy to think that even though baking wasn't my dream job, I was ridiculously content.

Wyatt had been the one to suggest that I take a job at the supernatural marketplace, working at a bakery during the day while he tended to SF business. I had to admit, it was an excellent idea. I'd never enjoyed a part-time job so much. Because not only was I allowed to constantly bake all of the recipes that swirled around inside my head, but I was also *paid* for it.

Eyeing the light golden color of the cookies, I was about to set them on the counter when the bell jingled on the door behind me.

My grip slipped, and the pan of cookies began to fall.

In a flash, I called upon the remnant of Verasellee's power that always hummed inside me.

The falling pan continued toward the floor, but slower, as if in slow motion.

I snatched it from the air and righted it on the counter before anything could hit the floor. A well of satisfaction grew in me. None of the cookies had been compromised.

Satisfied, I let time resume its normal pace as I regarded the cooked sweets.

The bell silenced, and I whirled around to greet my newest customer.

My eyes widened.

A woman with blue-black hair, startling cobalt eyes, and snowy translucent skin made me back up so fast, I nearly knocked the pan off the counter again.

Marnee ran a hand through her hair, her expression unsure. She wore jeans and a pink blouse, her skin healthy-looking with a subtle glow. "Um, hi, Avery."

My hand reached toward the pan. A part of me wanted to throw a cookie at her face, and the other part wanted to turn my back on her, but instead, I took a deep breath and said evenly, "Hi."

"I'm sorry to startle you like this."

My hand stopped its slow progression toward the pan. It would be a shame to waste the cookies after all.

The siren took another deep breath and slammed her hands into her pockets. "I'm returning to the SF to face whatever repercussions await me given my actions at Shrouding Estate." Her nose scrunched up. "I feel like such a bitch for how I treated you. It wasn't fair or right, and the fact that I drugged you and Nicholas is completely reprehensible. I'll accept whatever punishment the SF divvies out, but first, I wanted to see you in person so I could tell you how sorry I am."

My lips parted, my jaw coming unhinged.

"I don't expect you to forgive me, but I'd like you to know that I wasn't in my right mind when I did those things. I'd been away from the sea for too long, and it'd affected me. I know that's not an excuse, but I wanted you to know that."

I opened and closed my mouth like a fish, then finally found my voice. "You nearly got Nicholas killed. Wyatt attacked him because he was on top of me, and I nearly—" My lips thinned. "We both did things neither of us wanted to do but were forced to because of the drug you gave us."

She grimaced. "I know. I heard. All I can do is say that I'm sorry. I never would have done anything like that if I'd been thinking clearly."

"Have you been in the sea this entire time?"

She nodded. "I returned to land a few days ago in the fae realm, then came here. I knew the SF would have a warrant out for my arrest, and that I couldn't outrun them." She shrugged. "And I don't want to be on the run. I know I messed up. Like I said earlier, I'll accept the punishment that's coming my way."

I cocked my head. "What do you think will happen to you?"

"I'm not sure. I already reached out to Major Fieldstone and General McCloy. They said that if I turned myself in, the punishment wouldn't be as harsh, but as I was an SF member who left my squad and purposefully put civilians in harm's way, my behavior can't go unpunished."

I took a deep breath, the scent of cookies filling the air. Because so much time had passed since everything that had happened at Shrouding Estate, I didn't think I would ever see Marnee again. But the fact that she'd come here first to see me and apologize before accepting her punishment spoke volumes about the kind of person she really was. It wasn't her fault that her mind had become warped from being gone too long from the sea.

Tension left my shoulders, and I grabbed a small bag. "Would you like some cookies? They're fresh from the oven."

Marnee shrugged. "Um, sure. I've heard that you're quite the baker."

I dropped half a dozen into the small sack and handed it to her. She took it, but my hand lingered before letting go. "Thank you for coming to see me. That means a lot to me. It really does."

She opened the bag and peeked inside before closing it. "It's the right thing to do, and I wanted you to know that I'm ashamed of how I acted."

Any lingering anger or hurt I'd had over the way she'd treated me at Bavar's estate melted as rapidly as chocolate chips in the oven. "Thank you. All's forgiven."

She gave me a warm smile, then dipped her eyes to the mark on my neck. Her smile turned wistful. "He's a good man. You're lucky to have him."

I fingered the crescent moon shape near my collarbone, then felt inside for the bond that tethered me to Wyatt. He was working, currently in his third week with his newest batch of new recruits, so the emotions that strummed through our connection were the usual: determination and patience.

I dropped my hand. "Yeah, I am lucky."

She shook herself then scrunched the top of the cookie bag closed before turning toward the door. When she reached it, she paused and looked over her shoulder at me. "He's lucky to have you too. I can see that you're a worthy mate for him."

Before I could respond, she pushed through the door, the bell jingling above. For a moment, I just stood there, my mind reeling from what she'd said while also wondering what would become of her. I hoped her punishment wouldn't be too severe. After an apology like that, I now saw that her actions at Bavar's estate were truly because of her salt-deprived state.

Taking a deep breath, I began transferring the cookies onto a cooling rack when the bell on the door jingled again.

A flash of orange hair, a jeweled dagger strapped to a waist, and a delightful fairy grin greeted me when I turned to welcome my newest customer.

"Ah, I thought I smelled something that could only be created by the hands of Ms. Meyers." Bavar sauntered toward the counter, already appraising all of my baked goods on display in the cabinet.

I glanced out the window but didn't see any signs of the siren. "Did you see Marnee? She was just here."

The SF commander had his hands clasped behind his

back as he avidly perused the display of baked goods. "I did. She's on her way to headquarters now."

"Does that mean she won't be arrested?"

He raised his head, his expression contemplative. "No, she won't be arrested. She contacted me and Wes yesterday, letting us know that she was returning and would accept whatever punishment was deemed necessary."

I twisted my hands as his eyes lit up when he spotted my toasted hazelnut pastries filled with cream. "Ooh, I do love those little morsels. I'll take a dozen of those."

I sighed. "Bavar!"

He startled, a lock of orange hair falling across his forehead. "Yes?"

"How can you be thinking about food at a time like this? What if Marnee goes to jail?"

His eyes softened. "She won't go to jail."

"She won't?"

"No, she wasn't in her normal frame of mind when she committed those atrocious acts. And she's now had six months at sea and has returned of her own accord. The woman I spoke to yesterday is the Marnee I know and remember. She will go before a committee and undergo a rigorous mental exam, but I have no doubt that she will pass it."

"So nothing will happen to her?"

"I didn't say that. I simply said she wouldn't go to jail." He smiled when he caught my expression. "She will most likely be required to fulfill community duty for six months and will then undergo another mental examination before she's allowed to serve in the SF again, but I'm certain she'll do the service without hesitation. And as long as Marnee continues her soaks in the sea on a more regular basis, I have no doubt she'll be a valued SF member once again."

My death grip on the spatula eased. "I'm glad to hear it."

"Now, back to these delicious concoctions of yours . . ." Bavar leaned over the glass cabinet again and began pointing out which items he wanted boxed up. The fairy wasn't frugal in his spending, much to the delight of Mary, the bakery's owner.

I wiped the flour from my hands and began to place a selection of donuts, cookies, tarts, and cakes into a box when Bavar tapped on the cabinet. "Better add a dozen of those. Squad Three shall be here any minute as we decided to take our lunch break in the marketplace today. I'm sure all of them will enjoy whatever that tasty morsel is."

"That morsel happens to be my white chocolate truffle infused with raspberry. You may want to buy more than a dozen. Charlotte tends to inhale those."

His eyes glinted mischievously. "My, my, haven't you become quite the sales lady, but alas, you have twisted my arm. Make it two dozen."

I laughed and grabbed another piece of wax paper.

As soon as I finished boxing up Bavar's order, the door opened again, and the entirety of Squad Three poured into the bakery. Charlotte grinned when she saw me, Nick at her side. They were holding hands, as was the norm now.

As I'd come to learn after all of the chaos had died down following Lord Godasara's demise, Nick was confirmed as the "animal" Charlotte had slept with following the celebratory party after our new recruit graduation, when Wyatt and I had rushed to the Bulgarian libraries to find a cure for me.

She'd told me, in rather vivid details, why Nick was so good in bed. And apparently, he was enough of an animal that she was happy to keep him around.

So, for the first time in her life, Charlotte Morris was in a monogamous relationship. Eliza and I still loved to tease her about it to no end.

Charlotte sauntered up to the counter. "Hey, babe, what did you make this time?"

I grabbed the spatula and dished one of the hot cookies I'd just taken out of the oven onto a napkin.

"Just a new recipe I thought I'd try. Mary was nice enough to let me put them on display."

My boss had come to trust me and my recipes. She'd also gone so far as to offer me a permanent position, which I'd turned down. As much as I loved baking, the Supernatural Ambassador Institute was still calling me.

Besides, considering Wyatt and I both loved to travel, it seemed like the perfect solution for us once he finished training Elijah. Thankfully, the Supernatural Ambassador Institute had been incredibly understanding about everything that had happened to me. They were happy to hold my position until the time was right for me to join them.

Because of that, I wouldn't leave until after Wyatt finished training Elijah. Six months ago, that wouldn't have been an option, but since I'd—you know—saved the fae lands, I'd been cut a break once or twice, which also meant there would be no issues about my relationship with Wyatt once I started the new recruit program for the second time.

And luckily, that understanding had also extended to the fae lands' king and queen, Bavar's uncle and aunt. When it was confirmed to them that Squad Three and I had stopped Lord Godasara from wreaking havoc on their realm that would have undoubtedly collapsed their crown, they'd turned a blind eye to all of the laws we'd broken when I'd made Reese and Nick conduct the unlinking ritual.

"Are we still going out tonight with Eliza?" Charlotte asked as she bit into her cookie.

I scooped more cookies onto napkins for the rest of the squad. "Wouldn't miss it. See you and Eliza at six?"

"You can count on it, babe." She winked as Terry and Bishop snatched their cookies while Nick slung an arm around her shoulder. "I live for girls' night."

THAT NIGHT as I was getting ready, I stood in front of the mirror, curling my freshly washed and dried hair.

Wyatt's products still sat neatly on his side of the sink. One thing I definitely knew about him now was that he was actually neat and tidy. It wasn't just SF training that had made him that way.

I arched my neck, reaching for another long lock of hair behind my back, when my gaze landed on the crescent moon mark on my skin.

The bathroom door opened just as I twirled another group of strands around the curling iron.

Wyatt stood in the doorway. His nostrils flared as his gaze raked up and down my body.

I was wearing a dress that I'd purchased in the fae

lands. It was a shimmery bright purple, cinched in at the waist and stopping mid-thigh, with a square-cut neckline. My cleavage was on display, which I had a feeling Wyatt loved and hated at the same time.

Sure enough, he came up behind me, his hands snaking around my waist as he dipped down to kiss my neck. I shivered, heat pooling between my thighs.

The man could still get me hot with just a kiss.

"Do you have any idea how gorgeous you look?" he whispered when his head dipped again. He kissed his mark, his tongue licking it softly.

I shuddered, and my eyes rolled back. He knew how much I loved that. The claiming mark that he'd imprinted on me for the second time had become an erogenous zone. He knew damned well what those little flicks from his tongue did to me. Already my folds had slickened as a deep curling need rooted in my belly.

His nostrils flared, "You smell good enough to eat, Little Flower."

I clamped my legs together, as more liquid heat pooled between my thighs. "You're insufferable," I scolded, but a laugh still bubbled out.

He chuckled, the sound deep, and another shiver raced through my body to my toes. His hands drifted lower, to just below the dress's hem. His fingers trailed up my thighs, going higher and higher, and I wisely set the curling iron down.

"Are you wearing anything underneath this?" A low rumble filled his chest when his fingers met my bare ass.

"I thought you liked it when I didn't wear panties," I said innocently.

He growled. "Yeah, when it's just *me* you're with." His hands kneaded my hips before dipping down between my thighs. A soft swirl against my clit had me bucking under his touch.

He dipped his head again, his tongue finding his erogenous mark. "But if any of the guys tonight so much as get a *peek* of what's under this, you do realize that I'll murder them. *All* of them."

"Then I suppose you'll have to put some panties on me before I leave." I spun in his arms so that I faced him. I bit back a smile. I'd left my panties off on purpose. He always came home around this time, and I'd been hoping for a quickie before I left.

His hands traveled under the dress again until he grabbed my ass in both hands. My breasts pressed against his chest as my breaths quickened.

Glowing gold formed in his eyes as he hoisted me on the bathroom counter, my legs spreading automatically. "Were you really going to go out tonight without anything on underneath this incredibly tantalizing slip of fabric?"

I muffled a laugh when a territorial growl rose up in him. "No, I wasn't, and you *know* you have nothing to worry about. I'm one hundred percent yours. Always."

His hands went to his fly. In a blurred movement, his cargos had slid to the floor, his length hard and ready. It bobbed in the air when he shifted closer. "I may know that, but I'm still a jealous motherfucker. I don't like anybody to see or smell what's *mine*."

"Then you better fuck me now so I don't smell aroused when I go out tonight." I tipped my head back as I encircled his length with my hand, guiding him toward my center.

He groaned when his tip brushed against my moist heat. "Always so wet. Have I ever told you how much I love you?" He pushed into me, and I moaned in pleasure as he sank his shaft deep inside me.

"Only every day." I gasped as he began to move.

"Well, it's true." He pulled out, almost all of the way, then thrust back inside me again.

Gods, it was heaven when he did that.

I wrapped my legs around his waist, as he pumped into me again and again, his tempo rising with each thrust. Already, my climax was building. The man set me on fire.

He leaned down to nip at his mark. "I live for you, my love. Only you. Always and forever."

I arched against the back of the bathroom counter, my toes curling when a streak of pleasure bolted through me. Pulling him down again to my neck, I forced his mouth on the crescent moon.

He chuckled, nipped it again, and then began slapping into me hard and fast, his mouth latched onto his mark.

I moaned in ecstasy as the waves continued to build. Already I was on the verge of coming, my channel clamping around his shaft, the waves climbing higher and intensifying. From the harsh pants coming from my mate, I knew that he was close too.

It was crazy how much we craved one another, our need for each other only growing more and more each day.

He pulled back to look me in the eye, his irises like twin glowing stars.

A moment of sheer love pelted me. Gods, this man. He was my soul, my heart, my fire. He made me feel complete.

He thrust again, and I knew with his next pump I would come undone.

"I love you, my mate, my love," I said, pulling him

down as a climax threatened to shatter my soul. "Now, *kiss me.*"

His lips locked onto mine just as my release tore through my body. He swallowed my scream, his roar following, as our souls entwined throughout eternity and our mating bond burned bright.

KRISTA STREET'S
SUPERNATURAL WORLD

If you enjoyed this series, make sure you check out Krista's other books set in her *Supernatural World* - the same world Avery and Wyatt live in.

SUPERNATURAL CURSE
Wolf of Fire, book one
When her twin sister goes missing, Tala hires the Shadow Zone's most notorious dark hunter—a fiery hot werewolf with secrets that rival her own.

SUPERNATURAL COMMUNITY
Magic in Light, book one
A supernatural healer threatened by a deadly stalker. An alluring bodyguard she can't resist. And his secret that will shatter her entire world.

FAE OF SNOW & ICE
Court of Winter, book one
When Ilara's abducted by the hated crown prince, she's faced with an impossible choice—enslavement to her nemesis or war for the kingdom.

SUPERNATURAL STANDALONES
Beast of Shadows
His rogue beast craves her blood, yet his heart aches for her to save his soul.

Links to all of Krista's books may be found on her website:
www.kristastreet.com

ABOUT THE AUTHOR

Krista Street loves writing in multiple genres: fantasy, sci-fi, romance, and dystopian. Her books are cross-genre and often feature complex characters, plenty of supernatural twists, and romance in every story. She loves writing about coming-of-age characters who fight to find their place in this world while also finding their one true mate.

Krista Street is a Minnesota native but has lived throughout the U.S. and in another country or two. She loves to travel, read, and spend time in the great outdoors. When not writing, Krista is either chasing her children, spending time with her husband and friends, sipping a cup of tea, or enjoying the hidden gems of beauty that Minnesota has to offer.

THANK YOU

Thank you for reading *Kissed by Shadowlight*, the final book in the *Supernatural Institute* series.

If you enjoy Krista Street's writing, make sure you visit her website to learn about her new release text alerts, newsletter, and other series.

www.kristastreet.com

Links to all of her social media sites are available on every page.

Last, if you enjoyed reading *Kissed by Shadowlight*, please consider logging onto the retailer you purchased this book from to post a review. Authors rely heavily on readers reviewing their work. Even one sentence helps a lot. Thank you so much if you do!